SIF SIGMARSDÓTTIR

THE SHARP EDGE OF A SNOW FLAKE

Hodder
Children's
Books

HODDER CHILDREN'S BOOKS

First published in Great Britain in 2019 by Hodder and Stoughton

1 3 5 7 9 10 8 6 4 2

Text copyright © Sif Sigmarsdottir, 2019

The moral rights of the author have been asserted.

A CIP catalogue record for this book
is available from the British Library.

ISBN 978 1 444 93530 1

Typeset in Adobe Caslon by Hewer Text UK Ltd, Edinburgh
Printed and bound in Great Britain by Clays Ltd, Elcograf S.p.A.

The paper and board used in this book
are made from wood from responsible sources.

snowflake

1 – A flake of snow, especially a feathery ice crystal, typically displaying delicate sixfold symmetry.

2 – *derogatory, informal* An overly sensitive or easily offended person, or one who believes they are entitled to special treatment on account of their supposedly unique characteristics.

Oxford English Dictionary

Photo: A pink suitcase stands in a narrow, shoe-filled hallway.
Filter: Clarendon.

Possible captions . . .

Option one: Off on an exotic adventure **#myglamorouslife**
Option two: My dad just bought me this new travel bag. He doesn't know me at all, does he?
Option three: My whole life fits into a single suitcase. My mum's ashes fit perfectly on to the mantelpiece.
Option four: I committed a crime and now I'm being sent to a place of eternal punishment for the wicked.

Actual caption . . .

So long, and thanks for all the fish.

♥38

Chapter One

Hannah

As soon as the plane lands I take out my mobile. There's a message from Daisy.

Miss you already!

There's also one from Dad.

Got held up at work, will be around twenty minutes late.

Of course he will.

Dad had insisted on picking me up from the airport. I'd said I was fine with taking the bus. I always take the bus. But this time isn't like all the other times.

The plane is taxiing slowly on the icy tarmac towards the terminal. It skids a little. No one seems bothered. Compared to the violent turbulence during landing, caused by gusts of wind pounding the plane like the invisible fists of a giant boxer, this is a breeze.

The woman in the seat next to me keeps glancing at me and smiling. She's trying to engage me in conversation; I know she is. I stare down at my phone. *I don't want to talk.* I should have it printed as a slogan on a T-shirt, I've been saying it so frequently for the past three weeks, two days and six hours.

Notifications from different applications pop up all across my screen, numbers inside red bubbles, like traffic lights giving me an order: *Stop whatever you're doing and click on me.* I get a familiar rush of emotions; an addictive mix of expectation, excitement, dread and validation. I know I shouldn't feel those things. I know I'm being taken advantage of by greedy corporations out to improve their click-through rate and their bank balance. But under the circumstances it's a welcome relief from wanting to lie down and wait for the force of time to wipe me out like chalk from a blackboard.

I scan the numbers inside the bubbles, the never-ending appraisals that ebb and flow, as indifferent to our existence as the sea is to the shore: *How valued are you today? How loved, how sought after? Does anyone like you? Got any new friends? How about followers?*

I start by clicking on Gmail. Excluding promotions and notifications from various social media applications I've got two new emails. One is from someone called Stacey Callaghan. I've no idea who that is but I've got a pretty good idea what the email is about. The subject is 'Condolences'. I move it to the 'Read Later' folder with the rest of them. The other is from Granny Jo. She refuses to learn how to use messaging services and keeps sending me short messages in the subject line: 'Pick up milk on way home'; 'Working late, order pizza'. This time it's 'Call me when you've reached your dad's house'. I click on it expecting the body to be empty as usual. But it isn't.

3

My darling girl. I hope you've landed safely. I just want to ask you – beg you – not to ignore what I said to you this morning. You're not responsible for anyone but yourself now. Let yourself be free. Please, Hannah, I can't take another life wasted.

Love,
Granny

I try not to burst into tears.

It's less than five hours since I said goodbye to Granny Jo. Somehow it feels like an eternity.

I'd expected a talk from her before I left. But I wasn't prepared for what she had to say. She was asking too much of me. I'd told her I couldn't just start over as if my life was a story written in Word and all I needed to do was delete the old document and create a new one. Of all people, she should know that.

I press the home button on my mobile and Granny's message disappears. I'm digitally burying my head in the sand. I can't think about this right now.

As a distraction, I open Facebook. The only thing there for me is a single friend request from someone I'm pretty sure isn't a real person but a bot. Desperate for a fix of some digital love, I switch to Instagram.

That's better. The photo of my suitcase has thirty-eight likes and one comment. The comment is from Daisy: 'What gorgeous luggage!'

I get a slight buzz. Thirty-eight is good. Better than average.

The woman next to me is leaning into my line of vision. She's radiating a desperate need to talk; like a balloon that will burst if she doesn't let some air out. I pretend not to notice her. But some people just can't take a hint.

'I'm here to see my grandkids,' the woman chirps. She's so close I can feel her breath on my cheek. It smells of garlic and menthol.

I try to devise an answer that is just polite enough to keep her from thinking I'm an anti-social psychopath but curt enough to make it clear that I'm not interested in having a chat. 'That's nice.'

Either the woman is socially tone deaf or she simply decides to ignore my signalling. She offers me a Strepsil. 'Want one?'

I shake my head.

She puts the cough sweets into a weathered backpack along with her glasses and the book she's been reading. It's one of those Nordic noir crime novels, the latest accessory you have to have in your handbag to be considered on trend. It has the mandatory snowy landscape on the cover, tastefully peppered with drops of blood. It's murder, minimalistic chic style. Why do people like reading about fictional horror in their spare time? Isn't there enough awfulness in the world as it is?

The woman puts the backpack on the floor, straightens in her seat and flashes me a set of yellowing teeth, a threat of more small talk to come.

'Is it your first time here?'

I put my phone back in my pocket. It has failed to provide me with the solitude I crave. 'No.'

'Are you here on a holiday?'

A slight snort escapes my nostrils. I don't understand why anyone would come here on a holiday. Why would you travel willingly to the freezing cold end of the earth? I should say, *No, I'm not here for a holiday*. I should say, *I'm here as a punishment; I'm here as a prisoner of my own crappy fate*. But I simply say, 'Sure.' No one wants to hear the truth – even if they say they do. The truth makes even the so-called professionals uncomfortable – I found that out almost immediately.

The day after Mum died, the vicar from the church up the street came knocking on our door. I don't know why – one of our neighbours must have told him about us. We'd never been to church and neither I nor Granny Jo had ever before seen this man standing on the cracked pavement outside our house.

'Are you from Ocado?' Granny Jo asked, looking the man up and down. He looked young-ish, despite a receding hairline, and wore jeans and a big down coat to ward off a sudden burst of September cold. He could easily have been one of the delivery men who brought us our weekly groceries.

'I'm Dominic Johnson,' the man said, managing the perfect balance of not smiling while still giving off the vibe that he came in peace. 'I'm from Christ Church. Can I come in for a little chat with you and your granddaughter?'

Granny gave a loud, purposeful sigh. Saying that she was not a fan of all things God related would have been an understatement.

I followed as Granny took the poor man through to the living room, feeling curious as well as apprehensive. It was no coincidence that she had him sit down on her reading chair by the bay window. On the bookshelf right above the man's head was one of Granny Jo's favourite books – her Bible, you could say if you wanted to annoy her – grandly displayed in hardback, with the commanding title: *The God Delusion*.

Granny glanced down at the grey sweatpants she only wore around the house. She ran a hand over her shoulder-length hair, smoothing it out. It was grey with auburn strands – it used to be the other way around not that long ago.

It wasn't only the God thing that was irritating Granny, she also didn't like surprise visitors. With the exception of Daisy, she wanted to know in advance if we were having company. When people came over she always made an effort; ditching the sweatpants for suit trousers and a shirt, or even a dress, and making sure we had nice biscuits in the house. The other reason used to be Mum. Granny wanted us to appear normal, like any other family; mother, daughter and grandmother living happily under one roof. Mum, however, was to normalcy what an airport runway was to a quiet cup of tea. You never knew what state she'd be in if the doorbell rang at random.

Granny sat down on the sofa opposite the vicar. 'Hannah,' she barked at me. 'Get the man some tea.'

'There's no need,' the vicar said, still wearing his down coat. 'I don't want to intrude . . .'

'Well, you already have.'

I disappeared into the kitchen, happy to escape the awkwardness. But to my surprise, when I returned, the two of them were discussing the proposed redevelopment of the north-east corner of Highbury Fields, our local park, and they were in full agreement: the council's plans were the usual pandering to developers who thought of nothing but concrete and money, and the park should be left as it was.

I sat down next to Granny.

'So, how are you, Hannah?' the vicar said after his first sip of the tea.

Granny straightened, turning up her nose, alert but wary like a hyena that had just got a whiff of a carcass.

I shrugged. I didn't want to talk.

The vicar leaned forward in his chair, exposing a bald patch on the crown of his head. 'Even though she's gone, she will always be with you—'

'I'm sorry,' Granny Jo interjected. 'I hate to be rude.' (That was a lie; she loved putting people off their footing with her brusque manner and tell-it-like-it-is philosophy). 'But I'm afraid I can't allow such talk in my house.'

The vicar shifted his eyes from me to Granny, raising his eyebrows. He didn't appear at all fazed. 'And what kind of talk is that?'

'Talk of things, destinations, that don't exist.' Granny Jo's face turned hard. 'Look, Reverend—'

'Call me Dom.'

'Dom. Here we don't trivialise death by pretending it's anything but a final parting. Death serves a purpose; "it is the dark backing that a mirror needs if we are to see anything", a wise man once said.'

I'd heard her say this more times than I could count – and I knew what was coming next.

'The finality of life is what makes it precious,' Granny continued. 'It puts things into focus and gives you the urgency

8

you need to live life to the fullest. Why go on an adventure today, why go on a holiday, why learn a new language, read a book, fall in love today if you're going to live for ever? In endless time, all things can be accomplished. Thus, all things can wait.' Granny Jo sucked in her cheeks, suppressing a smirk. She was clearly pleased with herself. 'So, I will not have you belittle death in my house.'

The vicar smiled. 'That was a good speech. I bet you read it in a book somewhere.'

Granny's lips parted with an indignant gush of air. She looked as if she'd just been slapped. Granny Jo had worked as a librarian at Islington Central Library for thirty-two years. If I'd had to venture a guess, I'd have said around seventy per cent of our conversations were about something she'd read in a book.

The vicar struggled to raise himself up in the cushy reading chair. He took one more sip of his tea, then placed his cup and saucer on the coffee table. 'Let me tell you this, and I speak from experience: Death is so much more complicated in practice than in theory.'

Granny pouted her lips. She was a notoriously sore loser. 'Yes, well. I'm sure we'll figure it out. It's not like we have a choice.'

The vicar bowed his head; he was bowing out.

He got up. 'I'll leave you ladies in peace.' He reached into his pocket, took out his card and placed it on the coffee table next to his hardly touched tea cup, looking in my direction. 'Some of your neighbours were wondering if you'd be interested in having a little remembrance service for Ellen up in Christ Church. Feel free to get in touch if that's something you'd want. I'm just around the corner.'

Granny got up from the sofa to show him out. But she wasn't rid of him yet. Her back curled in disappointment when the vicar stopped in the living room doorway.

'Hannah,' he said and turned to me. 'Your mum sometimes stopped by at the church for a chat. I know she battled her demons, but on a good day she could really light up a room.'

A familiar feeling of mortifying embarrassment took over my entire being and I wished with all my heart that I would be swallowed up by the sofa cushion. To the outside world Mum's highs were endearing. Only to Granny and me, they served as a flashing siren in the darkness of her messed-up reality. Ecstasy/ agony: with Mum they were two sides of the same coin.

'I'm sorry for your loss, child. May God be with you.'

That last thing was what tipped Granny over the edge. If he'd only skipped that last bit, he would have got out unscathed.

'Let me tell you what God is. God is a meme – you know, like those silly pictures you see on the internet – with highly infective power. God is a cultural virus that is hard to eradicate. I prefer Darwin to your virulent meme, thank you very much.' Then she literally pushed the vicar out the door.

The plane stops in front of the terminal building. The woman next to me is banging on about taking her grandchildren to the pond to feed the ducks. I can't listen to her any more. It's nothing personal. It's just that hearing about other people's glorious mundanity makes it hard for me to breathe. It's the grief, I guess; grief for what I've lost, but even more for what never was. My greatest aspiration in life is normalcy. I can only hope for the mind-numbingly mundane. To me, boring is perfection.

I reach for my phone again to try to shield myself from the woman's chatter. I don't care if she thinks I'm rude.

Looking at my Instagram account, people might assume the following things about me:

I've got shiny, straight red hair and perfect skin.
I like cooking.
I'm into nature.
I love going out with my fun-loving girlfriends.
I'm normal.

They'd be wrong on all counts.

FIVE WEEKS EARLIER IN LONDON

Photo: A girl with long dark hair, sporting a pink floral dress and a beaming smile stands in a grey London street, like a sole ray of sunshine on a rainy day.
Filter: Rise.

Caption: Summer is a state of mind.

♥1253

What the caption should have been . . .

Option one: What do you see when you look at this photo?
#happiness #glamour #lovelife #instagood
Option two: Appearances can be deceptive **#fake**
Option three: I got paid two thousand pounds for posting this picture on Instagram **#ad**
Option four: This photo bears no relation to reality **#instalie**

Chapter Two

Imogen

Imogen Collins looks at herself in the mirror. Her skin looks really good today. Such a big change from a year ago when she spent every morning covering up spots and blemishes with a foundation so rich it felt like putting on wall paint. Maybe it's the anti-blemish night cream the people at L'Oréal sent her that did the trick. Or maybe it has more to do with stress hormones and distance in time and space between her and the Beast.

Shit. There he is again. The Beast. Always creeping up on her, cropping up in her thoughts, uninvited and unwelcome. It's been a year but the shadow is still there, even on a sunny morning like this one. Maybe she should see someone about this. Get some pills or something.

There is a creaking of floorboards. Imogen can hear footsteps on the other side of her closed bedroom door; they're light and considered. It's definitely Anna – Steph and Josh never bother to think whether the others are asleep when they get up early. That means there will be coffee ready in five minutes. Anna always makes extra for Imogen. Imogen loves Anna. If Anna were a man she would date her – hell, she'd marry her. Anna is the perfect person to live with. She's quiet, she cooks and she makes a mean mojito. What more do you need in a partner?

Imogen can think of three things: eyes, brown and penetrating; cheeky grin vibrant enough to single-handedly sustain a whole night of slightly embarrassing erotic dreams; and abs hard as rock (she'd touched them by accident when they both went for the pulldown station at the gym).

Her date with Callum is tonight. It had been Imogen who asked him out. She doesn't really know him. They've chatted a few times at the gym and Imogen is pretty sure they have nothing in common. He works as a bartender in the evenings and as a freelance tattoo artist during the day. But she is moving on, getting out from under the shadow, stepping into the light—

Stop it, Imogen. Why does everything always have to be about him? Why does everything have to be tainted? Why can't a date just be a date and not an attempt to *move on, forget, start over, find a new path* or some other shit like that? She should be fine. She should be happy. People keep telling her how fantastic her life is. 'I wish I could do what you do,' people say and tilt their head to one side, smiling as if they're just so happy for her without realising that their resentment is reflected in their stone-cold eyes.

Only yesterday an admiring girl stopped her in the street in Covent Garden.

'Are you Imogen Collins?' she asked. The girl couldn't have been more than ten, standing next to a woman who was probably her mum.

'Yeah that's me,' Imogen answered, giving the girl a well-honed professional smile that was meant to: a) look inviting (when it came to followers, retention was as important as gaining new ones); b) convey surprise (to make the girl feel special in thinking that she was the first person in the world to recognise Imogen in the street); and c) portray kindness (because no one wanted to follow the perfect life of a stuck-up bitch).

'Can I have a selfie with you?' the girl asked.

Imogen was running late on her way back to the office after her extended lunch break. 'Of course you can, sweetie.'

As Imogen walked down King Street afterwards, she heard the mum say, 'Who was that?'

Imogen rests her open palms on the dressing table and takes a deep breath. It's a trick she saw on YouTube to reduce anxiety. Sometimes it works. Sometimes it doesn't. The wood feels nice and cool against her damp skin. She loves that dressing table. It's made from walnut but has a contemporary feel to it; the mirror doesn't have a frame and the drawers don't have handles. She told her housemates that she got it at a thrift shop. She actually got it at Heal's and paid £3,299 for it. That's more than her housemates earn in two months. But Imogen can afford it. She could almost afford to live by herself in the four-bedroom house the four of them share in Bloomsbury. But she likes the company. She needs the company. Solitude doesn't agree with her any more. When she's alone the shadow grows bigger, darker—

Stop, just stop.

Imogen opens a drawer in her dressing table and takes out a jar of loose powder, a brush and mascara. People think she spends hours in the morning getting ready, putting on make-up and picking out clothes. But she doesn't. She's not even that interested in make-up and clothes – well, no more than the next person. Like so many things in her life, her social media career is something that she started on a whim and then spiralled out of control. When it comes to Imogen things always seem to spiral.

A high-pitched beep reverberates from the kitchen. One, two, three. The coffee is ready. Imogen quickly slathers on the mascara. It's lumpy. Whatever. She's taken all the Instagram photos she needs for the week.

She grabs her bottle of Coco Mademoiselle and sprays on a generous amount – the only fixture of her beauty regime; she never leaves the house without it. Then she opens up her laptop, resting on top of the dressing table.

Imogen tries to post twice a day – once before work and once in the afternoon. Before going to bed last night, she picked out this morning's photo and wrote a caption. It's a sponsored post. The photo is of her standing in a busy London street on a grey, rainy day wearing a beautiful pink summer dress from Topshop. The caption reads: 'Summer is a state of mind.'

It was taken last weekend. In the photo Imogen is smiling. It looks like she's having a fabulous day, but she remembers feeling miserable. She was cold and she had a massive hangover from too many of Anna's mojitos. In the photo Imogen is shielding herself from the bulging raindrops with a copy of the *Guardian* – when she got home it had turned into an unreadable paste-like lump. She always buys the *Guardian* on Saturdays. It reminds her of home. It reminds her of her mum and dad fighting over the Review section. She hasn't spoken with her parents in . . . what? Now it's August. They had their epic Skype fight in March. So: March, April, May, June, July . . . She hasn't spoken to her parents in five months. Blimey. She didn't realise it had been that long.

That's another thing the Beast took from her. Her parents didn't understand her decision. She didn't want to explain. So: They'd come to a stalemate.

Whatever. Her life is fabulous. Everyone wants to be her. Everyone wants to do what she does. She's lucky. She's strong. She's not broken.

But she will be fired if she doesn't hurry. She's going to be late for work if she doesn't leave the house within eight minutes. The walk to work takes her seventeen minutes; twenty in rush hour, when the streets are exceptionally busy.

Imogen gets up from her chair – a matching walnut stool, also from Heal's. She doesn't need to work. The revenue from her Instagram account alone is twice as much as her salary at London Analytica. But being a social media influencer isn't a career – at least not for life. It's like being a footballer. You've got a few good years in you and then you're out. One day you're a star, the next no one even remembers your name. But she'll be ready. That means she's in control – at least it makes her *feel* like she's in control.

The doors to her closet are ajar; it's so full of stuff they don't close properly any more. Ever since she reached the million followers mark she's been getting so many clothes sent from various retailers that she will probably never have to do laundry again.

Imogen picks out a top at random. A white pussy-bow blouse with red flowers. She rips off the tag, puts it on and grabs her jeans from the floor.

She's looking forward to that coffee. She might have to get it to go. A month ago, she posted a photo of her old travel mug on Instagram, a chrome-coloured cup from Bodum her mum had given her before her A-levels and Imogen had decorated it with stickers that revealed some of the embarrassments of what was now her past; things such as undying love of One Direction, Hello Kitty and Taylor Swift. Ever since the post she's been sent travel mugs from various companies around the world.

She buttons up her jeans. A slight buzzing sound breaks the morning silence. She leaves her mobile on low vibrate during the night. She's got fans all over the world, many in Australia and the United States, and sometimes she gets more than a thousand notifications in one night.

Imogen scrolls through the notifications. She once read a newspaper article about how the number of likes a person gets on social media affects their sense of self-worth. She totally buys it. The photo she posted last night, of the book she is reading before bed, has been a success. She feels her mood lift, the shadow grow lighter.

The best thing about her accidental social media success isn't the free stuff. It's not even the money. It's the buzz she gets when she wakes up in the morning and sees that she is seen, she is heard, she is loved. The feeling is more invigorating than coffee. And just as addictive.

The first thing she thinks when she sees a notification from Gmail, a single blip in an endless stream of Instagram, Snapchat and WhatsApp messages running across her home screen like a river of love and appreciation, is: *How quaint.* No one really contacts her through email any more except work, and this isn't her work email, this is her personal account. It must be from someone old. Only old people use email. People who are thirty-five and over.

Then she notices the name of the sender. Her excitement over this digital equivalent of a message in a bottle quickly turns into a tsunami of darkness. For a moment she believes there's a chance she has conjured up this ghost by thinking about him. She knows she's not being rational. But that's what he does to her.

What does he want? And why now? It's been over a year. Hasn't he taken enough from her?

She can't open this email. She won't.

She can see the subject in the notification.

Youth + Insecurities = A Shitload of Money

What does that mean? It doesn't make any sense. Is he taunting her?

Stop, Imogen, stop. She's not going to fall apart. He has taken everything from her. The fact that she's still standing is the only thing she really has. It's the only thing she really takes pride in. Everything else, all the free clothing, the fancy furniture, her bulging bank account, the admiring strangers, all the pretty photos – she'd give it all up for things to go back to how they used to be when her parents allotted her a meagre sum of pocket money every week, for things to go back to how they were two years ago. Before she went to uni. Before she encountered him – the one she calls the Beast.

Photo: Three police cars with blinking lights are parked at the side of a snowy road. Beyond them lies a vast lava field.
Filter: No filter needed.

Possible captions . . .

Option one: I have arrived to serve my sentence – kidding, they're not here for me. Or at least I don't think they are.
Option two: A part of me wishes they were here for me – prison seems preferable to the place I'm going to.
Option three: Why am I so obsessed with knowing what crime has happened here?

Actual caption . . .

A real-life Nordic noir.

:heart:12

Chapter Three

Hannah

The wet flakes of snow hit the car window like balls of spit. *Welcome to Iceland, Hannah*, I mouth and pinch myself on the thigh to stop myself screaming – or worse, crying.

It's freezing outside. Still, the car feels like a sauna. I've never understood people who like saunas – a lot of people around here do (although thankfully they don't roll around naked in the snow afterwards like some of the Scandinavians). The dry and hot air of a sauna makes you feel like you're being suffocated with an invisible pillow. Exactly like how it feels being inside this car.

I glance at the man sitting next to me clutching the leather-clad steering wheel – this man I call Dad. I don't feel like I can look directly at him, like it would be rude somehow, like staring at a stranger. I guess in a way that isn't a metaphor (or am I thinking of a simile? I always get the two mixed up). Although I see myself in parts of his face – in his narrow grey eyes, which have an unsettling piercing quality that make you feel like he's either looking into your soul, reading your innermost thoughts, or simply looking right through you; in his dimples, two cheeky paradoxes defying the permanent seriousness of his expression; in his wild, dark-blond eyebrows – he's pretty much a stranger to me.

We've been on the road for ten minutes without saying a word to each other. The journey from Keflavík Airport to Dad's house in Fossvogur, a suburban-looking neighbourhood of Reykjavík where all the houses are as identical as the inhabitants are conformist, should take around an hour. Under the circumstances an hour seems like an eternity.

'How's Rósa?' I ask, thinking that small talk might liven the mood. I turn out to be wrong.

'Don't be like that, Hannah,' Dad snaps at me, the slushy road bearing the brunt of his piercing stare.

'Like what?' Rósa is a sensitive subject. But I was genuinely just asking how she is doing. Or at least I think I was.

'It's the tone.'

Fine, silence it is then.

God, I miss London. I miss Granny Jo. I miss . . .

I can't even think it. Despite everything I miss her so much.

Eventually, it wasn't the curse that killed Mum (although we all thought it would). It was something much more mundane that got her in the end. Cancer. The most common one: breast cancer. Nothing special.

Given how many times she'd tried to leave this world, she fought death surprisingly hard. When it wasn't on her own terms, she 'raged against the dying of the light', as they say. She always wanted things the way she wanted them.

My phone buzzes. I pull it out of my pocket. It's a WhatsApp message from Daisy.

D: There yet?
H: Unfortunately, yes.

D: Oh, don't say that – you're letting negativity win. You should approach this like it's an adventure.

Daisy is the type who spews positive thinking without even realising there is such a thing as positive thinking. My theory is that her mum read too many self-help books while she was pregnant. We've been friends since reception and most of the time I love her positive outlook on life. But occasionally, I want to throttle her.

H: I don't care for adventures. Look at Alice.
D: Alice? That pimply girl with the braces who used to serve us at Nandos?
H: No, that's Alison. I'm talking about Alice . . . as in *Alice's Adventures in Wonderland.*
D: Oh, that one. She had fun, didn't she?
H: She nearly got killed by a crazed queen and almost drowned in her own tears.
D: Oh, I see. Well, I'm sure your rabbit hole will not take you to Wonderland.
H: No, you're right. My rabbit hole takes me to hell.

I'm not exaggerating. Not exactly. In the olden days people believed the door to hell was situated in Iceland.

D: Let's just focus on the positives. Here's one: it's exactly two months till Christmas!

That is not Daisy being Pollyanna; that is a proper positive. It has nothing to do with Santa Claus or Jesus or three-for-two on perfume gift sets at Boots or whatever it is that floats people's boats about Christmas. For Christmas, Daisy is going to visit me in Iceland.

Her mum got her the plane ticket the same day I was told I'd be moving here. I feel like I should burn in hell for the following admission (I can see myself to the door, since it's probably close by), but the truth is the truth no matter how horrible: throughout my life I've wished Daisy's mum, with her soft waist, home-made flapjacks, warm smiles and air of bland normalcy bordering on a cut out from a 1950s *Good Housekeeping* – I've wished she was *my* mum. Now that Mum is gone, admitting this feels more treacherous than ever.

The phone buzzes in my hand. I startle; I'm half expecting it to be a message from Mum telling me off for my betrayal from beyond the grave.

D: Can't wait to see you in December – along with those Northern Lights of course. Got to go study. I bet you wouldn't want to trade places with me now.

I still would. Daisy is studying for her A-levels at Highbury College. I was a week ago.

I miss Daisy.

I put my phone in my pocket. I wish I was back in London studying for my A-levels. The fact that I'm not is one thing I can't blame on Mum. No, that was all me.

When I started the school paper, the *Highbury Gazette*, it was merely an excuse not to have to go straight home after school. But then I got really into it.

26

There were twenty of us writing regularly for the paper, meeting twice a week in the news room (aka the school library) to decide on the week's content. Daisy was head of the marketing department, ringing up local businesses and charming them into advertising in the paper. People started coming up to me at school and talking to me about articles they'd liked. Then people started asking me if they could join up.

I loved it. I loved digging around, searching for newsworthy things to write about, like the nutritional deficiencies of some of the school meals, the highlights of the latest Ofsted report, the split in the drama club about the new play – half the club wanted to do a modern-day version of *Hamlet*, the other half wanted the production to be a traditional one. I loved conducting interviews with students who had been somewhere interesting or done something remarkable, and I got a massive kick out of doing exposés on things such as the damp problems inside some of the classrooms, which turned out to be a serious mould issue that could have had health implications for the students and the teachers.

The *Highbury Gazette* started out as a way to kill time but became my pride and joy. No longer was I simply Hannah, the rather plain girl who doubled as a carer for her weird mother, who sometimes showed up at the school gates wearing a nightgown with a Tesco's bag in hand bursting with cans of lager. I had suddenly become Hannah, the editor of the school paper, the bearer of truth, badass, somebody.

It was barely a week after Mum died and I just wanted to take my mind off things. I got the idea from reading an article in the *Guardian*, the paper Granny Jo bought every morning, about this female BBC Radio presenter who found out her male colleagues were being paid 50 per cent more than she was for the same work.

The headmaster sometimes let Daisy use his office to make her marketing phone calls and he let me do interviews there. One of those times I broke into his computer – or that's how he interpreted it. I wouldn't call it a 'break-in'; it's not a 'break-in' if you simply log in to a computer; it's not a 'break-in' if your password is your wife's first name (which I managed to guess on the third try, by the way). It took me two minutes to dig up the payroll information. I opened a browser, logged in to Gmail, attached the Excel sheet and sent it to myself.

I did the calculations when I got home. The school was paying its male teachers 23 per cent more than its female staff.

I didn't include my big exposé in the final proofs I had to show to Ms Thackeray, my English teacher, before I sent the issue off to the printers. After I got her approval, I changed the front page of the paper.

All hell broke loose. The parents went crazy. So did the board of governors. The headmaster had to apologise for the pay discrepancy and promise to fix it. The students loved the mayhem.

I was expelled.

Dad glances my way. 'I've got a surprise for you.'

A flight back to London? I want to say, but manage to bite my tongue. He's trying to make peace. I should go along with it.

'I've organised your first assignment.'

Oh, that.

Given the reason I was expelled from school, the irony of my punishment must make my former headmaster about ready to explode with fury: I've been sentenced to an internship at my dad's newspaper.

I glance at Dad. He has his eyes fixed on the road. There isn't much traffic and he's driving well over the speed limit.

'What's the assignment?'

Dad's face softens. 'It's an interview.'

Okay, okay, maybe this won't be so bad. I like doing interviews.

'With a famous social media influencer.'

I was wrong. This is going to be awful.

'I hate social media influencers,' I say and throw myself back in the car seat like a petulant four-year-old who isn't allowed a lolly. But I don't care. 'They're stupid, and they portray people my age as a bunch of airheads who think pouting for selfies is a real job, posting belfies on Instagram is an important form of self-expression and photoshopping thigh gaps is something you list as a skill on your CV.'

Dad ignores my statement. 'Her name is Imogen something or other. Ever heard of her?'

'There are millions of people who call themselves social media stars. Why would I have heard of her?'

'She's like you . . .'

I bet she's not.

'She's from the UK, but she has just moved to Iceland.'

I glance at Dad. I am starting to smell something fishy.

'She's taking part in Cool Britannia 2.0, a conference held by the British embassy to promote cultural relations between the

UK and the rest of the world. This Imogen is giving a talk about fashion, or make-up, or self-improvement . . . something to that effect.'

Something to that effect?

'In exchange for the interview she has agreed to help you out.'

There it is, that thing I'd smelled: an agenda that reeks as badly as *harðfiskur*, an Icelandic delicacy of dried fish which has the odour of an old garbage bag.

'Help me out with what?'

'Settling in. Moving to a new country.'

'I don't need hand-holding. I've been coming to Iceland every summer for my whole life.'

Dad tries to give a casual shrug but it comes out all stiff and contrived. He knows full well how lame he is being. 'It has all been arranged. The interview is tomorrow. You might as well make use of the opportunity to speak to someone about things.'

'I can't believe you did that. I can't believe you bribed some loser social media personality to talk to me.'

'Jesus, I was trying to do a good thing here.'

'A good thing would have been to let me do a proper interview.'

'It is a proper interview.'

'No, it's not. It's an ad. Since this Imogen is technically paying to have her event promoted in your paper – not with hard cash but with consultation – the interview isn't real journalism but an advertisement.'

'Why do you have to twist things?'

'Isn't it illegal to publish ads and pretend they are genuine journalistic content? It's illegal in the UK.'

Dad throws himself back in his seat. 'You always do that, Hannah.'

The sleet is turning into snow and the windscreen wipers rushing violently over the glass can hardly keep up.

'What? What do I always do?'

Dad's face is turning red. 'You always manage to make everyone feel bad about themselves.'

Wow. That's harsh – even for him. 'Do you seriously want to go there?' I ask as sixteen years' worth of toxic emotional waste stored away in the back of my brain starts spilling everywhere.

'Go where?'

I know exactly what to say; I've been practising this speech for years.

'The fact that you feel bad about yourself is not my fault.'

I hesitate. Is this really how I want my so-called new life to start? The answer is no. But my words are like a boulder rolling down a hill. They've started their journey into the world and I've got no power to stop them crushing whatever happens to be in their path.

'Even though my existence serves as a reminder to you of your inadequacies, your moral shortcomings and your selfishness, you have no right to blame that on me. It was your decision to leave Mum. It was your decision to leave me to deal with her shit. You made your bed. If you feel guilty, have a conversation with your conscience and leave me out of it.'

There. I've finally said it. My heart is pounding with a paradoxical mix of anger, anxiety and relief.

I wait for Dad to snap at me. But he doesn't.

The seconds tick by. They turn into minutes. *Shit*. The silence in the car is making my ears ring. I start to wish he *would* snap at me.

Did I go too far? I replay the speech in my head. I do it again. And again. With every repeat the volume goes up and the sting of my words becomes more ferocious. I'm beginning to feel guilty – even though it doesn't make sense. Why am *I* feeling guilty?

I can't take Dad's expressionless face any longer. That's so him. Never facing the issues, just letting grievances build up, fester and rot until they stink up the place so badly there's no way of clearing the air.

If that's how he wants this: fine. I turn away from him to face the side window.

The scenery that greets me is as cold and hard as Dad's silence. Some describe the landscape on the drive from Keflavík Airport to Reykjavík as magical, a view reminiscent of the landscape of the moon (a line probably made up by the tourist board). I only see wasteland: cold and barren lava fields formed in volcanic eruptions centuries ago.

It's a wonder that anyone actually lives here. The island has been trying to kill off its inhabitants ever since they first got here just over a thousand years ago. Time and time again throughout history, freezing weather, burning lava, earthquakes, floods, avalanches and plagues have stopped just short of eradicating homo sapiens from this volcanic piece of rock located just outside the Arctic Circle. In the eighteenth century they actually considered moving the whole country to Denmark after a string of natural disasters wiped out a large portion of the population.

I wish they had.

Dad's still not saying anything. Why am I here? There's nothing for me here. No one even wants me here. Not Dad. Certainly not Rósa. The twins barely acknowledge my existence, and Grandma Erla and Grandpa Bjarni go slightly pale every time I visit. I think they see Mum when they look at me. They will always think of her as the woman who almost ruined their son's life.

The snow is falling thick and fast now. The snow in Iceland is dangerous. People still die from exposure, even on the streets of the capital.

The traffic is slowing down. There's a car barely a metre in front of us but I can hardly see its outlines through the fog of snow.

'Bloody tourists,' Dad growls. He hits the brakes. We go from eighty miles per hour to twenty miles per hour in seconds. 'If they don't know how to drive in snow, they should take the shuttlebus.'

I push my cheek up against the window to better inspect the row of slowly moving cars. *Great.* Now this awful car journey is going to take even longer.

I spot something on the side of the road a few cars down. A flash of blue light. I don't think it's tourists with bad driving skills who are causing our delay.

As we draw closer I can make out police cars. There are three of them, parked on the hard shoulder. The sound of a siren fills the air. An ambulance is coming towards us, approaching the scene from the opposite direction.

Crime is rare in Iceland. I grab my phone and snap a photo of the action.

Suddenly we swerve off the road. I grab the dashboard in fear of my life, thinking Dad has lost control of the car on the ice.

He stops the car suddenly and shifts it into park. Without turning off the ignition, he opens the door.

'Where are you going?'

'I'll be right back,' he says and slams the door shut.

I watch Dad run towards the police cars. The wind is heavy and he has to lean forward to push through it. He looks as if he's breaking through a brick wall head first.

I notice four police officers and two paramedics walking across the lava field towards the road, carrying a stretcher between them. As a reflex I pull the handle on the door and jump out of the car. I'm gagged by a gust of wind. Struggling for breath, I run after Dad. His hair, neatly shaved at the sides and meticulously combed to one side at the top, is blowing in every direction despite the generous amount of hair gel I know he uses every morning.

I'm just about to catch up with him when a policewoman dressed in a black down coat with the police crest on the sleeve – a yellow star – steps out of one of the cars with the blue blinking lights.

'Stand back,' she says, waving her arms. Her plump face is red from the cold and her blonde hair is tied back into a ponytail that flutters in the wind.

Dad doesn't listen – he never listens. 'What's going on here?'

'Please, sir, I need you to stand back. And you too, miss.'

Dad whizzes around. 'I told you to stay in the car,' he shouts at me.

Why should I listen to you when you're not listening to the policewoman? This logic makes perfect sense in my head.

I try to distract Dad by pointing out the group of officers approaching with the stretcher. 'Look.'

It works. Dad turns back to the policewoman. 'Has there been an accident?'

'Please, sir. Step back.'

The officers and paramedics are clambering up a small, gravelly hill lining the road. The earth is made slippery by the falling snow. There is someone lying on the stretcher, draped under a burgundy blanket. The policewoman is busy blocking Dad's way. I grab the chance and rush past them towards the officers, who are struggling to get up the hill.

'Hey!' the policewoman shouts.

I slide my hand into my pocket, pull out my phone and, as discreetly as I can, I snap a couple of photos of the officers with the stretcher.

The woman grabs my shoulder and flings me around. 'I want the two of you out of here or I'll have you arrested on the spot.'

Dad scowls at me, as if the fact that we're not allowed to stay is somehow my fault. We scuttle back.

Once we're back in the car Dad grabs his mobile from the inside pocket of his skinny, dark-blue blazer. It's far from weather-appropriate attire. But in Iceland no one dresses according to the weather. If they did, they would wear snow

35

jackets and ski pants all year long, and Icelanders are far too fashion conscious to stray that far away from vanity towards comfort. If you see someone wearing walking boots in Reykjavík, you know they're a tourist. I've seen Rósa run on ice as smooth as glass in six-inch heels.

'It's Eiríkur,' Dad says into the phone. 'I'm driving on Reykjanesbraut and the police are here. Have you got any reports on what's going on?'

Someone is saying something on the other end of the line. I try to make out the words but they're too muffled. If they weren't, I'd understand. I speak Icelandic fluently – Dad and I always speak in Icelandic. It's a skill I sometimes resent. What a waste of brain capacity to speak a language that only around three hundred thousand people understand. It would be so much handier to know German or Spanish – or even Chinese. Although, now that I've been sentenced to life for my crimes and sent here like an unruly Russian to Siberia, I guess knowing the language comes in handy.

'Okay,' Dad says. 'Call our contact at the Reykjavík Met. I'll be back at the office hopefully within the hour.'

So, he isn't going to spend the day with me, help me get settled in, give me a hug and tell me that everything is going to be all right. What a shocker.

'Keep me updated,' he says and hangs up the phone.

Dad shifts the car into drive, makes a sharp turn and heads towards the road. As we wait for a car to give us a pass I take out my phone. I find the photos of the police officers carrying the stretcher.

We re-enter the slow-moving traffic.

'Do they know anything?' I look up from my phone as we drive past the incident. The police and paramedics are sliding the stretcher into the ambulance.

'No.'

'What do you think happened?'

'It's probably just some tourist who got hurt. Stopped his car to get some photos, wandered too far and slipped on the ice.'

'But there was no car.'

'Huh?'

'There wasn't a car at the side of the road, just the police and the ambulance service. A tourist would have driven a rental, wouldn't he?'

Dad looks over his shoulder.

And that isn't the only thing that refutes Dad's theory. I turn back to the photos on my phone. I zoom in on the stretcher. The burgundy blanket covers the entire length of it. You can't see a single bit of the person lying under it. This is not how you cover up a patient. This is how you cover up a corpse.

I flick to the next photo. At first glance it seems identical to the first one. But then I notice something white peeking from under the blanket. I zoom in on it. It's the corner of a towel, judging by the patterned selvedge. And then I see it. Bile rises to the back of my throat. I can see dark blue fingers poking from under the towel. *Is that what happens when you die in the cold?*

The traffic is moving back to a normal pace. I'm getting carsick from staring at the photo too long so I put my phone back in my pocket. I can't get the fingers out of my mind.

My brain keeps conjuring up different explanations for what has happened. It's like a search dog – alert, panting and drooling – on a mission which it won't stop until it has been completed.

Statistically, the explanation for all the police cars is highly likely to be a tourist who got lost and tragically died from the cold. But somehow, it doesn't sit right with me. I didn't see anyone at the scene from the Search and Rescue squads, the team of volunteers who are usually called in to look for wayward visitors. And the police officer was really intent on getting us out of there.

I am consumed with the need to know the truth. It's a familiar feeling, a feeling that I love. I feel invigorated, like after going to the gym (if I ever went to the gym). I feel like – suddenly and if only for a moment – I am me, the true me, and I'm exactly where I'm meant to be, doing exactly what I should be doing.

Where does this need to know come from? Why is figuring out the truth so gratifying?

Could it have been a murder? Hardly. Iceland has one of the lowest murder rates in the world. Murders almost never happen in Iceland. But sometimes – occasionally – things that 'almost never' happen actually do happen. That's a statistical fact.

I think back to the woman who sat next to me on the plane and the book she was reading, the Nordic noir crime novel with its snowy, bloodstained cover. Why do people enjoy reading murder mysteries so much? Is it because people get a kick out of uncovering the truth, like when I worked for the school paper?

When I was expelled I told the headmaster that it had been conviction that drove me to do what I did. But deep down I think it might have been something else. What that is, however, I'm not sure.

Instagram

Photo: A silver tray with bottles of Voss Artesian water and perfectly polished glasses standing on top of a meeting room table.
Filter: Juno.

Caption: Getting ready to give a presentation at work. So excited! **#lovemylife**

♥2409

What the caption should have been . . .

Option one: There are triggers everywhere. Today it was a glass of water. Tomorrow it will be something else.
Option two: I thought that my life was my own, that the path that I'm treading was my choice. I may have been wrong?
Option three: Today my prison is a fish tank that has been drained of water and I am the fish.

Chapter Four

Imogen

Imogen has heard her boss's sales pitch so many times she knows it by heart. Which is just as well. They've been preparing for this meeting for weeks – it's an important step in Ms Kendrick's mission to expand into the food sector – but Imogen can't for the life of her focus on what's taking place in the stuffy glass cage that they call the office meeting room.

'What we do here at London Analytica is cutting edge,' Ms Kendrick says, standing in front of the big flat-screen TV that's showing a carefully designed PowerPoint slide – white, futuristic font on a steely grey background – with five words on it:

Openness
Conscientiousness
Extroversion
Agreeableness
Neuroticism

Ms Kendrick is wearing black tailored, skinny trousers and her signature tweed Chanel jacket. She has a few of them, all in the traditional cardigan-style cut. This one is a mix of grey, black and pink wool with gold buttons. It's from the latest

‏ɔlection. The company must be doing well. Imogen looked it up online and found out the jacket cost five grand.

'Having one single marketing message for everyone is outdated,' Ms Kendrick says. 'It's so last century,' she adds, widening her eyes for effect. 'What we at London Analytica offer is the future of marketing.'

The clients sit at the far end of the long meeting room table, opposite Imogen and Mark, Ms Kendrick's second in command. They are two men, the CEO and the COO of a frozen seafood company. Both are bald and ashen, closing in on their sixties, wearing ill-fitting suits and surly frowns. Imogen has seen the type before. Owners of a business long past its prime, facing a last-ditch attempt to restore it to former glory. They say they're ready to embrace the future, that they're ready to step into the twenty-first century, but their faces say they really just want to curl up in the 1950s, have their advertisements printed in a good old-fashioned newspaper where they can admire them over a warm cup of tea while their wives put their frozen fish fingers in the oven.

'What we offer is psychographic microtargeting: a revolutionary marketing method which enables you to tailor-make a message for each and every one of your potential customers.' Ms Kendrick shifts on her feet. The men's scepticism is putting her off balance.

It isn't going very well. But Imogen is too distracted to be embarrassed for her boss. She can't stop thinking about the email. She opened it just before the meeting started. She knew it would mess up her concentration. But not opening it, not knowing what it said, was wreaking havoc with her work day.

'Immie,' Ms Kendrick is saying. 'Immie?'

It takes a while for Imogen to remember that's her. At the office she is Immie. She hates the nickname she was given when she started at the company. But she had no choice but to accept it. Imogen is also Ms Kendrick's first name, and colleagues needed to distinguish between her and the leading lady. They weren't about to mess with their boss's name.

Ms Kendrick is peering at her over her cat-eye glasses. How many times has she called out her name?

'Glad you're with us. If you could come up here, please, and tell the gentlemen a little bit about the mechanics of what we do.'

It's Imogen's job to explain the OCEAN model. The OCEAN model is the cornerstone of the company. It's actually nothing new. It's been well established within the field of psychology for decades. Imogen knew about it before she started work for London Analytica. The OCEAN model had been a part of the Introduction to Psychology paper at Cambridge. She loved it. Until she hated it. Until he ruined it.

She stops herself from going there. The email, the past, the Beast. It has to wait. She has to keep it together for the meeting.

Imogen gets up from her seat. Mark is sitting next to her. His chair is slightly too close to hers and as she tries to squeeze past him she hits her foot on one of the chair legs and stumbles.

'You okay there, Immie?' Mark says, offering her a steadying hand and saving her from falling flat on her face.

Mark is one of the co-founders of the company. But unlike Ms Kendrick, the company's success hasn't made him all stiff and intense, like a cat fresh from a visit to the taxidermist.

'Yes, peachy, thank you, Mark.' *Peachy*. Why did she say peachy?

Imogen walks alongside the meeting room table, towards the flat-screen at the front. The meeting room, the fish tank as they call it, gets really hot and stuffy during the summer and she's sweating. She wonders whether there's a sweat stain on the front of her blouse. She doesn't want to look and draw attention to it if it is there.

Imogen reaches Ms Kendrick, who hands her the remote for the slides. Ms Kendrick raises her thin, harshly painted-on eyebrows, a gesture with meaning as clear as day: Don't fuck this up.

'Thank you, Ms Kendrick,' Imogen says, sounding surprisingly upbeat considering that on the inside she feels like running straight home, putting on pyjamas, bingeing on pizza and Netflix and never leaving the house ever again. But instead of following her urges, she turns towards the clients and throws them a smile.

Their faces look mummified. Wow. This is going to be a long day.

'I'm Imogen Collins. I'm London Analytica's social media campaigns executive and I will be telling you a little bit about how we do what we do – the tricks behind our magic, if you will.'

Still not even a hint of a smile.

'Psychologists have found a way to measure people's personality according to five independent factors: Openness, Conscientiousness, Extroversion, Agreeableness and Neuroticism. These are known as the Big Five – or OCEAN.'

Imogen has committed her lines to memory. Every single word. She delivers her part of the presentation as if she were performing in a play, playing the role of a confident, up-and-coming, young woman, wise in the traditional sense but also with a finger on the pulse. Sometimes she feels like she goes through her whole life like a character in a play, playing the role of the girl who has it all and has it all figured out, when in truth she has no idea what she's doing, where she's going or why she's here.

'Until recently, targeted advertisements have relied solely on demographics. But organising an ad campaign around the demographic concept – on the idea, for example, that all women should receive the same message because of their gender – is plainly ridiculous.

'While most ad agencies still use demographics to get their clients' word across, we use psychometrics.

'We at London Analytica have developed a unique model that predicts the personality of almost every single consumer in the United Kingdom using the OCEAN system. We know people's hopes, dreams, needs and fears, and how they are likely to behave.

'So . . .' Imogen pauses for breath – but only a short one; she just wants to get the presentation over with. 'Two things you are probably asking yourselves: how and why?

'Let's start with the how. Our model is based on real scientific research. By using Big Data, we can map out people's digital footprint and determine their personality. Remarkably reliable deductions can be drawn from simple online actions. For example, on Facebook, one of the best indicators for heterosexuality in men is liking the band Wu-Tang Clan. Followers of the musician Lady Gaga are most probably extroverts, while those who like philosophy tend to be introverts.'

Judging by the bewilderment on the clients' faces, they have no idea who Wu-Tang Clan and Lady Gaga are.

'Each piece of information is too weak to produce a reliable prediction. But when you combine tens, hundreds or thousands of individual data points the resulting predictions become really accurate.

'It turns out you can evaluate a person better than their average work colleague on the basis of only ten Facebook "likes". Seventy "likes" are enough to outdo a person's friends, one hundred and fifty: their parents, and three hundred likes: their partner. More likes can even surpass what a person thought they knew about themselves.'

One of the suited men starts coughing. She's losing them. Or maybe she never had them. The only card Imogen has up her sleeve is to crank up the enthusiasm.

'You might be wondering what mapping out an individual's personality has to do with your business of selling frozen seafood. It has everything to do with you!' She realises she's speaking with the fervour of a squeaky cartoon character. But what else can she do?

'The reason is that it also works in reverse. Not only can psychological profiles be created from your data, but your data can also be used the other way around to search for specific profiles. With our model here at London Analytica, we can look for all sleep-deprived, anxious mothers and target them with the message: "Don't lose any more sleep over what to make for tea." Or we can single out introverted, obese men with messages such as: "Let the chippy come to you."'

The man starts coughing again. This time more forcefully. His round face is turning slightly red.

Imogen isn't sure what to do. She decides to keep on going. 'So, what our model essentially is, is a people search engine which allows us to—'

The coughing client raises one hand. 'Excuse me.' More coughing.

Imogen stops speaking, thinking he has a question. It turns out he hasn't – or at least not the type of question Imogen was expecting.

'Could you be a dear and pour me a glass of water?'

It's as if Imogen's world slows down, as if the fish tank becomes a real fish tank. She tries to lift an arm but it barely moves. Her brain is telling her to take a step forward but her body refuses. She opens her mouth but nothing comes out. She's drowning.

The expensive looking bottles of Voss Artesian water are right next to him. So are the glasses. He could easily reach out and get them himself. She is not his servant. She is not the company's coffee runner. She's the social media campaigns executive, for Christ's sake. She wasn't hired to pour water for old, self-important bastards too lazy to do it themselves.

The room is starting to spin around her. Or maybe it's her that is spinning, spiralling out of control again. *Imogen, calm down. What's the big deal? He's only asking for water.*

Everyone is looking at her. Ms Kendrick is probably fuming.

Outside the fish tank, Imogen can see some of her colleagues in the open plan office leaving their desks for lunch. Out of the corner of her eye she sees someone stop right by the glass meeting room. Did they stop to stare at her, watch her make a complete fool of herself? Are they all looking at her and laughing? Saying she was only hired for her looks, her long dark hair, her skinny arms and her cleavage. That she'd never been qualified for the job and would fail miserably.

Stop it, Imogen. She knows this isn't just about the client and the fact that he requested some water. Like everything else, it's about the email, the past, the Beast.

When Imogen looked at the email, it turned out, it wasn't actually meant for her.

When Imogen got the job with London Analytica, the hottest data-driven marketing agency in town, she took the fact that she shared a first name with the company's founder to be further evidence of this being her destiny. This was all part of a divine plan. Dropping out of uni after only a year of studying psychological and behavioural science was the right thing to do. Moving out of her parents' house in Cambridge and into a dilapidated house in London with three strangers was the right thing to do. Changing her lifelong plan to go into child psychology to seek a career in marketing was the right thing to do. Subsidising her income and raising her profile by becoming a social media influencer was the right thing to do.

Little did she know that this insignificant coincidence would – nineteen years after her parents decided on a whim to call

48

their new-born daughter Imogen – completely pull the rug out from under her.

The email hadn't been meant for her; it had been meant for Imogen Kendrick. Her boss.

Ms Kendrick's voice snaps her out of her trance. 'Immie. Did you not hear the man? Get him some water.'

Mark jumps out of his chair. 'I'll do it,' he says, even though he is the furthest away from the tray with the water bottles and glasses out of everyone in the room.

Imogen watches Mark walk all the way around the table to the other side where the clients are sitting.

'Still or sparkling, sir?' he asks.

'Sparkling,' answers the client, who is no longer coughing.

Mark reaches past the man, opens one of the cylindrical glass bottles and pours from it into a glass, which he places on the table in front the client.

The man takes the glass. 'Thank you,' he says, then presses his thin lips to the rim. He has white, sticky blobs of saliva at the corners of his mouth. He gulps down half the drink. His yellowing eyes water slightly because of the fizz.

'You're welcome,' Mark says and bows his head with what appears to be exaggerated servility.

Imogen wonders if it is a dig; a dig at the man who was so important he couldn't pour his own water, or a dig at her for not doing as she was asked. As Mark marches back to his seat Imogen gets her answer. When he gets to the end of the table he looks at Imogen, rolls his eyes and tilts his head towards the client, who is just finishing the rest of his drink. Then he smiles at her.

Imogen gets a lump in her throat.

Mark is always so nice to her. Not like Ms Kendrick and the other two co-founders, who barely acknowledge her existence. It's like they're so high up the chain of command they can't even see her. She's just a dot in the far distance to them. Mark, on the other hand, often joins the staff in their little kitchen where they go for coffee and the latest office gossip. He laughs with them, tells jokes and even drinks the awful instant coffee which is the only caffeine on offer. Ms Kendrick gets coffee delivered to her office twice a day from Pret A Manger.

The day Imogen started work for London Analytica, Mark told her if she needed anything she shouldn't hesitate to come to him. A couple of days into the job Imogen couldn't get the printer to work. She'd been hired as the young tech-savvy person every company needed and not managing to print out a simple sheet of paper was too embarrassing to admit. Mark had come over and joked that the printer was almost as old as a steam engine and operating a steam engine was not a part of Imogen's job description.

But even though Mark is always nice to her, Imogen makes sure she's never nice back. She's not rude, just professional. No unnecessary smiles, no laughing, no jokes. That's one of the lessons the Beast taught her. That's one of the scars the Beast left her with. She can't shake the feeling that what happened was somehow her fault. That she shouldn't encourage new male attention.

Ms Kendrick clears her throat. The noisy expulsion of phlegm is fraught with meaning. 'Could you please continue,

Immie. There needs to be time for Mark to go over the financials.'

Mark sits down. He nods at her encouragingly.

Imogen opens her mouth to continue her presentation. But nothing comes out. She tries again. Nothing.

She once learned that fish breathe by taking water into their mouths and forcing it out through their gills. Oxygen then moves into the blood and travels to the cells. Standing there opening and closing her mouth, pained and panicky, trying to get the words out, Imogen imagines she looks like a fish on dry land, gasping for breath and only minutes from death.

She can't live like this any more.

Imogen lets go of the remote for the PowerPoint slides. It falls to the floor with a hollow thud, the sound cheap plastic makes when it falls on to expensive solid-wood flooring.

'Imogen,' she hears Ms Kendrick say as she turns her back on the people sitting at the long table. Ms Kendrick hasn't called her Imogen since the job interview. 'Imogen, we're on a schedule here.'

Imogen stumbles towards where the door is meant to be. Its exact location is hard to find on a wall that is made one hundred per cent from glass.

'I'm sorry,' she mumbles, fumbling for the knob. She finds it, grabs it. The steel feels cool against her skin.

She thought she'd made the right choice. She'd thought that choosing to stay silent was empowering. But every time someone silently eyes her up on the Tube, every time an old fart like the one sitting opposite her in the meeting room asks her to get him a cup of coffee – or, in this case, a glass of water – it all comes crashing back down.

She's made a mistake. She's made a huge mistake.

Imogen rips open the meeting room door and runs out of the fish tank.

Photo: A photo of a photo; an old snap of a woman with burning red hair falling over her shoulders and a smile as bright as the sun on her slightly pale face. She's holding a rather wrinkly and frowning new-born baby.
Filter: Time.

Desirable captions . . .

Option one: #love
Option two: Miss you.
Option three: Mother and daughter – the strongest bond of all.

Possible captions . . .

Option one: I wish I remembered that.
Option two: I wish I could say that you were always my rock.
Option three: I wish I never turn into you. **#sorrymum**

Actual caption . . .

Once upon a time.

♥9

Chapter Five

Hannah

A Facebook friend of mine, a guy I don't really know but who goes to my school – or, I guess, my former school – just lost his grandfather. He has written a heart-warming post about what his grandfather meant to him, what he had learned from him and how much he is going to miss him. His words fill me with a sense of betrayal. I haven't commemorated Mum at all on social media.

If I were to commemorate her, I could write something like this: *I just lost my mum. She leaves the biggest hole imaginable in my life. I feel so empty now that she's gone.*

That would all be true. What to say next, however, is the tricky part. I could write: *My mum was my rock, my role model and my greatest supporter.* But that would be a lie.

If I were to write the truth, it would go something like this: *With the loss of my mum, I've lost the centre of my being.* That's nice, right? That's acceptable. But then comes the unacceptable part: *Since I was twelve years old I've been my mum's carer. Most of you don't know this. I've done my best to hide that part of my life from the outside world. Now that she's gone, I literally don't know what to do with myself. What am I meant to do with my time when I don't have to cook her meals, take her out for her daily walk, go to her in the middle of the night with a glass of water when she cries out for the voices in her head to stop; when I don't have to do her washing to make sure that if she leaves the house she doesn't smell of the alcohol she's poured down her top in a drunken haze; when I don't have to make her take her pills or coax her down from our rooftop when she's threatening to jump?*

But social media was not designed for you to share the truth about your life. No one types about their misery on Twitter, no one writes a post on Facebook of their deepest sorrows, no one posts a photo on Instagram of the time they spent two hours cleaning the bathroom floor after their mum did a number two all over it because she was so out of it she couldn't find the toilet.

So, what I do is this: I take a snap of the framed photo of Mum and me that I brought with me from London and post it on Instagram. It's the happiest memory I have of Mum. In the photo I'm only a couple of days old, so technically it can't be a memory. No one remembers their first days of life. But I allow myself to pretend it's a real memory because sometimes, when there is simply too much reality in your life, you need a little self-delusion to keep on going.

It's seven o'clock in the morning. I should be getting ready but I'm still in bed. For the first time in ages I slept like a log. The bed in Dad's guestroom is the cosiest bed I've come across in my life. It has a memory foam mattress and the duvet is warm but light as a feather – it is stuffed with Icelandic eiderdown.

I always stay in the guestroom when I visit. It's small with a single bed, a small chest of drawers and a tiny flat-screen TV.

This time Dad – or probably Rósa – has tried to liven it up. There are two moss-green glass tea-light holders on top of the chest of drawers that weren't there before. The bed has a new bedspread. On the wall above the TV now hangs a framed Moomins print.

I have to admit, the room looks nice. Less like a guestroom, more like someone's permanent bedroom.

Permanent. The word is like a punch in the gut which radiates angry swirls of panic through my body and tears me out of my tranquil post-sleep calm. It's starting to sink in: *This is my home now.*

I can hear Dad, Rósa and the twins upstairs preparing breakfast. There's the scraping of pans, the clatter of cutlery and laughter. I can smell bacon. These domestic attacks on the senses make me feel slightly defensive. In my old life I usually scoffed a quick bowl of cereal before leaving for school and Granny Jo just grabbed a coffee to go. Mum rarely woke up before noon.

I guess breakfast isn't always this homey. The family is preparing my welcome party. It's going to be at seven-thirty in the morning. It was the only timeslot available in the household's busy schedule of work, school and the twins' long list of extracurricular activities.

I get up, get dressed and go up to the kitchen at exactly seven-thirty. They don't notice me when I arrive and I stand in the doorway inspecting the scene. Rósa is standing over a noisy KitchenAid electric mixer she almost never uses but which is always on display on the counter, as proof of her keen eye for design. Dad is putting strawberries into a stemmed glass bowl shaped like a chalice. I recognise it as an Iittala, a designer glassware brand Rósa loves so much that the house looks like their production line. I'd bet my life on it that the tea-light holders in my bedroom are Iittala as well.

The twins are sitting at the kitchen table, each with an iPad in hand. And Alda is there. My heart skips a beat. Finally, a friendly face. Alda is Dad's older sister. As far as I can tell, they hate each other. Maybe that's why Mum and Alda always had a good relationship despite everything.

Alda looks up from the newspaper she's reading. She sees me and her make-up-free face lights up.

'Hey!' she shouts and jumps to her feet. 'Look who's awake.'

She rushes towards me and squeezes me so tight I swear I can feel a rib crack. It's only been a couple of weeks since I saw her last. She was the only one from Dad's family to show up for Mum's cremation.

'How are you?'

I just shrug. It's easier than saying, *My mum just died and I've been sent to live in this hellhole, but otherwise I'm fine.*

'Morning, Hannah,' Rósa says, turning off the mixer. She looks up and gives me a stiff smile. It's the sort of smile you give to a stranger who you catch looking at you in the street, in the hope he'll bugger off instead of talking to you.

Alda turns towards the twins. 'So how is it to finally have your big sister living with you?'

The twins don't even bother looking up. I guess I shouldn't take it personally. They're twelve. Ísabella and Gabríel. I secretly call them Wednesday and Pugsley because they're just like blonde versions of the children from *The Addams Family*. I've always found them slightly intimidating, even when they were smaller.

'You should feel lucky to have a big sister to look out for you,' Alda continues, despite the fact that the twins don't appear to be listening to her. 'Just like I look out for your dad. Everyone needs a big sister.'

Dad snorts. 'Yeah, like a hole in the head.'

Alda ignores him.

Dad puts the bowl of strawberries on the kitchen table. The tabletop is so white and shiny that looking at it hurts my eyes. Dad and Rósa's house is all about the white and shiny, straight clean lines, minimalism and chrome. It looks more like a museum than a place where people live.

He looks at me. 'Are you wearing that to the office?'

I'm wearing a white T-shirt, a leather jacket and skinny jeans. I saw a journalist wear a similar outfit on *Question Time* recently and thought she looked cool.

'And that purple stripe in your hair . . . Rósa has offered to take you to her hairdresser to have it fixed.'

Every time I allow myself to think, *Maybe this isn't so bad*, Dad goes and says something like this. I want to scream at him but I don't want to do it in front of the twins.

'You realise my hair is that way on purpose,' I say, with a forced smile. 'I wasn't out walking one day when a pigeon shat semi-permanent hair dye on my head that accidentally formed a line.'

Dad is always doing that. Criticising the way I look – not in so many words but rather with snide comments or a look of silent horror on his face.

'Have it your way,' Dad says and turns to fetch the rest of the food as if this is no big deal – it was just an innocent suggestion, and I'm totally overreacting.

The purple stripe had been a part of my attempt to find myself – obviously not in a metaphysical way, as in finding my purpose on earth or anything like that, but finding myself stylistically.

I'd deliberately attempted a few different looks in the past couple of years. The first was the fierce, bordering on gothic look. I dyed my hair black and wore red lipstick at all times. Next was the nerdy look. I bought fake round glasses from Topshop and wore a chequered skirt with knee-high socks. Then I tried out what I now call the 'clown look'. I'd seen people do it on Instagram: put on a mish-mash of clothes that technically don't go together but look fabulous as an ensemble on someone posing on a street corner in a photo posted on social media or published in *Now* magazine. On a person standing on a Tube platform waiting for the next train to arrive the look, however, is absolutely ridiculous.

Dad returns with a huge serving plate of scrambled eggs and smoked salmon.

'Everyone, take a seat,' he says and places the plate on the table. 'I called work and told them Hannah and I will be an hour late.'

Wow. Dad is really trying – and I don't mean that ironically. Dad loves nothing more than his work. Giving up part of his workday is the equivalent of donating an organ. When Dad and Rósa fight it's always about Dad's job. He didn't come home by the time he said he would. She had booked the babysitter but they'd missed Mahler's second symphony at the Harpa concert hall (Dad hates classical music and I suspect Rósa isn't into it either, but she demands that they go listen to the Iceland Symphony Orchestra play every other month because that's where people who want to appear cultured and important go to mingle with others who want to appear cultured and important).

I sit down next to Ísabella, who still has her nose buried in the iPad. Alda sits down opposite me. Dad keeps bringing more food to the table: pork liver pate, sheep rillette, bacon, blueberry skyr, muesli. In Iceland, when you have a party there is always ten times more food than you need to feed the number of mouths present.

'So, Alda,' I say, loudly enough for the whole room to hear. 'Do you think I should maybe take Rósa up on her offer to take me to her hairdresser?' I'm trying to match Dad's gesture by sounding upbeat and conciliatory.

Alda just shrugs. 'Do. Or don't. Whatever.' Judging by the state of her tousled grey hair that reaches all the way down to her waist, and her knitted mustard sweater vest over a crinkled shirt, she hasn't been to the hairdresser or a non-charity store once in her life.

'I mean, I want to fit in,' I say – which is the truth but it's also a statement meant to cater to Dad's allegiance to conformity. 'Maybe I should use this opportunity to reinvent myself. No one knows me here. I can be whoever I want.'

Alda groans. 'Why are young people today so obsessed with who they are? Instead of always trying to be somebody, just try to be. Just let your different selves flow through you; let each of

60

them surface, naturally, organically, when they want to. You need to stop trying to be somebody and learn the art of being nobody.'

Alda reaches for her brown leather satchel on the floor. She's had it ever since I can remember. If I didn't know better I'd assume she'd bought it to signal her job as a professor of history at the University of Iceland – but I know it's just a random choice. To Alda, looks, clothes and accessories don't hold meaning.

Alda takes out a cigarette from her silver case and places it between her lips. Before she can light it, Dad intervenes.

'How many times do I have to tell you we don't allow smoking in here?'

'Fine, fine.'

Dad brings the whipped cream Rósa was making to the table. 'And who even smokes any more? Don't you know it's the twenty-first century? Don't you know it can kill you?'

Alda makes a face. 'You sound like Dad.'

'How would you know what Dad sounds like these days? When did you last visit our parents?'

'Piss off, Eiríkur.'

I feel my body go stiff. I know it's stupid. This is nothing. This is just how Dad and Alda speak to each other. But it's this place, the memories of the screaming rows my parents had when they fell out of love and me and mum left, moved from Iceland back to London, when I was four.

I need an excuse to move away from the tense atmosphere. I reach for an empty glass on the decked table and grab it. I get up from my seat.

'I need water.'

I head to the sink to fill it up from the tap. But on my way back the sleek glass somehow slips from my hands. It falls to the floor, and with soul-shattering noise breaks into a million little pieces.

I get my wish as silence fills the kitchen. Everyone is looking at me: Dad, Alda, Rósa, who is standing by the coffee maker with a scoop full of ground coffee hovering above the funnel. Even the twins look up from their iPads.

'I'm sorry, I'm so sorry.' There is glass and water all over the nice white-oak, sand-brushed kitchen floor. I bend down and start picking up the pieces of glass with my fingers and place them on my open palm.

Rósa shouts out, 'Don't!' She rushes over. 'You'll cut yourself.' She takes my hand and turns it over so the glass I'd picked up falls back to the floor. 'I'll get the vacuum.'

I know what they're thinking. It's the curse.

I know the symptoms: hallucinations, delusions, confusion, social withdrawal, lack of motivation, irrationality, false beliefs, voices in your head. I know the facts and the figures: late adolescence and early adulthood are peak periods for the onset of the curse; in forty per cent of men and twenty-three per cent of women diagnosed with the curse, the condition manifests itself before the age of nineteen. And I know the causes: they can be both genetic and environmental.

But I can do all the research in the world and be no closer to knowing whether I have it or not.

When I was expelled from Highbury College, Dad didn't say it but I know he thought it. This was it. It was starting.

Getting expelled from school was exactly the kind of trouble Mum would get into.

Mum's spontaneity, her erratic behaviour and her unpredictability was what Dad liked about her when they first met. Then it became what he feared in her. Then what he loathed about her. At least that's how Granny Jo describes it.

Rósa returns with the vacuum cleaner.

I stare at the shards of broken glass lying in a puddle of water. They look like glaciers floating on a vast sea. One precursor to the curse is clumsiness.

Rósa mops up the water with a huge bundle of kitchen towel.

Dad reaches for the radio at the end of the table and turns it on.

'Dad,' Ísabella says, in a whiny drawl. 'Can you buy me the new iPhone? Both Sandra and Guðrún have the new iPhone.'

Gabríel grabs a strawberry from the stemmed glass bowl. 'If Ísabella is having a new phone, I want a new bike.'

'Shush!' Dad snaps at them and points to the radio. It's eight o'clock and the news is starting. No one is allowed to talk when Dad is listening to the news.

A lump forms in my throat. The contrasting smells of the sweet strawberries and smoky, slightly burnt bacon are making me feel sick. I can feel a slight stinging sensation in the palm of my right hand. I open it. It's bleeding from the cut glass.

Dad turns up the radio. The noise is like a power drill to the head. 'Prime Minister Sigmundur Benediktsson has responded to recent claims that he and his family tried to hide millions in offshore accounts.' Why does Dad always have to listen to the news at the loudest volume possible?

'And on to international news,' the newsreader shouts – or that's what it feels like. 'A Russian cyberattack on the British government's Department of Health and Social Care was disrupted by UK military intelligence.'

I need to get out of here. I'm going to my room. I've turned on my heel when the newsreader falls silent. There's a short pause before he continues.

'News has just come in on the man found dead in a crevice in Hvassahraun yesterday.'

I stop in the kitchen doorway. A man was found dead in Hvassahraun? That's the lava field we drove past from the airport.

'He has been identified as forty-two-year-old Mörður Þórðarson.'

'No way!' Alda shouts out. 'I know him. He works at the university. He has his own lab called DataPsych or something tacky like that.'

'Shush,' Dad says.

The newsreader goes on. 'He lived in Reykjavík and leaves a wife and two young children. The police are treating the death as suspicious.' Another pause. 'And now to the weather.'

I return to the kitchen table and take a seat. *It has to be murder, right?* What other kind of death could be considered suspicious?

The smell of burnt bacon and volume of the radio don't bother me any more. I hardly notice Alda's excessive chewing on her nicotine gum. I ignore the bickering of the twins. As if reading a whodunit, I distract myself from my own worries by connecting the dots, trying to get to the truth; I pave over my own misery with someone else's.

Photo: An empty whisky tumbler standing on a worn tabletop.
Filter: Gingham.

Caption: When life gives you lemons . . . you order a whisky sour.

❤937

What the caption should have been . . .

Option one: My first Instagram post ever was of a pint I was having in the Union Bar at Cambridge. The beer was lukewarm and the table I was sitting at with a group of freshers was old and wobbly. But still, everything felt as fresh as a leaf in spring.

I only had twenty followers on Instagram, but seconds after I posted the photo I got my first Instagram like. As the little red heart lit up with a notification I felt my own heart flutter. I was being seen. I was being heard. The acknowledgement seemed to enhance the moment. It gave it significance. It made it more real somehow. After my first fix of Instagram love I was hooked.

Option two: Am I addicted to the validation of strangers?

Option three: Or do I do this for the money?

Chapter Six

Imogen

The closer Imogen gets to the bottom of her whisky sour, the more convinced she is that her decision is the right one. She's just going to delete the email and pretend she never received it. It's not her problem. No one came to her rescue when she was the target. Why should she risk everything for people she doesn't even know?

Imogen is sitting at a wobbly table in Freud, a cocktail bar in a dark concrete cellar below the pavement of Shaftesbury Avenue, ignoring the sunshine outside and waiting for Callum to arrive. She nearly cancelled the date, but decided instead to arrive early and get a couple of drinks in her beforehand for courage, and to forget about the awful day she had at work.

Ms Kendrick had come to find her after the meeting.

'Into my office, now.' No sooner had Imogen closed the door than Ms Kendrick had started shouting. 'What the hell was that?'

Imogen mumbled something about suddenly feeling unwell. 'It must have been something I ate,' she said.

'You'd better not be pregnant,' Ms Kendrick snapped.

Imogen was shocked. Who did she think she was? Her mother? Was it even legal for her to say that to an employee?

Imogen didn't answer. She wasn't pregnant – of that she was sure. But the status of her uterus was none of her boss's business.

The awkward silence was finally broken by Ms Kendrick.

'This better not happen again,' she said and sent Imogen back to her desk.

Mark had come to her later during the day.

'Don't worry about the meeting,' he'd said with a casual shrug. 'We all choke from time to time. Those guys were jerks.'

But Imogen did worry. She couldn't lose her job. This job was everything to her. It was what made her get up in the mornings. This job was real, unlike her influencer career which always felt pretend, somehow. This job was what her self-worth rested on. It gave her self-respect. When she put on work-clothes – a shirt and maybe a blazer – and walked into the office she felt dignified. When she stood up in a meeting and – unlike today – gave a good presentation, she sometimes even thought: *Maybe he's wrong; maybe I'm not a stupid, worthless, good-for-nothing slut.*

Imogen takes a photo of her almost empty glass standing on a worn wooden table. The black paint is flaking off. The photo looks good. Arty. She opens Instagram and posts it with the caption: 'When life gives you lemons . . . you order a whisky sour.'

She scrolls through her Instagram photos. There are photos of her posing in various outfits, wearing accessories she has been paid to promote, holding books she hasn't read, pointing at pretty food in a restaurant she didn't order and lots of photos of her with her housemates. The earlier snaps are more playful. Trees, flowers, a photo of her wellies covered in mud. Those are the ones she posted for fun – not money.

As Imogen skims through a filtered version of her life over the past couple of years, she comes across a photo of her posing outside the offices of London Analytica. Anna took it on her first day of work. Imogen remembers how excited she was – she hadn't been this happy since she left uni. She knows her happiness was genuine. The photo reflects it. Even though no one else sees it, Imogen can tell her real smile from her fake one.

Imogen glances at her watch. It's seven o'clock. She looks up and sees Callum walk through the door of the bar.

Imogen has only ever seen him in his gym clothes, all sweaty and frazzled. She wasn't sure what to expect but he looks good. His chestnut hair is combed back and his face is shaven. He's wearing light-green chinos, brown suede loafers and a white Ralph Lauren Polo shirt. Maybe he is Imogen's type after all.

But then she sees the tribal sleeve tattoo peek from underneath the shirt and she remembers the epic dragon tattoo that covers the whole of his right leg. And she remembers that he only works as a bartender and he never went to uni and he probably didn't manage a single A-level and . . . *Stop it, Imogen.* She hates when she does that, when she turns into her mother: snobby and judgemental.

Callum sees her. He smiles. He's got a beautiful smile. His teeth are very white. Perhaps slightly too white, like *Love Island* white. *Stop it, Imogen.*

Imogen gets up from the table. She always hates this part of a date: the hello. Do you go for a hug or a peck on the cheek? And if it is a peck on the cheek, is it a single or a double?

The panic rises within her as she watches Callum approach the table. He's almost there. What's she going to do? *Hug? Peck? Hug? Peck?*

She can't move; she's completely frozen with indecision.

'How are you?' Callum says and puts one hand on her shoulder.

It has to be a peck. If he were going for a hug, surely he would take her by the shoulders with both hands, wouldn't he? She leans in, pouts and aims for his right cheek.

Somehow, she finds herself facing him. What is he doing? Is he going for her left cheek? Who starts with the left cheek? It's like shaking someone's left hand. It just isn't done.

They end up smashing their faces together, giving each other a clumsy peck on the corner of the mouth.

Shit. That was the worst hello in the history of humanity. Imogen feels her cheeks go red. Callum blushes a little too.

'So,' he says, quickly shaking off the embarrassment with a clap of his hands. 'What can I get you? I've heard they make a mean daiquiri here.'

Imogen looks down at her glass. It's almost empty. That means she's already had two cocktails. She shouldn't have any more. But then she remembers the day she's had.

'A daiquiri sounds great.'

Imogen inspects Callum from behind as he stands at the bar waiting to be served. It might just be the two whisky sours but he is absolutely gorgeous. He's tall, confident and broad-shouldered – well, he should be considering all the shoulder presses she's seen him do at the gym.

Callum turns around. He's holding a cocktail glass in each hand and a bag of crisps between his teeth.

Whisky or no whisky, he *is* gorgeous. Imogen is still wearing the sweaty shirt she had on at work. She wishes she'd had time to change.

Callum manages to transport the drinks to the table without spillage. He places one of the glasses in front of Imogen. The drink is yellow and has a citrusy smell. Imogen has no idea what's in a daiquiri – and she doesn't care. Alcohol is alcohol, and with every sip of it she draws further away from her awful day had into a mist of indifference.

'Nice to see you outside of the gym,' Callum says and sits down opposite her.

'And you,' Imogen replies. 'Cheers.' She lifts her glass and takes a sip. The cocktail is both sweet and sour and the alcohol, which she guesses is rum, burns her throat. Heat travels from her mouth to her soul.

'So, Callum.' She relaxes in her chair. She hopes he doesn't notice, but this is big for her. This is her first date since things went down with the Beast. She takes another sip of the daiquiri. She's happy she didn't cancel. 'Tell me something about yourself. Other than the fact that you like going to the gym, I know nothing about you.'

Callum smiles such a gorgeous smile that the room lights up – or maybe it's his teeth. *Stop it.*

'I grew up in Reading. I'm an only child. My mum's a music teacher. My dad is a software developer. I moved to London two years ago.'

'After your GCSEs?'

'No.'

'A-levels?'

'No. After uni.'

So he did go to uni.

'I did a creative arts degree at Bath Spa. I have a small studio in Hackney. I sell paintings at pop-up art fairs. It doesn't pay the bills. Hence the job as a bartender and the gig at the tattoo shop.'

Imogen leans back in her seat and stares at him. 'How old are you?'

'I'm twenty-three. How old are you?'

'Nineteen.'

'I thought you were older.'

'Oh, great, thanks.'

'I mean in a good way.' Callum starts blushing again. 'You seem so . . .' He stops to consider his words. He seems to realise he's in a tight spot. 'I don't know . . . Wise.'

'Wise!'

'Okay, wise is perhaps not the right word. Independent. Sure of yourself. Like you know what you're doing, where you're going. Am I making any sense?'

Imogen bursts out laughing. 'Well, thank you for the compliment. I'll take it. And here's one for you: You don't look a day older than twenty-one.'

'Ouch. And here was I going for my best mature grown-man look.'

'Well, I guess we're even then.'

Callum leans on the table. Imogen loves the mischievous glint in his brown eyes – he looks like someone who doesn't take things too seriously. That's just what she needs.

'So, what about you?' he says. 'You said something about taking a break from Cambridge.'

Was that what she'd called it at some point? She can't remember all the stories she's told. She has learned that the main reason you shouldn't lie is that lies are hard to keep track of.

'I studied psychological and behavioural science for a year. I loved it. But one of my professors recommended me for a job with a seriously innovative company here in London. It was an opportunity I couldn't turn down.' She hopes she sounds convincing. It isn't the truth – but it's close enough.

'Wow. Sounds exciting. And what does the company do?'

'It's a marketing agency.'

Callum raises his eyebrows. 'Oh, I thought you said it had something to do with innovation.'

A surge of irritation puts Imogen off balance. 'On the face of it London Analytica is just a marketing company,' she snaps. She doesn't mean to sound so defensive about her job but old habits die hard. 'But what we're actually doing is ground-breaking in the field of psychology, in the field of data analysis, in the field of computer science . . .'

Her words fade out. Who is she trying to convince: Callum or herself? Maybe her mum.

She grabs her drink and takes a sip. It soothes her. She smiles at Callum.

'What we do is use data enhancement and audience segmentation techniques to provide companies with psychographic analysis of potential customers.'

Callum closes his eyes and rubs his temples theatrically as if he has a headache. 'You use what to what?'

He's cute *and* funny.

Imogen gives out what's meant to be a flirtatious laugh but she fears sounds more like a pig's snort. 'It sounds more complicated than it is. Say you have a company that sells – I don't know – frozen fish fingers.' She should have thought of a different example. The idea of fish fingers makes her go cold after today's meeting. 'Not every person on the planet is your audience. Most likely the company operates in a certain area, let's say the UK. Not everyone there is likely to buy frozen fish fingers so you need to narrow down your market.

'Who buys fish fingers? Busy mums for their kids. Single men who don't know how to cook. But you're still left with a huge number of people. At London Analytica we use psychological profiling to identify who your potential clients are – who's likely to buy your product. But not only that. We help you target these individuals with tailor-made messages.'

'What do you mean, tailor-made messages?'

'People who look similar on the surface often want and respond to completely different things. And people who might look totally different on the surface are deep down driven by the same needs and want the same things. We go beneath the surface and learn what people really care about. You could say that we map out people's identities so companies can navigate their personalities better.'

'All this work, for what? In order to sell them stuff.'

'Yes!' Imogen replies enthusiastically, only registering Callum's cynical tone of voice after her exclamation.

'So, you identify people's weak spots, their hopes and dreams and fears, to use against them to sell them things.'

Just shit all over my life, why don't you?

'We call it behavioural microtargeting,' Imogen says, hoping that giving what she does at work a scientific-sounding label will restore some of her self-dignity.

Callum has touched a nerve. How did she end up doing this for a living? She thought she knew:

- *He* got her the interview.
- She was offered the job.
- She couldn't say no.

But she has wondered lately whether she jumped or was pushed. He'd made it sound like he was doing her a favour. But did she ever have a choice?

Callum is sitting opposite her in petulant silence. She needs to change the subject.

'Did you know that research shows that memories aren't stored in your brain like books in a library, but each time you recall a memory the brain rebuilds it?' She'd only read it this morning.

Callum forces a smile. He's trying to look interested but he clearly isn't. This date is so dead.

'So memories can change with every recollection; the act of remembering can be influenced by various things: knowledge, beliefs, goals, mental state, emotions, the people around you, your surroundings, your imagination ...' She's babbling. *Shut up, Imogen.*

Callum is gulping down his drink.

Imogen looks down at the table. The cracks in the paint look like hidden canyons in a landscape. *Did she jump or was she pushed?* Memories are unreliable. But recently she's been leaning towards pushed.

Callum puts down his empty glass. 'Fascinating,' he says, even though his sunken pout clearly indicates he does not think it's fascinating at all.

Imogen doesn't really care. She has other things on her mind. What is she doing with her life? She went into psychology because she wanted to help people. Now it's her job to hurt them.

How can they even consider doing that? Can't they see how wrong that is?

The email. She'd told herself she would delete it. She'd told herself she'd forget about it. But she just can't stop thinking about what it said.

It should have come as no surprise that the Beast was emailing Ms Kendrick. It was, after all, the Beast who'd got Imogen the job interview with London Analytica. She knew he was collaborating with them on a regular basis.

When Imogen started uni, she hadn't even heard of psychometrics, the data-driven, sub-branch of psychology. But Imogen became fascinated with the idea that by analysing big data she could get to know a person better than that person knew themselves. Even though she'd only just started the course she'd decided that she was going to do her thesis on psychometrics.

The Beast had been so supportive. He'd offered to become her supervisor. He'd involved her in his research, looking for new, more efficient ways to analyse the massive amounts of data he'd gained access to.

Everything people did, both on and offline, left a digital trace. Every purchase they made with their debit and credit cards, every search they typed into *Google*, every movement they made when their mobile phone was in their pocket, every 'like' on Facebook was stored. It was their job, his and hers, to connect the dots, draw deductions.

One day, after class, the Beast told her about this start-up in London's Shoreditch he was working with. They wanted to offer data-driven marketing based on his models. He asked her if she wanted to assist him in setting it up.

She'd been so flattered. There she was, only just starting uni and she'd already found her place in the world. She'd thought she was so smart. So capable. So grown-up. But what she'd been was smug. How arrogant of her to think she was something special; how naive of her to think that she was anything other than a silly girl with no work experience, no qualifications, no special knowledge.

Callum reaches out his hand and places it on Imogen's. 'I'm sorry. I didn't mean to insult your job or anything. It's just that I don't support things like that.'

The distaste with which Callum delivers the apology makes it sound more like a non-apology. 'Things like what?'

'You know: marketing, branding – just consumerism in general.'

Imogen tries not to laugh. Says the guy in the Ralph Lauren Polo shirt which cost ten times more than a regular polo shirt just because of branding.

He goes on. 'Marketing is all about making people feel bad about themselves. Then some company can swoop in and make some money from selling you something that is meant to fix you – even if you're not broken.'

Imogen's stomach turns. She thinks she might throw up. She's had too much to drink. But it's not just that.

What the Beast proposed in the email. It wasn't just marketing. It was dangerous. Someone could get killed.

Imogen replied to the email with three words: 'The wrong Imogen.' He didn't reply. Imogen assumed he'd send the email again to the right Imogen: Ms Kendrick. She got her confirmation just before the end of work when Ms Kendrick called Imogen into her office for the second time that day.

'I need you to do a stint abroad. We've got a new project. Slimline.'

Imogen nearly screamed with excitement. She'd always wanted to travel for work.

'I need you to go to Iceland for a couple of months and work with our big-data psychologist.' She stopped. 'Oh, of course you know him. Mörður taught you at Cambridge, didn't he?'

Imogen went from ecstasy to sheer terror in a fraction of a second. This wasn't happening. This couldn't be happening. The fear shot through her like poison squirting from her heart through her veins – burning, blistering, tearing her to shreds.

'I can't.' She couldn't see him again. She'd thought she would never have to see him again. She had to get out of this.

Ms Kendrick narrowed her eyes. She looked angry, almost feral, with her thick-rimmed, cat-eye glasses dwarfing her narrow face.

'It's my mum,' Imogen lied. 'She's sick. I need to be here for her.'

Ms Kendrick appeared to believe her. At least she let her off the hook.

Imogen had managed to hold it together in front of her boss but as soon as she stepped out of her office it all came crashing down. The world around her seemed to evaporate. Imogen was transported back in time to the place of her nightmares. She felt the hand grab her waist and push her up against a hard concrete wall. It wasn't a real hand, just a memory, but the effect it had on her was as real as anything. Her heart was racing, the blood was pounding in her ears as she sensed the hand slip underneath her top and slide up the side of her body, over her ribcage, towards her left breast. There was a pinch. Imogen screamed out. *Shut up – someone might hear.* She couldn't move. She couldn't breathe—

'I'm going to get another drink.' Callum is getting up from the table. 'Would you like one?'

Drink. She needs a drink. 'Yes, please.'

'What are you having?'

'Anything.'

Imogen watches Callum squeeze through the crowd lining the bar.

A sudden anger rises inside her. She's mad at herself. She should just forget about everything. Look at her – here she is, living in London, one of the greatest cities in the world, on a date with a cute guy, with a job all her friends envy, a wardrobe full of expensive clothes, a make-up bag with all the latest cosmetics and a million adoring fans on Instagram – she has it all.

Except she doesn't. The two photos she tries to post on Instagram a day feel like a noose around her neck. She gets anxious just thinking about how to pose, what to wear and what image to project. Even writing the caption makes her want to crawl into a dark hole and never come out. Even though she lives in a house with three other people, she has never felt as alone in her life. She used to know where she was going, she had goals; she was going to finish her studies, then go into clinical psychology, become a counsellor or even go into research. But now she has no path to tread, no plans, no direction. She just lives one day to the next without a hint of purpose.

The one thing she did like, however, was her job. Until today. Even that is a part of a reality someone else constructed for her. Reading the email that morning, she realised that even her job isn't what she wants to be doing. What they're asking of her . . . she doesn't even have words to describe how repulsed she is.

The Beast broke her. He used her youth, inexperience and her insecurities to lure her into a trap and then he ruined her. And now he is about to use the same manipulative tactics to ruin the lives of thousands of girls all over the UK, all over the world, with the help of London Analytica – and Imogen.

The Beast needs to be stopped.

She's got an idea. The muscles in her thighs contract as she prepares to get up. But then she changes her mind. She can't. Facing him would be like tearing off her skin as her soul was smothered to death.

Imogen notices a guy standing in the queue for the bar. He's looking at her. As a reflex, she smiles politely. The guy suddenly puts one finger in his mouth and slowly pulls it back out. Then he winks at her.

Imogen feels like she's about to throw up.

The Beast doesn't only need to be stopped. He needs to be punished. The consequences for what he did have to be harsh – and permanent. He should never be allowed to ruin anyone again like he's ruined Imogen.

She gets up. Her movements are brusque as she grabs her bag from the floor and tugs her coat free from the back of her chair where it has got tangled.

She can see Callum standing at the bar, waiting to be served. She doesn't say goodbye.

As Imogen climbs the steps from the dark basement bar into the bright, busy London street she's light with relief. She's going to remember this moment. This is it. This is either the beginning of the rest of her life. Or: the beginning of the end.

Photo: A fresh notebook sits on top of a snow-white table next to a ballpoint pen.
Filter: Moon

Possible captions . . .

Option one: My first day at the office **#myfabulouslife #dreamjob #news #journalism #ontopoftheworld**
Option two: I woke up this morning thinking there was one thing in life I was good at. It turns out the number is zero.
Option three: What happened next? You can read all about it in tomorrow's paper.

Actual caption . . .

Tabula rasa.

♥13

Chapter Seven

Hannah

I scan my notes on Imogen Collins in the car on the way to the office. This is the first day at my first real job and I'm so nervous I think I might throw up all the eggs, bacon and waffles loaded with jam and whipped cream I had at my welcome breakfast party. I shouldn't have eaten so much but it was just so good.

'You shouldn't read in the car,' Dad says. 'It'll make you carsick.'

Yes, well, he should have left me more time to prepare for the interview rather than springing it on me less then twenty-four hours ago.

I don't say anything though. I don't want him to think I'm not qualified for the job. Journalism is all about being quick, about fast turnarounds. News is only news for about five minutes – after five minutes people move on to something else: a new scandal, a different celebrity's cellulite, a new tragedy, a new murder. (Was it murder?)

I turn my notes over to the profile of Imogen Collins I created before bed last night:

Imogen Collins. A social media influencer with more than a million followers on Instagram. Age: nineteen. Birthday: 29

November. Grew up in Cambridgeshire. Has a younger sister. Mum is a GP. Dad is an accountant. She went to an all-girls school in Cambridge city centre and then did a year at the University of Cambridge, before putting her studies on hold after being offered a job with an up-and-coming start-up in London – a boutique marketing agency offering services based on the latest scientific research in the field of data-driven psychology and artificial neural networks . . .

Whatever that is. It sounds like one of those farcically pseudo-scientific facial cream ads: inspired by DNA technology.

I tried to figure out why Imogen Collins became internet famous. What is her brand look? What is her message?

Every article on the internet advising people on how to become a social media influencer says you need a niche, a brand. You can choose between things like fashion, make-up, books, furniture, travel and self-improvement. Imogen, however, seems to include it all.

There's a photo of her posing in a beautiful white maxi-dress, clearly made for a summer holiday on a beach somewhere, on a grey London street; there's a photo of her smiling in a restaurant making a pair of frogs' legs smothered in butter and garlic do ballet; there's a photo of her putting on make-up; there's a photo of a book on top of a nightstand; there's a photo of a beautifully crafted walnut dressing table; there's a photo of a sunset with a quote written on it: *Twenty years from now you will be more disappointed by the things you didn't do than by the things you did* – Mark Twain; there's a photo of an apple pie with another quote: *If you want to make an apple pie from scratch, you must first create the universe* – Carl Sagan.

She chooses filters at random. She's breaking every rule of social media success. The one common theme is the captions. They're snarky, sarcastic. Reading them almost makes me like her.

Googling Imogen Collins last night, I found two mentions of her in the mainstream media. She appeared in a listicle a couple of years ago in *The Times* titled 'The Top Ten Influencers to Watch' and in an article in the *Guardian* titled 'Social Media and the Death of Creativity'. In the latter, Imogen is quoted as saying: 'I don't think social media poses an inherent danger to creativity. Like everything else, it's about quantity. Too much of anything is bad for you. If you eat too much broccoli, I bet it can kill you.'

There was an interview with her in *Varsity*, the University of Cambridge student newspaper. The reason for the interview was the fact that she had the most Instagram followers of all the students in the school. She didn't make much of it. 'I do it for fun,' she said. 'I have no aspirations to become a social media phenomenon. If anything, I try to convey with my posts the absurdities of social media, the fakery that characterises that world. My posts should be viewed as parodies.'

Her influencer status was a total accident. I start to hate her again. She looks like a person who gets everything handed to her on a silver platter.

I barely feel my phone buzz in my pocket. I'm wearing Rósa's woollen cape from MaxMara. It's minus seven degrees Celsius outside and she made me put it on over my leather jacket. The fabric is so thick it almost completely absorbs the shock from the vibrations.

I take out my phone. It's Daisy. I had called her last night to fill her in on my first night in hell, and about the Imogen article. Daisy is a sucker for social media and knew exactly who I was talking about and wanted to help me with my research.

D: Morning.

H: Hi!

D: Did you see this?

It's a link to a Twitter thread. I click on it:

Julius Thornton @j_thorn

Just heard that if you sleep with your professor you can get a job with a fancy start-up in London. So much for meritocracy. @Cambridge_Uni.

Oliver B. Johnson @ollie_the_awesome

Who's the cow? @j_thorn

Alexa Sanders @alexa_02

What makes you think it's a woman? @ollie_the_awesome

Oliver B. Johnson @ollie_the_awesome

It always is.

Julius Thornton @j_thorn

@ollie_the_awesome It's a certain socia media sensation with a massive cleavage and a voluptuous butt. Fingers on buzzers.

Alexa Sanders @alexa_02
@j_thorn @ollie_the_awesome Do you realise how offensive
you're being?

A.C. Robinson @acrobinson
@j_thorn 'A voluptuous butt'. Glad to see that your daddy is
getting his money's worth paying for your English lit studies.
Man Booker Prize, take note.

Julius Thornton @j_thorn
Fuck you.

A.C. Robinson @acrobinson
And the eloquence continues.

Oliver B. Johnson @ollie_the_awesome
Back to the cow: Is it @susanna_shines?

Julius Thornton @j_thorn
Guess again.

Oliver B. Johnson @ollie_the_awesome
Is it Theresa Reid?

Julius Thornton @j_thorn
Guess again.

Oliver B. Johnson @ollie_the_awesome
Is it Imogen Collins?

Julius Thornton @j_thorn
We have a winner.

Alexa Sanders @alexa_02
I thought she quit school after failing her exams.

A.C. Robinson @acrobinson
I heard a rumour about her sleeping with numerous teachers
and then being expelled.

Oliver B. Johnson @ollie_the_awesome
I always knew she was a slut.

Wow. The cruelty of the internet never ceases to amaze me. Do
people not realise that people can see them? Do they not realise that
people who read their words judge them as if they were saying these
horrible things out loud? Why do people not think of the internet
as part of the real world? Why do they approach it as some sort of
safe space for being a dick? I start to feel sorry for Imogen Collins.
But I also feel curiosity tickling at my core. What happened there?

My phone buzzes.

D: I bet none of it is true. You know how rumours can spread
like wildfire on the internet.
H: You're probably right – good research though!

Or is she right? Imogen Collins seems so squeaky clean on
the surface. But I guess it's hard to see the truth through what
Imogen herself has called 'the fakery' on social media.

The car has stopped. We're parked in front of the headquarters of *Dagblaðið* but it feels like we're in the middle of nowhere. The paper's offices are in a huge building situated on a deserted moor on the outskirts of Reykjavík.

The building is constructed out of what looks like huge concrete Lego blocks and glass. The blocks are in various shades of green – sage, mint, emerald – and grey. During the summer the building disappears into the subdued colours of the surrounding grass, moss, shrubs, and low-growing vegetation. But during wintertime, when a blanket of snow rests over the dormant nature underneath, the building stands out as a reminder of the seasons to come.

'Ready?' Dad asks, which I think is rather sweet and unusually sensitive of him. Maybe he does care about my wellbeing.

It turns out, however, that I'm reading too much into things.

'Do you really need to wear your Dr. Martens to the office? It's important to look the part and more professional-looking shoes would be preferable.'

That's the dad I know and . . .

I open the car door. My whole body stiffens as I'm attacked by freezing cold wind. The wind in Iceland has a strange suffocating quality to it. When it hits your nose and your mouth, it feels like someone has thrown a whole bucket of ice water right in your face with the force of a jet engine. You lose your breath. There are more than one hundred different words to describe wind in Icelandic. The same goes for snow.

Dad and I run towards the glass entrance of the building. The sliding doors open quickly, then close again. We both sigh with relief to be indoors.

A woman is sitting in the reception inside a round booth-like desk reminiscent of a spaceship. 'Morning, Eiríkur.'

In Iceland people go by their first name. No one is addressed by their surname. Even the president is just Guðni and not Mr Jóhannesson.

'Morning, Sigríður,' Dad says without reciprocating the smile. We walk past the woman, mount the stairs and reach a vast open-plan office. As far as the eye can see there are desks with wooden tabletops and steel legs that can be adjusted according to height. It's like a factory floor but instead of an assembly line there are people typing away at desktops.

Dad strides towards his office. I follow him. No one pays us the slightest bit of attention.

'We'd usually start the day with an editorial meeting at nine where the content for tomorrow's paper is decided and I hand out assignments,' Dad says without turning around. 'My deputy handled it today because we were so late. But you will attend the meeting tomorrow.'

'Wearing the right professional-looking footwear,' I add as a joke but Dad doesn't laugh.

Dad's been the editor of *Dagblaðið*, an old-fashioned printed newspaper, and its only slightly more modern website, Dagbladid.is, for twelve years. I won't be writing for either. I've been hired as the second staff writer for its newly launched English-language website, *IceNews*. It's mostly aimed at tourists as well as the growing number of immigrants living in the country.

We're about to step into Dad's office when I think I hear someone calling out my name. I turn around.

'Hannah!'

I suddenly see a hand shoot up, out from the desert of journalists. A head follows. It's a man. No, a boy. No, a man. His dirty blond hair is slightly messy and styled in a quiff. He's got on glasses with thick, square rims and he's sporting exceptionally well-trimmed stubble.

He's walking towards me. I have no idea who he is.

'Long time no see!'

I just stare.

The man-boy smiles.

'It's me. Kjarri. Don't you recognise me?'

'Oh, my God.' It's Kjartan. Kjartan Tómasson. 'I haven't seen you in . . . what? Ten years?'

'Eight. We moved out of Fossvogur eight years ago.'

Kjartan, or Kjarri for short, used to be my best friend in Iceland when I was growing up and was forced to spend two months every summer with Dad. Kjarri lived next door to Dad and Rósa with his mum and dad and little sister. He made the summers in Iceland bearable. But one time when I arrived at Dad's, Kjarri and his family had moved away. I asked Dad to help me track him down. Dad said he would when he had the time, which turned out to be never.

'Wow.' I can't help it. I look Kjarri up and down. He's changed.

His hair used to be blonder. And so unruly. I remember his mum complaining about never being allowed to cut it. He used to be short – shorter than me – but now he's as tall as a tree. His teeth always appeared slightly too big for his mouth but now they fit perfectly. His eyes are still the same: blue woven with strands

91

of grey like playful waves ruffling the surface of the otherwise perfectly still sea on a sunny day. His cheeky smile is still there too. We used to get up to mischief when we were kids: we put spiders through the neighbours' letterboxes; we took the bus down town without letting anyone know, so once Kjarri's mum had to call the police – she was convinced we'd been abducted.

The recipe for cherry pie pops into my head. I used to make it for Mum – she loved pie, but it was also a reference to her favourite TV show of all time, *Twin Peaks*. As you make the pie – clumsily pit the cherries; battle the dough, which keeps sticking to the rolling pin; carefully place it in the pan but still it breaks apart – the ingredients look like they're going to result in a parody of a pie, at best. But then, after fifty minutes in the oven, when the crust is golden brown and crumbly, when the sweet juice from the cherries is bursting through the cracks in the pie lid, by some kind of miracle everything comes together the way it's meant to. Kjarri is all grown up, like a pie that has come out of the oven just right.

I've been staring so intently at Kjarri for so long I start to blush. I have to say something before things become too awkward. 'What are you doing here?' I stutter.

His smile bursts with enthusiasm. *Just like a cherry pie*. 'I work here.'

'You do?'

'Your dad is so awesome.'

He is?

'I did a year at Menntaskólinn í Reykjavík—'

'Hey, that's the school I'll be going to!' Menntaskólinn í Reykjavík, or MR, is the junior college both Dad and Grandpa

Bjarni went to. It was established in the year 1056 and Dad says it's the best school in the country. I'm dreading it, but I do want to finish my A-levels.

'I liked the school but I kind of needed a break from studying. I ran into your dad a few months ago and he told me that *Dagblaðið* were setting up an English-language news site and were looking for a staff writer. I lived in the States for a few years after we moved out of Fossvogur – Mum did a master's degree in finance in Boston – so I speak English fluently. I suspect that's the only reason I got the job. It's been a learning curve but I think I'm getting the hang of it.'

Kjarri grins at Dad, who's standing in the door of his office typing on his phone. 'Right, boss?'

Dad not listening to anyone doesn't seem to bother Kjarri like it bothers me. He continues talking to me.

'I sometimes contribute articles and interviews to the paper as well. Mostly things for the lifestyle section. That's why we'll be doing the interview with Imogen Collins together.'

'Together?'

'Yes, didn't your dad tell you? We'll conduct the interview together. I'll be writing one up in Icelandic for the paper and Dagbladid.is, and you'll be writing one in English for IceNews.is.'

I feel both relief and frustration. Does Dad not trust me with this? Does he think I need handholding? But this turn of events also means I can stop worrying. This is my first assignment and it is pretty big. If I mess it up, someone will be able to pick up the pieces.

Kjarri glances at a huge, round clock hanging on an exposed concrete wall at the back of the newsroom. 'Imogen will be here in an hour. Shall I quickly show you around and then we can go to the cafeteria, grab some coffee and prepare a few questions for the interview?'

I look at Dad, who has disappeared into his office. He's sitting at his desk, talking on the phone through a headset and typing on his computer. He has disappeared into his own world again. I wonder whether he even remembers that I'm here.

I turn back to Kjarri. I'm so grateful that he's here – a raft in the middle of a sea of cripplingly cold indifference and paralysing uncertainty – I almost jump on him and wrap my arms around him to keep myself afloat. Thankfully, I manage to restrain myself. I'm sure I will provide him with plenty of reasons to doubt my sanity in the future – there's no need to jump the gun. So, I simply shrug and reply as casually as my limited acting abilities allow. 'Sure. Sounds cool.'

It's an Oscar-worthy performance.

We're sitting inside the meeting room waiting for Imogen Collins to arrive. Three of the walls are stone-grey concrete, and the fourth wall is glass from floor to ceiling. I feel like Kjarri and I are actors playing journalists on a stage and the people walking past in the long hallway outside are the audience.

'I heard about your mum,' he suddenly says. 'I'm sorry.'

Before I can say anything, his mobile, which is sitting on top of the round meeting room table, buzzes. He jumps up from his chair.

'She's here. I'll go down to the lobby and get her.'

I wait for a good few minutes before I see him, along with our interviewee, appear again at the end of the hallway. They make their way leisurely towards the meeting room. She is saying something. He is laughing. For some reason I am fuming. *Don't rush on my account.*

Even before they're close enough for me to see Imogen's features properly I recognise her radiating beauty. Her legs are long, her waist is tiny, her hair is voluminous and she moves with the elegant softness of the tide on a sunny Mediterranean beach. I instantly dislike her.

As they walk in I can tell Kjarri is at the end of a story that is meant to impress as well as entertain. 'I'd barely played a note on the guitar when the stage tipped and I fell off it straight into a pile of cow dung below.'

Kjarri is speaking to her in English with a thick American accent. It's cute.

But Imogen doesn't laugh. Instead, she glances over her shoulder. Kjarri's cheeks go slightly red, two half suns reaching up from the edges of his stubble.

I get up from my chair. Proximity does not diminish Imogen Collins's beauty. Quite the contrary. She's wearing a leather pencil skirt and a simple nude cami under a white blazer. Her elegance is understated yet overpowering. Her cheekbones are higher than Everest. Her brown eyes have an emerald tinge to them. Her dark hair is so shiny I'm tempted to touch it as I reach out my hand to greet her.

'Hi. I'm Hannah.'

She doesn't shake my hand. She just turns back to stare through the glass out into the hallway where a man is standing looking down at his phone.

'Who's that man? What's he doing here? Did he follow us up the stairs?'

The man is wearing a checked shirt that is tucked into loose-hanging jeans.

'I can't have people following me around in here. I thought this was a safe building. This is not acceptable.'

What's her problem? The man might look a bit scruffy but this is a newspaper office – scruffy is the universal uniform of journalists.

I glance at Kjarri. The playfulness on his face has been replaced by sweaty embarrassment.

'Erm . . . I don't – I don't—'

I suddenly remember: When we were kids Kjarri used to stutter when he was nervous.

'I don't think he followed us up here,' he manages on his third try.

I suddenly feel all protective of him. Who does this Imogen think she is? Does she think the man in the hall is some crazy fan of hers? He doesn't look it. She might be internet famous but she's not exactly real world famous. You wouldn't read about her in the *Daily Mail* alongside the Kardashians or anything.

Imogen reaches into her grey leather shoulder bag. I'm not excessively good with brands but I'm pretty sure it's a Birkin bag. She pulls out an iPhone X in rose gold. 'I think we need to call the police.'

The threat of the police shakes Kjarri out of his fumbling state. He successfully gathers himself and heads for the door. 'I'm pretty sure this guy just works here. I think he's in the ad department. Let me just ask him.'

Kjarri walks out into the hallway and exchanges a few words

with the man, who looks into the meeting room at me and Imogen, then starts walking away, towards the newsroom.

Kjarri returns. 'I was right. His name is Daði. He's actually the paper's sales executive.'

Imogen lowers the hand that's holding her phone. She draws a breath. I think she's about to apologise. I think she's about to come up with an excuse that would explain her irrational behaviour – she's tired, she's stressed – but quite the contrary.

She slams her bag on the meeting room table, pulls a chair from under it and slumps down on it with a dramatic sigh. 'I have to be somewhere in an hour. Let's get this thing over with.'

Kjarri shoots me a side look and widens his eyes.

Wow, I mouth.

Imogen Collins is everything I expected her to be: beautiful, stylish, elegant and a total cow.

Kjarri and I sit down at the table. Our handwritten notes are on there as well as a scattering of pens and a pile of fresh notebooks with Dagblaðið's logo on them.

We both take our phones out. Kjarri offered me a digital recorder while we were preparing. I turned down the offer. I already have a recording app on my phone from my work at the *Highbury Gazette*.

I open the app, press record and place the phone on the table. I reach for a fresh notebook and a pen.

'Thank you for taking the time to meet with us,' Kjarri says and puts his phone down next to mine. The stutter is gone. He's himself again. 'It's a pleasure to—'

'I really don't have much time,' Imogen snaps.

Kjarri's face crumples slightly but he manages to stay calm. 'So, the first question has to be this,' he says, his signature cheeky smile crossing his face. 'How do you like Iceland?'

I can't help but roll my eyes. Icelanders have a pathological need to ask foreigners how they like the country. I can't decide whether the question is the result of an inferiority complex of a small nation or megalomania – whoever asks the question always seems to expect a glowing review of the beautiful nature, the quaint towns, the spectacular Northern Lights and the hospitality of the inhabitants.

Imogen shrugs. 'It's nice. Quiet.'

The brief answer seems to derail Kjarri. I use his silence to take over.

'A lot of people dream of doing what you do; a lot of people want to become influencers. How did your success come about?'

'I never wanted to become an influencer.'

I wait for Imogen to elaborate, expand on her answer, but she lapses into a sulky silence.

I guess it's my go again then. I try not to let my frustration show. 'But now you have achieved success you do enjoy your social media work, right?' I feign a smile.

'It does have some perks, yes.'

Jesus! Is that it? I grind my teeth. 'Such as . . .'

'I don't know.' Her eyes wander towards her Birkin bag sitting on the shiny, white table. She points to it by lifting her chin. 'This bag, for instance. It costs more than ten thousand pounds – and there is a waiting list of people who want to buy it – but I got it for free. And no waiting. I guess you can call that a perk.'

As interview subjects go, Imogen Collins is a living nightmare. I want to quit; just put down my pen, get up and walk out of here. But of course, I can't allow myself such luxury – if for no other reason than not to give Dad yet another cause to doubt me.

Okay. Next question.

'What will your talk at the Harpa conference hall be about?'

'I guess it will have to be about how to become a successful social media influencer. Isn't that why the event is sold out? Everyone wants to be famous.'

'Do you have any advice for those who do want to become influencers?'

For the first time since the interview started Imogen actually seems to be mulling over the question. 'I think the most important part when it comes to success just generally in life is: love what you do. You can work hard on something, you can be calculated, you can make a strategy, analyse the Excel sheet, do and say the things you think people want to see and hear – but success is random. You never know where lightning will strike next. Life is about the journey – not the destination. If you love what you do you've achieved success.'

The hair on my arms starts rising. A buzz, reminiscent of the feeling you get after drinking a can of Red Bull slightly too fast, shoots through my veins all the way to my brain. I'm not only awake, I'm not only alert, I'm alive. I'm in the right place, at the right time, doing exactly what I'm meant to be doing. It's a good answer. An interesting answer. I can definitely work with that answer. I don't have to look at my notes, the next question comes to me like divine inspiration.

'Looking through your Instagram account, I don't get a strong sense of identity. I don't see a theme in your posts. What's your niche? What's the message you're trying to convey to your followers? What do you stand for? Who is Imogen Collins?'

'Identity is an illusion.'

'What do you mean by that?'

'It's a fictional construct. At least in the wider sense.' Imogen pouts as she contemplates her words. Her cheeks are starting to colour and her face is softening. Her stare is less intense. It looks like she's beginning to relax.

'Say I reach for my phone, right here, right now, and take a selfie. That's me at a moment in time. Say I write a song, or a poem. That's me, my thoughts, my emotions, at a moment in time. Five minutes later I'm not the same person. We're in flux, constantly changing, for the better, for the worse and sometimes neither. The truest thing I can offer my followers is this flux.'

Kjarri raises his pen, trying to squeeze in a question. 'Imogen, if I could just ask you—'

But I don't let him. Every good journalist should be able to recognise when a conversation is on a roll, when it's going somewhere. You don't interrupt an interview with some random pre-planned question when it's flowing so naturally towards a clearly enigmatic destination.

'I get the sense that you are conflicted about your status as an influencer. Are you apprehensive about the ever-increasing power of social media in our society?'

'Not really. I think it's narrow-minded to dismiss social media as something solely destructive. Some people always fear novelty. Once, the novel was considered to corrupt young minds. Once, the radio was bad for you, then it was the TV, then the VCR, and now it's the smartphones. There's always something.'

'But what about the cult of personality that has become a side product of applications such as Instagram? Don't you think all this self-obsession is unhealthy?'

I'm hoping to rile her up a bit. She doesn't take the bait. She doesn't take the question as it is meant: as a personal accusation.

'I don't know why that should be a problem. Almost since the beginning of man, we have relied on myths to give meaning to our lives. What people are doing in applications such as Instagram is creating a personal myth. Consuming those myths, creating them; how is that any worse than admiring a god, an actor, a writer, a philosopher – or preaching to a congregation, or writing a book for people to read?'

'So, you don't have any qualms about social media then?'

'There certainly are some unsavoury aspects to social media, some dark alleys you can go down.' Imogen is looking past me, through the glass wall out into the hallway. 'Social media can be used to manipulate people, control them, exploit them—'

Kjarri suddenly leans on the table, forcing himself into Imogen's line of vision. 'I'm sorry to interrupt, but as we don't have much time I have to ask you this: What brought you to Iceland?'

Imogen jerks back as if she'd forgotten he was there, as if he'd jumped at her from a bush as she walked along a quiet country lane.

'I'm sorry, I didn't mean to startle you.'

Imogen glances from side to side. Her eyes grow darker as her pupils dilate. 'I heard something. Did you hear something?'

Why is she so on edge?

She blinks and turns to Kjarri. 'Sorry, you were saying?'

'What – erm – what – what brought you to Iceland?'

Imogen is sitting up straight. Her face has turned stony again. 'Work.'

Silence.

'Erm . . . What type of work?'

'Marketing.'

More silence. This is excruciating.

'Erm . . . okay . . .' Kjarri is trying so hard not to panic but he is breathing heavily and he keeps stroking his stubble – clearly a nervous tic. 'You work for a company in London, don't you?'

'Yes.' Imogen glances at her wristwatch: a gold Michael Kors bracelet watch.

'Why does a London-based company need to have an employee in Iceland of all places?'

Imogen gives a sigh and looks at Kjarri with the pained expression of a toddler who has reluctantly decided to give in to a parent's constant nagging about tidying up their room and eating their broccoli.

'London Analytica is a cutting-edge company that seeks to adopt the latest technology and make use of the latest science wherever that is found in the world. In Iceland we work with one of the world's most highly revered and sought-after data psychologists and his team to provide our clients with a unique way to reach their customers.'

Imogen's monotonous sales pitch is delivered with the complete lack of conviction of someone who is reading from a piece of paper with a gun to their head.

'The good team at the DataPsych research lab does all our data analysis using algorithms they developed especially for marketing—'

'Wait!' It takes me a couple of seconds but I suddenly realise I've heard that name before. 'Did you say DataPsych?'

Imogen doesn't answer.

'Did you know Mörður Þórðarson?'

She looks down at the table and clamps her lips.

Kjarri starts stroking his stubbled chin with twice the vigour. 'I think we should stay on topic.'

It's blatantly apparent that Kjarri does not have a nose for news in the slightest. I decide to ignore his plea. 'You must have known Mörður.'

Imogen is staring at the table with such intensity she looks like she's trying to cut it in half by shooting laser beams out of her eyes. 'I'm really not here to talk about my work for London Analytica. I'm here to talk about my event tomorrow.'

'So you did know him!' I yelp triumphantly. 'Do you know how he died?'

Kjarri finally catches on. 'Are you talking about the guy who was found in Hvassahraun? That professor or whatever?'

'A lecturer,' Imogen snarls.

I can tell I've hit a nerve. She knew him. 'Do you have any idea how he died?'

'I said I'm here to talk about the event tomorrow.'

'Do you know what is happening with the investigation? Have the police spoken to you?'

Imogen looks up. She turns her fierce laser glare on me. She looks furious. 'Why would the police speak to me?' She spits out the words.

I don't allow her to put me off balance. 'I mean, speak to you and the people who worked with him. Do they know how he died? What did the staff at DataPsych think of him? Was he liked? Did he have any enemies at the office?'

Kjarri looks at me like I've lost the plot.

Imogen breathes in and then out. 'I have to leave in a few minutes,' she says with exaggerated politeness. 'Your dad wanted me to chat to you about moving from the UK to Iceland. I haven't moved here, I'll only be staying for a few months, but I can tell you a bit about the things I found the hardest when I arrived – like knowing what milk to buy, knowing which cheese is the closest to cheddar, figuring out how the buses work—'

I shake my head. 'I don't need any advice. I'm half Icelandic. I've been coming here every summer most of my life. I'm not bothered about the cheese.' She's not getting off the hook this easily. 'So if I could just ask you a little more about Mörður and DataPsych.'

'I really can't . . .'

Imogen pushes her chair back.

'No, wait!'

As she gets up she sways slightly.

'Are you okay?'

She steadies herself on the table. She grabs her bag, turns around, runs towards the door and flings it open.

I watch her waver along the hallway until she disappears down the stairs.

I'd done my research. I'd constructed an image of Imogen Collins in my head. I'd formed an opinion about her. But something doesn't add up. A piece of the puzzle is missing. Who is Imogen Collins? Influencer, social media star, natural beauty, total cow. Yes, she is all of those things. But there is more to her story. I can just feel it in my bones. Imogen Collins is a mystery to be solved.

I suddenly remember Kjarri. I look around. He is standing in the doorway. He has his back to me. His hands are buried in his hair. It's like he's pulling at it. I need to teach him a bit about journalism. Before the interview I'd been so relieved that he was going to be there to hold my hand for this first assignment. As it turns out, it's actually he who should be thankful I was there holding his.

Kjarri suddenly flips around. He's glaring at me with wide eyes. His face is burning red, making his stubble appear lighter in colour than before. His lips part. I think he's about to thank me for my good work. I imagine him saying that he's very impressed, that I'm clearly a natural, that my future obviously lies within journalism and he's going to tell my dad how well I did. How wrong I turn out to be.

His words are as sharp as needles and their sting as painful as a dog's bite.

'What. The. Hell. Was. That?'

FOUR WEEKS EARLIER
IN REYKJAVÍK

Photo: A girl wearing briefs, a thick woollen sweater and matching woollen socks is leaning close to a mirror while pouting and applying cherry-pink lipstick.
Filter: Juno.

Caption: The good people at Studio X sent me this new lipstick to try. It's the perfect shade for my new adventure. Feeling bold. **#fab #makeup #ad #instabeauty**

❤2936

What the caption should have been . . .

Option one: How do you feel when you look at this photo? Fat? Ugly? Insignificant? Does it make you feel like your life is lacking? Does it make you think: 'Why am I stuck at home drowning in dirty laundry and credit card bills when everyone else is out there having fun, meeting up with friends, drinking, dancing, smiling, hugging and having a fabulous time while wearing fabulous lipstick?'

Option two: This is how I feel when I look at this photo: Please don't notice the cellulite on my thighs. Please don't notice the three pounds I gained in the past week and a half. My hair looks frizzy. I should have used a hair straightener. Is the flesh on my right ankle bulging over the top of my sock? Should I have Botox? Should I have liposuction on those ankles? I could have the fat transferred to my boobs or my cheeks. God, that sounds disgusting. But maybe that's exactly what I need to become complete.

Chapter Eight

Imogen

Imogen is standing in front of a white door, willing herself to knock. She can see her own reflection in its high-gloss finish. Her face looks drawn and her outlines are blurry, vague, like she's barely there, like she's about to vanish from the world. She can't remember why she ever thought this was a good idea.

There's a clock on the wall behind her. Looking at its mirror image in the door's sheen, it's as if time is going backwards. They say time is the best healer. If that's true, time has been standing still for the past year of her life. Her wounds are still as raw as the day she received them. And the hurt is just as bad, if not worse. Some people talk about closure. The only thing time has given Imogen is resentment.

Imogen raises her hand, planning on tapping on the door. Instead she simply stands there with her arm raised in the air.

In the social science building on the University of Iceland campus half an hour earlier, Imogen had seen a group of students who, judging by the expressions on their faces – slightly fearful but also frantically excited – were beginning their first year at the university.

Imogen remembered that time well. Only two years earlier she'd been in their shoes: at the start of something new, dwelling in possibility.

She can't do this. Her whole body is paralysed with fear. Why did she ever think she could do this?

Facing the freshmen, Imogen had felt jealous. She wanted to shout at them: *You don't know anything*. Watching their clueless little faces, she felt ancient – like she could be their mother. They reminded her of what she was missing out on. They reminded her of what she had lost, what she'd never be able to get back.

Imogen's rage kicks her arm into action. Her eyes are watering with fear. But she's not letting him get away with it. He needs to be stopped.

The knocks are sharp and aggressive. The door opens immediately. But sometimes in life, what lies behind closed doors isn't what you expect.

The face that greets her makes her stumble backwards in shock.

Imogen had prepared herself for the hungry scowl of a man-eating lion. Instead she's got the human equivalent of a smiling kitten.

It isn't the Beast who is standing in the doorway.

Imogen forces her head to move away from the image it had expected and process what her eyes are actually seeing.

Male.

Around her age.

Hair: Blond, with darker roots, scruffy and comes down to his shoulders.

Eyes: Watery blue.

Wearing: Unbuttoned checked lumberjack shirt over a white T-shirt and jeans.

Shoes: Dr. Martens boots with laces untied.

Style: Grunge – although it feels accidental, as if the guy's shirt is genuinely washed out instead of its worn feel being part of the design; as if he'd be wearing exactly the same thing if the grunge period wasn't having a stylistic comeback with Topman selling tattered jeans and tired-looking T-shirts with photos of Kurt Cobain on them.

The guy smiles at her. He looks a bit like Kurt Cobain on all those T-shirts with his piercing blue eyes. Imogen has never been able to decide whether eyes like that epitomise deep artistic genius or simple cheekiness.

'Imogen,' the Cobain lookalike says. 'So nice to meet you.'

Imogen is confused. She's still coming to terms with reality. 'How do you know my name?'

'I'm Orri. We've been in touch via email. I helped you organise your accommodation.'

Oh my God, she must be coming across like a total idiot. Of course it is Orri.

Accommodation in Reykjavík had turned out to be in short supply during the summer because of all the tourists who descend on the city. When she mentioned this in one of her emails to the lab while they were preparing for her arrival, Orri had contacted her and told her that there was a room going at his mum's house which she sometimes let out to foreign students. It was cheap and close to the university campus. Imogen jumped on it. One less thing to organise.

'So sorry,' Imogen says and gives an apologetic laugh. 'I don't usually act like a paranoid weirdo, I promise.'

'Come in, come in,' Orri says, waving her through the door with a slight bow as if he were welcoming royalty.

Imogen steps into the lab. It's a small room with no windows, three mismatched desks with small steel storage safes underneath, three old desktops, three plasticky-looking chairs: the office equivalent of the house of the three bears. That must make Imogen Goldilocks.

'How are you settling in?' Orri asks and closes the door behind her.

Imogen is deeply grateful to him for resuming normal communication and pretending that she isn't behaving like a madwoman.

'Thank you so much for organising the room for me.'

'I hope my mother is behaving herself.'

'She's been wonderful,' Imogen says. *Wonderful and kooky.* When Imogen arrived yesterday, Sigurlína had kindly made her lunch – a smorgasbord of Icelandic delicacies: smoked lamb and flatbread, herring and rye bread. Then they'd had coffee in the back garden, where Sigurlína introduced Imogen to the invisible elves. They were living inside a stone the size of a car she'd saved from a lava field the authorities were paving over to make houses and roads.

'This will be your desk,' Orri says and points to a wobbly little thing in the corner. 'This one is mine,' he says, gesturing towards the slightly bigger one next to it. All around the computer monitor stand *Star Wars* figurines.

'Cute.'

'Well, sometimes you just need to recruit the help of an army from a galaxy far, far away to help you with your work.'

'And I guess it helps if the Force is with you.'

Orri looks at Imogen with those watery blue eyes and she feels as if she's being submerged in cold water.

Oops. Was that rude? She didn't mean to be rude. She was just trying to be funny.

Orri continues with his tour of the desks, which suddenly feels as gruelling as eating all three bowls of porridge from the story of Goldilocks.

'And this one belongs to—'

A soft clicking sound echoes from the other end of the room. Imogen shoots around as urgently as if she'd heard a gun go off.

She notices another door at the back of the room. The doorknob turns and a crack opens in the door. She can hear whispers: hushed, angry voices. There are two of them, both male, and they're speaking in English. Imogen picks out words and phrases – *this is unacceptable, you said you'd do it; I didn't realise the context; you can't back out now* – but the context eludes her. One of the men is speaking with what sounds like an Eastern European accent. The other is speaking English with an Icelandic accent. It's a voice Imogen would recognise anywhere.

Hearing it makes her feel dirty. Worthless. She suddenly feels the memory of his tongue sliding up her neck. His stubby fingers fumbling in places where they shouldn't be.

The door opens slowly, slowly. Coming here was a mistake. She's changed her mind. She doesn't want to face the past. She simply has to try harder to bury it. She's going to turn around, run out of here, go straight to the airport and back to London. Run, run, run. Run for ever, never stop running . . .

But it's too late.

There he is, standing in the doorway – the embodiment of evil, looking remarkably mundane in the yellow fluorescent lights of the lab – the Beast.

The day Imogen's life fell apart started out like any other. She didn't have classes until ten so she didn't get up until ten past nine. Her mum and dad had already left for work and her sister for school, but the kitchen still smelled of toast and coffee. She loved having the mornings to herself with only the residue of company. It was like being alone but knowing that you weren't alone. It was solitude without the danger of loneliness.

Imogen watched an episode of *Friends* on her phone while she ate a bowl of chocolate Weetabix. Then she went back upstairs to get dressed.

With the enthusiasm of a child who just got a new toy she cut the tag off a white ribbed top with floral embroidery she'd been sent earlier in the week. She'd just started getting sent free stuff to promote on her Instagram account – she'd already got three tops, a coat, a scarf and a fancy towel with her initials embroidered in the fabric – and the novelty of it was thrilling. Getting dressed in the mornings had suddenly become creative and purposeful.

Imogen had matched the shirt with cropped wide-legged blue trousers and a pair of brand-new Adidas trainers her mum had bought her as a good-luck-with-your-exams present. She put on her Coco Mademoiselle and looked at herself in the mirror. Something was missing. She grabbed a fiery-red lipstick from her nightstand and put it on. There.

She reached for her phone, opened the curtains, positioned herself in front of the mirror, turned her shoulders to the left, tilted her head to the right and took a snap. She quickly opened Instagram, chose the Clarendon filter, wrote 'In bloom' as the caption and clicked 'share'. That was how much thought she put into her Instagram posts in the beginning. When it was just a bit of fun, it was actually fun.

She grabbed her school bag from the floor, ran back down the stairs, put on her big red woollen coat, which had earned her the nickname Little Red Riding Hood, and headed off, oblivious to the existence of the Big Bad Wolf waiting for her in the woods.

It only took her ten minutes to walk to school. Her parents had persuaded her to live at home instead of on campus to save money on accommodation and expenses. It made sense – although sometimes Imogen felt she was missing out on a part of the university experience that came with freedom from your parents. Little did she know.

The first class of the day was Psychological Enquiry and Method. After two fifty-minute lectures it was time for lunch. A bunch of students were going to the main dining hall but Imogen had plans to help out at the lab.

Mörður was alone. 'Imogen,' he called out excitedly when she walked in. He didn't take his eyes off the computer screen. 'You've got to come see this!'

She loved being part of a research group. There were five of them working with Mörður on his research project: Dr Richard

Simmons, a research associate; Samuel Pearce and Aalia Khan, both post-grad students; and Candy and Imogen, both in their first year at Cambridge. She felt that she was a part of something important. The work gave her a sense of belonging and she got a massive kick from seeing that what she was studying, the things she read about in textbooks all day, had an actual practical use.

'Look,' Mörður said, pointing at the screen.

Imogen placed herself behind him, looking over his shoulder.

'I'm trying out new software. Datajuice. It lets you upload raw data and create interactive reports and publish them online instantly.'

That was impressive. Usually it took them days to copy and paste data from one program to another before they could even start analysing it and writing their reports.

'Will you look at this!'

On the monitor was a bar chart in various colours. As Mörður clicked on a drop-down menu and chose a different viewpoint the chart changed.

'The user can play around with the data without any special training.'

That was even more impressive. It had taken Imogen months to learn how to use SPSS, the statistics software used all over the psychology department for analysis. She still hadn't got the hang of it properly. All the students hated it.

'Think of the possibilities. Our clients are going to love this. This will give them so much more insight. This would be perfect for London Analytica.'

'What's London Analytica?'

Mörður got up from his seat. As he did so he accidentally bumped into Imogen. His shoulder hit her in the boob.

Was that an accident?

He headed for the table with the kettle and the teabags – the drink station, they called it. Mörður didn't drink tea. He mostly drank Diet Coke, but he also brought his own instant coffee to work. The kettle started simmering.

'I'll explain about London Analytics in just a moment. Would you like some coffee?' he asked, giving Imogen one of his smiles.

'Sure, thanks.'

Mörður was only slightly younger than her dad but he looked much younger somehow. Imogen wasn't sure whether it was his physique – he was slim and muscular; the way he dressed – he always wore skinny jeans or chinos and a tight T-shirt, often with a superhero on it; or his eyes which were unusually vibrant – as if they were giggling. His dirty blond hair was cut short and always had product in it and he wore sweet and peppery aftershave, like autumn leaves and cinnamon. Mörður was far removed from the old, awkward professor-type that could be found all over campus wearing an ill-fitting shirt and smelling of antiquity and arrogance.

'Fleeing the textbooks already?' Mörður asked, grabbing two mugs and pouring what appeared to be a random amount of coffee granules into them.

'That would imply that I've already started.'

'Ouch.' Mörður laughed as cheeky kindness spread from his eyes, through the crow's feet across his face. 'You'll be fine.'

Imogen's heart fluttered in her chest. She felt as if she'd suddenly grown taller. The waves of self-doubt inside her calmed. Here was a world-renowned psychologist saying that she was smart. A world-renowned academic who'd published more than thirty papers and written a whole book actually believed in her. He was helping her to reach her potential and plot out the grand arc of her career. Her face blushed with pride.

The last thing she thought before her life changed for ever was: *How lucky am I?*

How stupid she'd been.

It came out of nowhere. Or at least that was what Imogen thought at the time. One minute she was standing idly by the drink station listening to the kettle wheezing and staring out of the tiny lab window at the sunbathed back lawn. The next she was pinned up against the cold lab wall, her face squashed against the rough concrete painted a neat white.

It took her a while to realise what was happening. First, she had thought she'd tripped. But why would she trip? And why couldn't she move? Had there been an earthquake? Had the roof caved in and she was now trapped under it? But why was she up against the wall?

Suddenly, without her moving a muscle, her body spun around. It was as if there had been a shift in gravity and it had cheekily decided to make her do a twirl. With a thump, her back slammed against the wall.

An arm pressed hard on her chest, holding her firmly in place. It was Mörður. What was he doing? But then she felt something cold and sharp digging into the flesh on her waist. His fingers. How could his fingers feel like claws when they looked so manicured and innocent?

After that everything became a blur. Things happened furiously fast and unbearably slow.

His hand travelled up her body, across her breasts, his fingers pinching her so hard she screamed out.

'Shut up! Someone might hear.'

The hand slid up her chest, to her face. She could smell salt and clementine and it made her want to vomit. Mörður was always snacking on clementines and leaving the peel all over the lab. Imogen had thought it endearing. Now she thought it was the most disgusting thing in the world.

Pressing his whole body up against hers he used his hands to unbutton her trousers before turning his attention to his own.

Imogen couldn't move. She was frozen, hard as a statue. *Wake up, wake up,* she told herself, but it was as if she'd been stripped of all her power. She curled up inside herself.

Suddenly the door to the lab opened.

Samuel Pearce was standing in the doorway. 'Mörður?'

Mörður quickly let go of Imogen.

In a flash she was back in her body. She could move again. As she bent down to pull up her trousers her fear gave way to a shame so intense it felt almost as suffocating as Mörður's grip moments before.

Imogen straightened. Samuel Pearce was still standing there. Tears began rolling down her face. Every place on her body Mörður had touched was burning as if her skin was blistering.

Imogen's eyes met Samuel's. They stared at each other for a moment. *Help me*, Imogen pleaded with him. Samuel was still holding the doorknob. When he let go of it Imogen thought he was coming inside. She thought he would call in the head of the department. Then the police.

With one single step backwards Samuel was out of the room. Like magic, he was gone. Poof.

The betrayal was the last blow. Imogen's legs started to wobble. She reached out for the drinking station to support herself. She accidentally knocked over one of the coffee mugs. Coffee granules spilled everywhere.

Mörður scurried back, zipping up his jeans. 'Nothing happened,' he barked at her, sounding as if he was telling her off.

Imogen started tucking her top into her trousers. If she looked at his red, swollen, greasy face, she would throw up.

'If you tell anyone, I will make sure you'll never be able to call yourself a psychologist,' he hissed through clenched teeth. 'You won't graduate as one and you won't work as one. All doors will be closed to you.'

Looking down at the floor, Imogen began shuffling past him, making sure not to touch him, not to face him.

Mörður grabbed her by the arm.

A quiet yelp escaped from Imogen, like a cry from a wounded, helpless animal locked inside a trap.

'And anyway,' Mörður said, squeezing her arm so hard she could feel the bruises coming on already. 'If you do tell anyone, I'll deny it. No one will just take your word for it.'

Mörður doesn't notice her at first. He's deep in conversation with a stocky man with troll-like features wearing a baggy leather jacket.

Imogen wants to look away but she doesn't allow herself to. She's been burying her head in the sand for too long.

Suddenly, it's as if Mörður senses her presence, like an animal smelling prey nearby. Or perhaps an animal picking up on looming danger? He stops mid-sentence and turns his nose up. His eyes shoot towards Imogen in a sideways glance. His head follows.

They stand and stare at each other. The silence between them is swollen, bursting with meaning, pounding.

He's wearing his signature outfit: a snug superhero T-shirt, chinos and bleach-white Adidas trainers with three black stripes on the side. He's grown a beard since Imogen saw him last – not the old man type but the type you'd see on someone who works as a graphic designer in Shoreditch. Even with the beard he looks years younger than forty-one – or forty-two. He'd be forty-two now.

'Imogen. Lovely to see you. You look well.'

To anyone else the greeting probably sounds sincere. But to Imogen it sounds strained, pained and heavy with history.

Mörður turns to the short and rather angry-looking man, who's shifting impatiently from one leg to the other.

'Stan, this is Imogen. She will be helping me with data analysis for the next few months. She's from the UK.'

Stan gives a brief nod, then turns back to Mörður. 'I will speak to you soon.' It's definitely an Eastern European accent. Russian maybe?

The man's leather jacket creaks as he rushes past Imogen, then past Orri out the door.

The silence he leaves behind is awkward, cold, dangerous.

Mörður breaks it with a sharp cough. 'Orri, could you run to the cafeteria and get us some of those delicious salted caramel muffins?'

'Sure thing.'

'I'll come with you,' Imogen says, but a little too late as Orri is half way out the door and now she is left alone with Mörður.

'Step into my office, will you, Imogen.'

Mörður disappears into the back room again.

Imogen doesn't want to go in there. She can't go in there. But she has to. She has to act as if everything is okay. She can't do anything that might make Mörður suspicious.

Mörður is sitting behind a desk. There are two cans of Diet Coke on the table. Imogen suddenly recalls how rotten his breath was when he . . .

'Take a seat,' he says and points towards a feeble little chair on the other side.

'Ms Kendrick says that you're the most intuitive recruit she's seen for some time.' His golden lion trophy is standing proudly next to his computer – just like in Cambridge. 'So, I was very pleased when she insisted on sending you here to work with us on the Slimline project – we can certainly use the extra pair of hands.'

Her head is screaming: *Do you know what you did to me?* But her lips are clamped shut.

Imogen swallows bile. 'The pleasure is all mine.'

Mörður smiles a youthful, relaxed smile. This is the Mörður she thought she knew; cool, laid-back, friendly. A hipster with thick-rimmed glasses, a collection of superhero T-shirts and a Herschel backpack. He looks friendly. Harmless. Fun. He looks like someone you'd want at your party. But Imogen now knows it's an act. It's a disguise. His casual appearance is designed to lure you in, make you trust him.

This time Imogen is not falling for it. This time, the roles are reversed.

Imogen returns his smile. She's not sure what her plan will bring her. She doesn't know if it will open any of the doors she feels have closed to her. She doesn't know if it will reduce her sense of loss. But there is one thing she's sure of. If she's successful, her plan will guarantee her one thing: revenge.

Photo: Feet wearing black Dr. Martens surrounded by locks of red and purple hair scattered on the floor.
Filter: Gingham.

Possible captions . . .

Option one: #newlook #newme #makeover #newbeginnings #whothefuckaml
Option two: Sucking up to Dad.
Option three: Still looking for the real me.

Actual caption . . .

At the hairdresser.

♥22

Chapter Nine

Hannah

It's the day after the interview with Imogen Collins. I'm in a fancy assembly room in the British Embassy in Iceland. I stand next to an old-fashioned oil painting hanging on a wall in an ornate gold frame, holding a glass of sparkling wine. I left my Dr Martens at home and borrowed heels and a cocktail dress from Rósa.

I take out my phone to escape the awkwardness of being alone at a party. I've got two notifications: three people have liked the photo of me having a haircut on Instagram and I've got an email from Granny Jo with the subject: 'Read your interview. Wonderful job. You should have the Pulitzer'.

I open the email. Empty.

I spot Kjarri squeezing through the crowd of party guests. I give him a wave. He trudges over and stops in front of the oil painting. It's of a dark burning mountain – the landscape equivalent to the end of the world. He gives it a disapproving look before taking a step towards the wall and leaning up against it, his face as sullen as the ashen oil sky. He remains silent. I guess he's still mad at me.

I take a tiny sip of my sparkling wine, which I'm holding only as a part of my camouflage – I'm trying to fit in. It tastes yeasty. I usually don't drink alcohol. I'm never going to do drugs. I even avoid caffeine. I don't take any chances with things that mess with my central nervous system; I don't take any chances with things that mess with my head. I don't touch anything that could be the trigger that turns me into Mum.

I can see Imogen Collins standing at the other end of the room, drinking red wine and talking to a scruffy-looking guy. She looks radiant in a red midi scuba skirt and white Peter Pan collar shirt: professional chic – perfect for her talk at the Harpa conference hall later.

The guy she's talking to however, is anything but chic. He looks Imogen's age and he's wearing black skinny jeans tucked into an untied pair of Dr. Martens, and a denim shirt. But it's his shoulder-length hair that makes him really stand out at the party. He's the only man with long hair attending this gathering, which would most accurately be described as seriously la-di-da. The two of them are deep in conversation. They look like they're talking about something serious: the International Criminal Court in The Hague, or climate change. Maybe they're debating whether the inventor of the skinny jean should be brought in front of a tribunal. Those things are criminally uncomfortable.

Kjarri gives a loud sigh from where he's standing by the glum oil painting – next to each other they look like two bad omens. I should say something to him, maybe apologise again. But I'm too engrossed in Imogen's conversation. It's getting heated. Imogen clenches her fists. She hisses at the guy. He doesn't reply, just stands there, looking down at his shoes, shaking his head ever so slightly.

Her behaviour is so predictable. Because she's successful and beautiful, she treats people like they're her servants. She thinks she's so much better than everyone else. Just like when we did the interview.

The interview was in the paper this morning. Dad had been so pleased with it he'd brought it up at the nine o'clock editorial meeting. 'I loved how the piece painted a picture of a conflicted diva,' he said. 'Well done, Kjarri.'

'I don't deserve the credit,' Kjarri had replied sulkily. 'Thank Hannah. She's responsible for the line of questioning.'

I'd said I was sorry, but judging by his pouting – it's as if he's trying to mimic the mood of the harrowing oil painting next to him with his facial expression – it hasn't done the trick.

The sound of a microphone howling into life makes the party guests wince. On a raised platform, beyond the buffet table laid out with British delicacies such as cocktail sausages, soggy sandwiches and crisps, the UK ambassador to Iceland, Gerald Boothby, is smiling apologetically.

'Sorry, everyone, sorry,' he says but there's nothing apologetic about his presence. He speaks in the manner of someone who was born in a stately home and is distantly related to the queen. As opposed to the rest of the suit-wearing attendees, most of whom look like they're heading to the office of their used-car dealership, the ambassador has the air of a Hollywood actor going to the Oscars. His hair is dark with a few grey strands, his jaw is square and his light-blue eyes contradict his dark, voluminous eyebrows.

'Modern technology eludes me. I got an Alexa for Christmas and for the first few weeks I thought it was a paperweight.'

There is a ripple of laughter.

'I won't keep you long. We need to start making our way down to Harpa soon. I want to thank you all for coming here today to mark the start of Cool Britannia 2.0, a week-long conference and festivities to promote and celebrate Britain's creative industries such as music, fashion and art.

'Funnily enough, it was during the original Cool Britannia era, in 1997, that I first visited Iceland. I came here with a group of friends to see the band Blur play. It was an unforgettable experience – one of the best weekends of my life. I fell in love with the country and vowed to come back – although some of my colleagues at the Foreign Office asked what I was being punished for when I was shipped here.'

More laughter.

The ambassador smiles. But then his face turns serious.

'It isn't I who should be standing here and telling you about all the wonderful things we have planned: all the concerts, all the talks, the fashion show on Friday, the light installation by Damien Rust at the National Gallery of Iceland. All this is Sara's doing. Sara Gunnarsdóttir, our event's organiser, is a force of nature. Unfortunately, she can't be with us tonight. Most of you have heard about the tragic events . . .'

The ambassador's words fizzle out. I look around. People are nodding, their faces sombre. Some are bowing their heads. I have no idea what he's talking about but the urge to know feels like a chasm opening up in my chest.

'Our thoughts are with Sara and her family.'

I whisper to Kjarri. 'What's he talking about?'

He shrugs. He looks like he's barely listening to the ambassador's speech.

A voice whispers in my ear. 'It's her husband.'

I turn. It's an old lady wearing a pink satin jacket and a matching hat. She's standing next to me holding an almost empty glass of bubbly.

'Her husband?'

The woman pouts. Her red lipstick is pushed into the wrinkles circling her mouth like a river of blood coursing through a riverbed. 'Her husband is Mörður – or was Mörður, I should say. The dead university professor who's been in the news.'

What? I feel like this man is haunting me. I drive past the crime scene when the police find his body; the first person I interview for my new job as a journalist worked with him. And now this.

I suddenly hear voices hissing by the door to the assembly hall. People are looking. I stand up on tiptoe. It's Imogen. She's growling at a short and portly man. He's around fifty with pockmarked skin, wearing a shirt and a tie underneath a rather ill-fitting leather jacket. The slightly scruffy – or trendy, I can't decide which – friend with the longish hair is standing next to her.

Imogen notices that people are staring at them. She smiles apologetically and the crowd turns back to the raised platform where the ambassador is banging on about the monetary value of culture as an export.

I keep watching them. Imogen starts putting on her coat. The man in the leather jacket says a few words to her while she glares at him. He reaches into the inside pocket of his jacket and pulls out a chunky brown envelope which he extends to Imogen.

Imogen jerks back with a look of horror on her face as if he'd handed her a pile of dirty underwear. She refuses to take the envelope. The man tries to shove it into her hands, but she turns her back on him and strides out of the room. Imogen's scruffy friend hisses at the man before following after her.

That was weird – although not out of character for Imogen. She has a strange, distant and cold demeanour. It's as if she's always on edge. Or maybe it's just that she's got a stick up her arse. Perhaps she's on drugs like lots of other social media stars probably are. I've heard people who do cocaine can be very irritable when coming down from a high.

The ambassador has stopped talking. People are beginning to leave the party for the main event. After the interview, the company doing the PR for the programme gave Kjarri and me tickets for Imogen's sold out talk. I didn't really want to go but Daisy said I wasn't allowed to miss it.

I turn to Kjarri, who's still standing by the oil painting sipping wine. I intend to say, 'Shall we go to the hall?' but seeing his sulky face alters the course of my message.

'Why are you still pissed with me? I said I was sorry. I didn't mean to mess up the interview.'

He flinches. 'I'm not pissed with you. I'm pissed with myself.'

'Oh.'

'I shouldn't be here.'

'I'm sure everyone feels like that at a fancy embassy reception like this one. Unless you were born in a place called Downton

Abbey, or some crap like that, at a time when Britain had an empire on which the sun never set, you don't belong here.'

'I don't mean literally here. I mean I'm a phoney. I'm not a journalist. I haven't got a fucking clue.'

Kjarri has clearly helped himself to a bit too much of the free booze. He's slurring his words.

'Look at you,' he says and points at me with a wave of his glass of red wine, which threatens to shoot out and ruin the beautiful black A-line dress I borrowed from Rósa. 'You turn up for work on your first day and you ace the interview.'

I'd clearly misunderstood the situation. I thought Kjarri felt I'd messed up the interview.

Kjarri takes a big swig of wine. 'What the fuck am I doing with my life? Mum said it was a mistake to quit school. But I had to. It was all just too much.'

Somehow, I feel guilty about Kjarri doubting himself, as if it's my fault. I want to make it up to him. I want to make him feel better.

'You don't become a journalist overnight.'

'You did.'

'It was just beginner's luck.'

'I bet it wasn't.'

'I worked on my school paper. I've had practice. You can learn to be a good journalist.'

'I just wanted her to like me.'

'Who?'

'Imogen. You asked all the good questions, all the hard-hitting ones, while I was busy worrying about what she thought of me. I have an incurable need to be liked. I can't ask a person a question I know is going to make them annoyed with me. I'm not ruthless like you.'

Ruthless? Was that meant to be a compliment or a criticism?

Kjarri finishes the rest of his wine. 'We should go if we don't want to be late.'

I watch him stagger towards the door, suddenly struck by his public display of self-doubt. When I met him yesterday he'd appeared so relaxed, comfortable in his skin. He'd looked content and confident. Happy. But I guess that, just as you can't judge a book by its cover, you can't judge a person by the width of their smile.

The moment Kjarri and I step into Harpa someone grabs my arm.

'Oh, good, you're here. I've been waiting for you guys.'

I look up and get the feeling I'm hallucinating. It's Imogen Collins. And she's speaking to me as if she knows me.

'I want to apologise,' Imogen says.

I just stare at her, unable to speak.

'During our interview, I came across a bit ...' Imogen searches for the right word. 'A bit unhinged. I'm so sorry. I know it was your first assignment and I hope I didn't put you off the job. You're good at it. You should definitely keep it up. It's just that I have a lot going on. Oh, God, that sounded so lame. Sorry, again. There are just some things that I can't talk about. But you'll know soon. After my lecture you'll understand.'

She suddenly draws a breath excitedly. 'I know. To make up for what a bitch I've been I'll give you an exclusive. Let's meet up later tonight. I've got a good story for you. A scoop. It will put you on the map. Your dad gave me your number. I'll text you after the talk.'

And then she's off as quickly as she appeared.

Kjarri takes out the Snickers bar we got from a shop we passed on the way from the embassy to Harpa and starts to unwrap it.

'What was that?' he says with his mouth full.

'I have no idea,' I say and watch Imogen disappear into the crowd of people filling the lobby. But whatever it was it made me feel good.

Maybe Imogen isn't the cow I thought she was after all.

Kjarri and I take a seat in the auditorium. The seats are soft black leather, the floor is brushed concrete and the walls are covered with thin vertical timber panels with gaps between them and icy blue lights behind them. The atmosphere in the auditorium is mysterious-chic.

It's five minutes until the start and every single seat is occupied. The audience is mostly female, between the ages of sixteen and twenty-five. The title of Imogen's talk, 'The Accidental Influencer: How to Attract a Million Followers Without Giving a F***', seems to have inspired a lot of interest. Or maybe, despite being British, Imogen has a large following in Iceland. The internet and the world of social media aren't exactly confined by state borders.

I take out my phone and snap a photo of the empty stage and the name of Imogen's talk, which is being projected on to the back wall. I send the photo to Daisy. I get an immediate reply.

D: Wow! Looks amazing! Wish I was there. Have fun :)

The blond, slightly scruffy guy, Imogen's friend from the embassy party, is setting up a little camera on top of a tripod in front of the stage. She's probably going to stream the event live on her Instagram account or something glamorous like that.

The lights dim. I turn off the sound on my phone. The room jolts when a man's voice thunders through the speakers of the auditorium like the voice of God from the heavens – if God spoke with a slightly cheeky American accent. 'Please give an enthusiastic welcome to the wise, funny and fabulous Imogen Collins, marketing expert, trendsetter and Instagram sensation.'

Music starts playing. Imogen walks on to the stage. The room erupts in applause. I feel a burst of irritation. She looks like a flower burning with life in her white shirt and red scuba skirt against the cold concrete of the stage. Her walk is relaxed, her body language is open, her eye contact with the audience is inviting. Her smile is confident, yet humble. She looks like someone you'd want to be friends with. Gone is the tightly wound, rude diva Kjarri and I interviewed the day before.

'Thank you, everyone, for this warm welcome,' Imogen says and places her palms on her chest as a gesture of her gratitude and sincerity. 'It's an honour to be here with you tonight. Truly.'

Man, she's good at this. I suddenly feel all small and insignificant. It's strange how another person's accomplishment can diminish your whole existence. It's like you're only as good/worthy/talented as the next person is crap. Granny Jo says that comparing yourself to others is healthy; it keeps your fighting spirit alive. 'Whenever a friend succeeds, a little something in me dies,' she sometimes says, apparently quoting some dead American playwright.

Imogen casts her eyes downwards as she adjusts her headset microphone. When she looks up I immediately notice something has changed. Gone is the smile and the aura of friendliness. Instead she glares into the audience with the warmth and the charm of a stone wall.

'Success.' Imogen spits out the word as if she's bitten into something foul-tasting and she needs to get rid of it. 'You're all here to hear a talk about success. Or, as it's put in the programme —'

Imogen raises her arm and holds up a shiny little booklet. It's the Cool Britannia brochure we were given when we arrived at Harpa.

'*Come and hear about how Imogen Collins became one of the UK's most successful social media influencers and learn how you can do it too.*'

She lowers her arm and drops the brochure, which falls to the floor with a feeble thud. She looks down on it with something that resembles contempt on her face.

'You're here because you want to know how to pout successfully for a selfie; you want to know what filter is the best for ironing out your imperfections. Because no one wants to see the truth. No one wants to see a photo of you in bed eating a whole box of Dunkin' Donuts because your girlfriend or boyfriend broke up with you over text; no one wants your misery splattered across their Instagram feed.'

Kjarri leans towards me and whispers. 'She is mean.'

It's like Imogen Collins is two different people. This is the Imogen Collins Kjarri and I interviewed.

'I'm going to tell you my story. How it came about that I ended up here – on this stage, in this country. And in doing so,

I'm going to show you the one thing you don't want to see: the truth.'

Imogen stares at the people sitting in their soft leather seats sloping towards the stage. 'What do you think when you look at the photos on my Instagram account?'

Her tone of voice is accusatory and no one dares to answer.

'I bet you see a young woman living it up in London, wearing glamorous clothes, surrounded by fabulous friends, having the time of her life. I bet you see a life you wish you could have.'

A woman sitting in front of me whispers to her friend. 'I thought this was going to be a workshop.'

Imogen ignores a quiet discontent emanating from the audience. 'When I scroll through my old photos, that is what I see. But I know better. The photos of me smiling with a colourful cocktail in hand, wearing an outfit hot off the catwalk – I know that what I'm looking at is a lie. I know that I'm looking at a girl who's confused, desperately lonely and afraid.'

Imogen pauses for a breath. The whispers have died down.

'Everyone is talking about technology; how harmful mobile phones are to young people; how social media has ruined a whole generation; how technology makes us stupid, shallow and self-obsessed.

'For the past two years, I've made a career as an influencer. Many aspects have been a pleasure. Like engaging with people I would never have met. At the beginning, I loved taking photos, feeling creatively challenged and having an outlet to express myself. Sometimes I still do.

'But there are negative aspects of being an influencer. I have cried myself to sleep on numerous occasions because I'm convinced that no one likes me based on the number of hearts I've received on a photo on Instagram; my self-worth has been tied in with engagement, follower retention and the rise and fall of blue lines on graphs in Google Analytics.'

The audience is eating out of Imogen's hand.

Imogen takes her phone out of a discreet pocket at the front of her red scuba skirt.

'Let me just read you a little passage from a book that was written in 1898.'

Imogen's face is bathed in white light from the screen. She looks angelic.

'The abuse of letter-writing is one of the greatest trials of the epoch,' she reads. 'Everyone cries out and insists upon your listening. They write events while they are only happening. People unknown intrude upon your time and take possession of it. Enmities and friendships thousands of miles away scold or caress.'

Imogen looks up from the screen with an expression of mild amusement. 'Sounds familiar. Sounds like Facebook. But so wrote the British novelist Amelia E. Barr at the end of the nineteenth century.'

Imogen is smiling at the audience. Some people are giggling. The mood is lightening. Imogen's blond friend on the camera is looking at her with a crooked – adoring? – smile. I'd bet my right arm on the fact that he fancies her.

But suddenly Imogen's mood darkens again. 'Of all the self-loathing social media has caused me, of all the tears that I have shed, of all the sleep I've lost, nothing has caused me as much grief or as much damage as a certain face-to-face human interaction, an abuse of power as old as man – an incident which took place in the so-called real world, a world that is held up as a wonderful place of innocence and kindness compared to the alleged ruthlessness of cyber space. It is that incident which has brought me here, to your cold and raw but beautiful island . . .'

I hear the doors to the auditorium open behind me. I don't think anything of it until Imogen stops talking. She's looking up towards the back of the room, shielding her eyes against the burning-bright spotlight.

I turn around. People are flooding into the auditorium. I can't see them very well. But then the ceiling lights turn on. It's the police. At least eight police officers are rushing down the stairs that run along the seating area towards the stage.

Panic spreads like wildfire through the crowd. People are jumping up from their seats, some are ducking down behind them.

I instinctively grab Kjarri's arm. My mind is racing. *Fire. Terrorist attack.*

The voice of the announcer from earlier echoes through the sound system. 'Please remain calm. This is not an emergency. Because of technical difficulties we will not be able to conclude tonight's talk. We ask the audience to please remain seated until further notice.'

The first police officers are stepping on to the stage.

Imogen looks at them approaching. I try to read her face. Does she know what's going on? Or is she as confused as the rest of the people in the auditorium? There's no way to tell.

A female police officer walks up to Imogen and says something to her.

Imogen's reply is audible through the headset microphone she still has on. 'I'm sorry, could you please speak a bit slower? I don't understand Icelandic very well.' She doesn't sound shocked. She doesn't sound frightened. She sounds – polite.

One of the policemen still running down the stairs calls out to a group of people gathering in the doorway behind him. 'Could someone please turn off the mic.'

Imogen's friend leaves his camera and rushes up to the stage.

I let go of Kjarri and get up from my seat.

He slides forward. 'What are you doing?'

'My job,' I say and start squeezing past the people sitting in my row. 'Excuse me, excuse me.'

I can hear Kjarri following close behind me.

I reach the stairs. They've turned off the mic; Imogen's lips are moving but I can't hear what she's saying. She's surrounded by a group of police officers.

Her friend is trying to get to her but is being held back.

I run down the stairs and on to the stage.

One of the police officers stops me. 'Who are you?'

'I'm from *Dagblaðið*.'

'There's nothing to see here.'

'Clearly there is,' I say and shoot past him. He tries to grab me but Kjarri arrives and distracts him.

Tall as a tree, he towers over the policeman. 'Hi, man, what's going on?'

I tap the guy trying to get to Imogen.

'Do you know why the police are here?'

He shakes his head frantically. His hypnotic blue eyes look like they're about to pop out of his head. 'No idea.'

'Does she have a lawyer?'

'What kind of question is that?'

He's right. This isn't some cop show on TV. Why would she have a lawyer?

The blond guy is standing on tiptoe trying to get a glimpse of Imogen in the crowd of police officers.

'Fuck! They're cuffing her.'

I look over my shoulder. Kjarri is still talking to the police officer. 'We need to call someone,' I say to the guy, who is now pulling at his hair. 'Does Imogen have any family here? Any friends?'

'I can call my mum.'

Why would he call his mum? 'I think we need someone relevant who can help.'

The guy suddenly lets go of his hair. His arms shoot triumphantly up in the air. 'The ambassador. Imogen is a British citizen. Surely he's obligated to help.'

'That's a great idea! Is he in the audience?'

'I think he's at the Benjamin Britten opera in Eldborg, the auditorium upstairs.'

Of course he is. 'Go get him then.'

The guy spins around.

As I watch him mount the stairs I notice a face in the audience. It stands out for the same reason the ambassador is listening to Benjamin Britten and not a teenaged social media influencer. It's the face of a man – the audience is ninety per cent women. The man is also clearly well above the average age of twenty-five – probably more like fifty. And judging by his neatly pressed white shirt and the condescending smirk on his face, he considers himself far too cultured for this event.

I suddenly realise something. I've seen the man before. It's the man from the party. The one who tried to shove an envelope into Imogen's hands. He's taken off his oversized leather jacket but I'm one hundred per cent sure it's him.

He's talking on his mobile and staring at Imogen. My heart jumps when the man emits a gush of bellowing laughter. What's wrong with him? Does he think this is funny? Some people are simply soulless.

I turn away from the stocky little man and his arrogance. I try to squeeze closer to Imogen. I get a glimpse of her in between the officers, who are acting like a human wall, blocking the audience's view of the celebrity they paid to see. The policewoman who was the first to approach Imogen is holding her by one arm. Imogen looks remarkably composed. She's talking to them and nodding her head.

I reach into my bag and take out my phone. I need a picture for the paper. This is definitely news. I take a few snaps. I don't know if any of them are any good.

I manage to push closer. I raise the phone again. *Yes.* This is going to be good.

I suddenly notice Imogen's face go white.

'What?' she shouts. 'You're arresting me for what?' Her superhuman calm is gone. She's shaking. 'I didn't do it!' She's shouting so loudly the whole auditorium can hear her. 'I could never murder anyone! This must be some sort of a joke.'

Her eye catches mine.

'Hey! Hey, Hannah?'

Stupidly, I wave at her.

'You need to help me. Come here.'

I try to go to her but my path is blocked.

'Hey! She's my friend. Let her through.'

The police officers look at each other.

'Surely I'm allowed a hug from a friend under the circumstances.'

Imogen has a commanding presence. There she is, under arrest in handcuffs and ordering the police around.

Frozen with indecision, the police officers' defences are down. I seize the opportunity and push two of them aside and run towards Imogen.

Before the police realise I've broken through their wall, I link arms with Imogen, like I'm fettering myself to her. We're not friends. She doesn't want a hug. Something else is up.

Imogen shakes her other arm free from the policewoman's grip, turns towards me and pushes her body up against mine. I wrap my arms around her, hugging her tight. She rests her head on my shoulder and whispers in my ear: 'My phone is in my pocket. Take it.'

I know I shouldn't. I know I'm probably tampering with evidence or something. But as I release Imogen from my embrace, I reach into the pocket of her skirt, pull out her mobile and slip it into the black feather shoulder bag Rósa let me borrow to go with her cocktail dress.

I'm so frightened I'll be found out that I can't move. But no one seems to have noticed anything. The group of police officers starts moving away and the female officer takes Imogen by the arm and leads her off the stage.

Shit. I suddenly realise something. The phone. It must be password-protected.

Imogen suddenly looks over her shoulder and shouts at me. 'Wish my mum a happy birthday for me!'

Yes. The password must be her mum's birthday.

The audience is getting restless and more people are rising from their seats. Some are filming Imogen being led out in cuffs on their phones. I spot the old guy, still smirking with his leather jacket over his arm.

Kjarri is coming on to the stage with his phone to his ear.

'Who are you calling?'

Kjarri shushes me and soon I realise he's talking to my dad, explaining what's happened. 'She's been arrested for murder.' Brief silence. 'No, we don't know who.'

Kjarri is right. We don't know who it is Imogen is meant to have murdered. But to me it's as clear as day.

ONE WEEK EARLIER

Photo: A plate of rather poorly presented scrambled eggs with burnt toast on the side.
Filter: Lark.

Caption: Yummy.

❤1004

What the caption should have been . . .

Option one: I once got paid four thousand pounds for showing up at a seafood restaurant and posting a photo of myself eating a bowl of mussels. I didn't taste one bite as I'm allergic to shellfish. Was that wrong of me?
Option two: This is not an ad.
Option three: I haven't been asked for a sponsored post in almost two weeks.
Option four: I feel rejected.

Chapter Ten

Imogen

Imogen has got used to waking up to the sound of Sigurlína making scrambled eggs for breakfast from the hens she keeps in her garden, and the smell of burnt toast. But one morning, three weeks into her stay, the sound of people shouting rouses her from a dreamless sleep.

'It's not working!' It sounds like Orri. He's speaking in Icelandic. Imogen has been studying the language. She's beginning to understand a few words and phrases.

'Do you hear me? It's not working.'

This can't be Orri. The voice sounds too angry. Orri hasn't raised his voice once in the weeks they've been working together. He didn't even get annoyed when Mörður wrongfully accused him of jeopardising the whole Slimline project, when it was actually Mörður who gave him the wrong data-set to work with. Imogen suspects Orri of possessing some secret stoic superpowers.

'I've tried to bury it.' It's definitely Orri. 'I've tried to do what you told me and forget about it. But it's just making things worse!'

'Shush, Imogen is asleep.' It's Sigurlína. Imogen suddenly feels guilty. It's like she's listening in on a secret. Orri always acts so confident around the office. He probably doesn't want her to know this vulnerable side of him.

Orri raises his voice. 'This thing keeps haunting me,' he snaps. Or at least that's what Imogen thinks he's saying.

'Sweetie, you need to stop letting it control you like that.'

'I went out with my friends last night and after a few beers I found myself crying in the bathroom like a baby.'

'Oh, darling.'

'This is turning me into a freak.'

Sigurlína's voice is turning from soothing to strained. 'I can't understand why you're letting things get to you like this.'

Orri's anger rises. 'You can't do this to me any more. You're supposed to be my mother. You're supposed to concern yourself with my welfare. How can you not care?'

'I do care. You know I care. I'd do anything for you. I'd give you my right arm if you asked for it.'

'I'm not asking for an arm.'

'I know. You're asking for something that's not mine to give.'

The next thing Imogen hears is the front door being slammed shut.

Imogen gets out of bed. She puts on the long woollen cape Sigurlína let her borrow. The house is cold in the mornings.

It's an old timber house, clad with corrugated iron painted bright red, and it looks like something from the Sylvanian Families toy collection. It's more pretty than functional and the cold Icelandic wind constantly sneaks through the cracks with quiet whispers. Sometimes, when the breeze touches her cheek, Imogen imagines that it's the invisible elves from the stone in the garden stroking her with their long, skinny, freezing fingers.

Sigurlína says the elves, who are called *Huldufólk*, the hidden people, are devastatingly beautiful creatures – tall and graceful – but they can also be cruel. Imogen is fascinated and creeped out in equal measure by their alleged existence.

Imogen steps out of her room and walks the four steps it takes her to get to the kitchen. The house is only marginally bigger than a toy house. Sigurlína is sitting at the kitchen table staring into a yellowing porcelain coffee cup covered with drawings of blue violets. After decades in bloom it looks as if they have started to wither. She's wearing a golden silk nightgown with Chinese letters peppering the fabric. Her hair, which comes down all the way to the small of her back, is blond like Orri's, except hers is slightly streaked with silver-grey. Her eyes are narrow in a probing sort of way and they have the same translucent quality as Orri's. The irises look polished, glazed over almost, like frosted glass, and they dwarf the pupils with domineering intensity. But while Orri's are watery blue, Sigurlína's are light grey, like a still but infinitely deep lake.

Imogen sits down opposite Sigurlína. 'Everything okay?'

Sigurlína hadn't noticed Imogen approaching and she looks up from her cup, spilling a bit of coffee, startled when she realises she's not alone. She quickly covers the quiet vulnerability that has softened her face with a mask of solid pride. 'Yes, of course, love. Everything is fine.'

She's faking it. 'I heard you and Orri earlier.'

'Oh.'

'Is anything the matter?'

Sigurlína sinks back in her chair. 'I don't understand how my son turned out so square. I always tried to nurture his sense of adventure; I encouraged him to be creative and go wherever inspiration took him. Apparently, inspiration led him into a square box of mathematical equations where nothing matters unless it adds up.'

'You don't approve of his career choice?'

'Of course I do. Knowing how to work a computer is the surest way into a steady, well-paying job. No, the cracks in our relationship have nothing to do with his choice of profession – even though I have no idea what it is that he actually does. They're all because of his obsession.'

'His obsession?'

'Orri is obsessed with knowing who his dad is.'

'Why doesn't he know who his dad is?' Imogen blurts out but immediately regrets her intrusion.

Sigurlína doesn't appear at all offended or embarrassed. 'Orri is the result of a short and passionate love affair which was never meant to last. His dad was recently married. And I wasn't going to ruin that.'

'So his dad doesn't know that he has a son.'

'He does. At the time I told him I was pregnant and that I was keeping the baby but that he didn't have to be a part of our lives if he didn't want to. He was young. Younger than I was and people had high hopes for him. His future was all mapped out. A child out of wedlock could have ruined more for him than just his marriage. I offered him a way out. He took it.'

'And Orri can't accept that?' Imogen could easily understand why he couldn't.

'It's all about self-discovery. He says he can't know who he is until he knows who his dad is.' Sigurlína shakes her head. 'I keep telling him that his dad has nothing to do with it and he can be whoever he wants, it's for him to decide. But he snaps and says, 'Ever heard of genes, Mum?"

Imogen wants to say something encouraging, like: *He'll come around*. But how can she make a statement like that when she hasn't spoken to her own parents in six months? Maybe Imogen will never see her parents again and only on their deathbeds will they be crushed with regret from never having reconciled.

Despite being in a foreign country where she doesn't know anyone, where the wind is always blowing up a gale and the milk tastes different, Imogen doesn't miss home. She became good at not letting herself think about her family in Cambridge a long time ago. And she's so engrossed in the task ahead of her that she hardly ever thinks about London, the office in Covent Garden and her housemates. Imogen has a sudden realisation that she is living her new life as if it's real and not just a means to an end.

She's become fond of Sigurlína, who cooks for her, washes her clothes and lets her hog the remote when they watch Netflix together in the evenings. Imogen enjoys having someone take care of her like that. She'd almost forgotten what it feels like to have a mum. From the start Imogen has got the sense that the feeling is mutual; Sigurlína likes taking care of her. Now she understands why: Orri is slipping away from Sigurlína and she's grateful to have someone else to mother.

Imogen wishes she could stay in the small kitchen all day, chatting to Sigurlína in between Sigurlína painting in her studio, but she forces herself to get up from the kitchen table.

'Are you off, sweetie?'

'Yeah, I can't be late.'

'I'll put some eggs into a Tupperware for you. You can have them at your desk.'

Imogen fights back the tears. She wishes she didn't have to go. Every day, going to the office is like getting up, getting dressed, leaving the house and voluntarily walking into a torture chamber. It's like stepping into a lion's den with only crossed fingers for protection, fearing that it's only a matter of time before the animal attacks.

The only thing that makes the whole thing bearable is knowing that in the end it will all be worth it – Mörður will get what he deserves. In the meantime, she tries to contain her fear and enjoy the only positive thing at the office: Orri's company. She feels like she has known him her whole life. She can relax and be herself around him. Or almost herself. She has to be careful. She can't reveal her true self to Orri or anyone else in Iceland before she finishes what she came here for. She just hopes he will forgive her.

When Imogen arrives at work she can't see Mörður anywhere and feels relief wash over her. He isn't in his office, which doubles as a meeting room, nor in the shared open-plan workspace.

'He's working away from the office today,' Orri says from the 'kitchen' – a small corner table where the coffee maker stands next to a cracked plate of biscuits and under-ripened fruit, and a tiny fridge which holds nothing but Mörður's cans of Diet Coke.

Orri reaches for one of the biscuits. Imogen has observed that he only eats the ones with chocolate on top. How cute.

The lab is cosy when it's just the two of them. Orri told her that the number of staff fluctuates depending on how busy they are and how easy it is to get students to donate their time. At the moment there's only the three of them.

'It's been happening more lately,' Orri says with his mouth full.

'What has?'

'We call it *skreppa* in Icelandic. Mörður is suddenly always popping out; saying he has personal errands, saying he'll be right back. Sometimes he disappears for hours. He never used to leave the office. But for the past couple of weeks he's been more absent than he has been for the whole two years I've been working with him.'

Thunderous clouds gather on the horizon of Imogen's day. *Is it because of her? Is he avoiding her? Does he suspect something?*

'I know he's working on a side project. Maybe he's working on more than the one.'

Maybe it isn't about her.

'Is he allowed to do that?'

Orri shrugs. 'I don't know. He's got a full-time position at the university. And the lab just signed another huge contract with London Analytica, which takes up a lot of his time. He also has two kids, so I don't see how he has the time to take on more work.'

He has kids. Imogen had forgotten about that. All of a sudden, her plan seems heartless. Cruel. She shakes off the thought. It's not her problem that he has kids. He should have thought of that before he . . .

Orri saves her from spiralling down into the dark hole that is her past. 'What do you say we make use of the fact that the boss-man isn't here?' he asks. 'We could go out for drinks? Cocktail hour starts at four at Kaffibarinn. It's two pints for the price of one. We could even grab some dinner afterwards.'

Imogen stares at him, slightly confused. Is he asking her out on a date?

'Come on, you can't spend all your evenings watching Netflix with my mum.'

She should say no. She likes Orri. It would only complicate things. It would make her betrayal so much bigger.

But there's a rebellion going on inside her, a ray of light which penetrates the darkness. Imogen throws caution to the wind.

'Sure.'

Orri gets up from his desk at half three. 'You ready to go?'

Imogen turns off her computer. She's so ready to go. She hates every minute of her work day. The job itself isn't bad. She likes turning numbers into stories, analysing data in search of narratives hidden in the endless spreadsheets. It's knowing the effect her work will have that makes it unbearable.

If things go according to plan, however, the project will never go live. But if they don't . . .

She's already contacted two journalists working for two separate newspapers back in the UK. One never replied. The other one said it wasn't for them. She sent out a third email today. *Third time's the charm*, she'd told herself.

But what if no one's interested?

Imogen stands up. She can't contemplate that possibility right now. 'Let's do this.'

Orri is putting on a bomber jacket. 'I just have to make a quick stop at the British Embassy. Hope you don't mind.'

'The British Embassy?'

'I help them out once in a while with their computers. They're absolutely clueless. They barely know how to restart a computer or turn on a printer. It's a nice gig – flexible and it pays pretty well.'

'Do you have many side jobs like that?'

'Just this one. I've been doing it for well over two years now. Ever since I met the ambassador in a pub. He'd just been posted here and was out on the town celebrating with a few of the embassy staff. We started talking and it turned out they were in desperate need of a computer guy.'

They lock up the lab and thread their way through the crowds of students filling the hallways of the social science building. They walk past the cafeteria, where the air is crackling with the smell of grilled ham and cheese sandwiches and coffee, and down the stairs.

Orri pushes open the heavy wooden front door.

'After you.'

Imogen walks out into an afternoon that feels as bright as the flash of a nuclear explosion. The colour of the sky in Iceland is different from the UK. It's got a raw intensity to it which can feel like driving daggers into your eyes and gives the world a filter-like tinge. When it's cloudy the world turns strangely white, like all the colour is being sucked out of it, but when the sky is clear – sharp like a scream, all the colours are exaggerated, every detail magnified – it feels as if you've been sucked into an overly developed Instagram photo. Icelanders, Imogen has noticed, have slightly crumpled, angry expressions and her theory is that this is the result of generations of people living under the harsh Icelandic sky.

Imogen and Orri walk in silence past the university's main building, a domineering stone structure overlooking a circular lawn with a statue of a man battling a seal. Orri's very good-looking in an ungroomed kind of way. He isn't very chatty; he uses his words efficiently, as if there is a quota for the day. Usually, Imogen goes for the more outgoing guys. Used to go for them anyway. Like Damien, her boyfriend at uni, the life of every party – as in *all* the parties; he frequented them as if attendance was mandatory. In the end, Imogen couldn't keep up with him and after a few months they parted ways.

They cross the busy road which separates the university campus and the old town and reach the walking path that circles Tjörnin, a cute little lake where Imogen has often seen children feeding the ducks bread.

'This is nice,' Orri says and draws a breath.

Imogen isn't sure what he's referring to – the crisp autumn air, the lake, the fact that they left work early, the company – but whatever it is, she agrees with him.

They walk up the slight hill into Þingholt, one of the oldest neighbourhoods in Reykjavík. It is cluttered with small detached timber houses painted in bright colours, and look like they belong in a cartoon rather than on a real street.

The embassy building, however, is uninspired. A modern concrete slab, painted white. In front of it stand three flagpoles. On one flaps the Union Jack, on another the flag of the European Union and on the third the German flag.

Imogen turns to Orri. 'Why the German flag?'

'The UK shares the building with the German Embassy.'

They walk up the few steps that lead to the front door. Orri presses a buzzer and the door clicks open.

Imogen follows Orri into a foyer where a receptionist greets them and lets them into the building. They walk a long corridor until Orri takes a sharp turn through an open door into an office.

Behind a desk sits a rather striking woman, probably in her forties, with a blonde bob and red lipstick. When she sees Orri she jumps to her feet and runs towards him.

'*Takk, takk, takk,*' she says in Icelandic. Despite her very limited ability to speak or understand Icelandic, Imogen knows this means 'Thank you, thank you, thank you.'

The woman wraps her arms around Orri and plants a kiss on his cheek. Her red lipstick leaves a mark.

A small bubble pops inside Imogen and bitter resentment travels through her body. She identifies it as jealousy. How ridiculous. Imogen has no claim on Orri. Besides, the woman is far too old for him.

But Imogen's dislike of the woman doesn't last.

The woman is about to shake Imogen's hand when she suddenly jumps back.

'Oh my God,' the woman squeals, switching to English.

Imogen stands there with her hand hanging limply in the air.

'I know you! Your name is Imogen.'

Before Imogen can answer the woman starts bouncing up and down with the energy of a child, chanting, 'Yes, it is! Yes, it is!'

She then turns around and grabs her mobile from her desk. 'My friends are not going to believe this! I need proof.' She extends her hand holding the phone towards Orri. 'Could you take a photo of the two of us?' Then she changes her mind and pulls it back.

'I'm so sorry, Imogen, I'm being rude. I'm not mad. I know you don't take a photo of a person without asking. It's just that my friends and I love you on Instagram. And I just had coffee. Coffee doesn't agree with me, it makes me antsy, but I love it so I drink it anyway. My poor colleagues kindly put up with me. So does Orri. But he has the temperament of a Buddhist monk – nothing seems to rattle him.'

Orri is grinning. 'So, I guess you follow Imogen?'

'Everyone does. You're huge in Iceland. Look at this.' She rolls up the sleeve of the black, oversized sweater dress she's wearing, revealing a golden wristwatch. 'I bought this after seeing you wear it.'

Imogen remembers the watch. She got paid three thousand pounds to post a photo of herself wearing it. She got to keep the watch but she never put it on again. She would never post about anything she didn't think was half decent, but can it be considered a recommendation when she's being paid to promote it? Imogen tells herself that business is business. Her fans are free to follow her or unfollow her – which has been happening a little more lately. Her engagement is down. So are her sponsorships. It's her own fault. She hasn't been posting as frequently as she should have since she left her real life behind and arrived in Iceland.

The woman rolls down the sleeve again. 'But I don't just follow you for your great taste in fashion. Your account is so much more than just the photos and recommendations. The captions make it more interesting, you know? Like, not stupid. I'm not saying that every influencer is stupid . . . I'm ranting now. God, I sound like some crazy stalker who's obsessed with you. I'm just following you, not stalking you. Wow, I just realised how following people is much like stalking. You're spying on a person's every move, analysing what they're wearing, what they're eating, what their house looks like. Ew . . . Okay. I'm shutting up now. I'm coming across as a total weirdo.'

Imogen is trying not to laugh. 'Not at all. I'm very flattered.'

The woman takes a deep breath. 'There. I'm calm. So, what are you doing in Iceland, Imogen?'

Imogen has noticed that most Icelanders speak English with an American accent. But the woman has a distinct British drawl.

'I came here for work. I work for a marketing agency in London.'

'Wow! How glamorous.' The calm that had just started to settle on the woman's face evaporates. 'Oh, my God. I just had an idea. Imogen, I'm going to ask you something. Please, say yes. You have to say yes.'

Orri touches Imogen's shoulder. 'Run. Run for your life.'

'I'm organising a conference for the embassy. It's to promote cultural relations between the UK and the rest of the world.

The events are all connected to Britain's creative industries, such as music, fashion and art. There are exhibitions, workshops, talks – you name it.' The woman grabs both of Imogen's hands as if they are long-lost friends in Victorian times. 'Would you please be a part of it?'

Orri lets go of her. 'I told you to make a run for it.'

Imogen wishes his hand was back on her shoulder. He has the softest touch.

'I desperately need you.' The woman is insistent but endearing at the same time. 'What I've got is all just a little bit too stuffy, conventional, respectable, predictable.' She pulls a face. 'It's all just so . . . old. Like the ambassador. Don't you dare tell him that.'

Orri snorts. 'Isn't he your age?'

'How dare you, Orri? He's three years older. Besides, age is just a state of mind. Please, Imogen.'

The woman is like a human hurricane; she could blow a person in whichever direction she set her mind to.

But Imogen is going to say no. Her trip to Iceland is meant be an in-and-out operation. She isn't here to meet people or make friends. When she returns to the UK she needs to be able to sever all ties with this strange island.

'Please, save my conference by making it cool – it's actually called Cool Britannia 2.0, and ironically the cool is completely absent at the moment.'

Then again, what harm can it do? Orri is right. She can't spend every evening for the next couple of months on the sofa with only Sigurlína and Netflix for company.

Before she knows it, Imogen is nodding her head. 'I'll do it.'

'Thank you!' The woman stretches out a hand. 'I'm Sara, by the way.'

Imogen shakes her hand. 'Imogen Collins.'

It's the right decision. This is turning out to be a good day. Unusually bright. It's as if a soft lightbulb has gone off somewhere inside her, driving away the shadows.

Sara turns to Orri. 'Thank you for bringing me this saviour. How do you know each other, by the way? Are you dating? Please say you're dating.'

Orri blushes and sweeps back his blond hair from his eyes. 'We work together at DataPsych.'

'Oh, so you must know my husband,' Sara says to Imogen.

'Oh? Who's your husband?' Imogen asks out of politeness. She doesn't know him. Apart from Orri and his mum, she doesn't know anyone here.

'Mörður. Mörður Þórðarson.'

Imogen is unable to speak. She just stands there with her mouth half open, willing herself not to throw up. It had been such a promising, bright day – but now, the light inside her is out.

Photo: Crowds of people huddled outside Harpa conference hall under the dark Icelandic night sky.
Filter: Moon.

Possible captions . . .

Option one: I can't see a thing. Where are those Northern Lights when you need them?
Option two: The dark may play to my advantage. I may have just done something that does not bear the light of day.
Option three: Did I just commit a crime?

Actual caption . . .

Adventures in the dark.

♥29

Chapter Eleven

Hannah

The paper arrives through our letterbox just after seven. I run out into the hall to get it. Imogen's arrest is on the cover with the headline: *Social Media Star Arrested on Suspicion of Murder*. It's accompanied by a huge photo of Imogen wearing her red scuba skirt, white shirt and a petulant frown. One of the paper's photographers happened to be outside Harpa when Imogen was led out in cuffs to a police car. The photo might just as well have the word 'Guilty' printed on it.

I take the paper into the kitchen, where the twins are eating Coco Pops for breakfast and watching cartoons on the iPad. I sit down opposite them.

'You're not allowed to read the paper at this table,' says Ísabella. 'Mum says it leaves ink stains.'

I ignore her and turn the page. There's a whole spread dedicated to Imogen's arrest. Half of it is photos. One is a photo I snapped on my phone of Imogen speaking to the police on the stage at Harpa. I feel a little buzz from being at the right place at the right time.

I start reading the article.

Last night, Imogen Collins, a British social media influencer, was arrested for the murder of Mörður Þórðarson, professor at the Faculty of Psychology at the University of Iceland.

I knew it.

Imogen Collins has been living in Iceland since this summer. She's believed to be an employee of the research lab DataPsych, of which the deceased served as CEO.

Dad steps into the kitchen. He's fully dressed for the day ahead, his shoes already on and laced up and his hair gelled. There is a strong smell of sweet aftershave wafting around after him.

'We're leaving in five minutes.'

I get up and run downstairs to get ready. I'm still in my pyjamas.

I can't help but feel sorry for Imogen Collins. Everyone's eyes are on her, judging her. I know what it feels like to want nothing more than to blend in, disappear into a crowd, be like the rest of them.

I was five when I realised that there was something different about my mum. It was a few months after Mum and I left Iceland and moved in with Granny Jo in London. I'd just started reception when one of the kids came up to me and said: 'Why is your mum not normal?'

I went home and asked Granny Jo, 'Is Mum not normal?'

'Hannah,' she snapped, sounding angry. 'Normal is an ugly word. No one should aspire to be normal.'

But through the years, as I watched and dealt with the consequences of Mum's antics, being normal became my greatest aspiration.

'Two minutes,' Dad calls down to me.

I quickly put on jeans and a white shirt. I haven't told anyone about Imogen's phone. I'm trying to decide what to do with it. I guess I should take it to the police.

Lying in bed last night, I had a sickening feeling that the phone probably contains the evidence which will prove her guilt. I'm probably being used to hide the evidence from the police.

The phone is still in the black feather shoulder bag from yesterday. I take it out and put it in the pocket at the bottom of my backpack. I know what my lunchbreak will be spent doing: cracking that password.

The moment Dad and I walk into the office my phone buzzes. A message from Daisy.

D: Imogen Collins was on the news this morning.

When I got home last night I called Daisy and told her about what had happened at Imogen's talk.

D: They're saying that her victim is some college professor.
H: That's what the papers are saying over here too.

D: I refuse to believe it. She's too pretty to kill anyone.

H: I guess pretty people can be murderers too.

When I get upstairs Kjarri is pacing the floor of the cubicle we share. He's wearing a fitted black cardigan and a T-shirt, jeans and trainers. He looks more casual than usual. I like it.

'What's wrong?'

Kjarri jumps. He hadn't seen me coming.

'The police were here,' he says, stamping his foot and shooting me a ferocious look, as if that is somehow my fault.

Shit. Could it be my fault?

'They can't find Imogen's phone.'

I go cold.

'Witnesses have stated that she had it with her on stage last night. I remember it too. She read from it during her talk. But the police say it wasn't on her when they got her to the station.'

I feel light-headed.

'Did you take it, Hannah?'

'Why would you ask that?' I say, trying to wriggle my way out of trouble by turning the accusation around.

'Did. You. Take. It?'

I don't answer.

'Fuck. Are you crazy?'

The last word stings. I know he doesn't mean it literally, but when you live in constant fear of the curse the word's meaning is always literal.

'No,' I say looking down on my toes.

Kjarri is fuming. 'A man has been murdered, Hannah. He

168

has lost his life. He's dead. Do you get that? Do you realise what that means? A mother has lost her son. A wife has lost her husband. Children have lost their father. This is not a crime novel. This is not some silly cop show. This is not a puzzle for you to solve for your own amusement. This is not a pleasant pastime. This is a murder case.'

'Tell it like it is, why don't you?' I mumble, trying to sound indignant but instead sounding like a balloon deflating.

He has hit a nerve. But his harsh words are not enough to take all the air out of me.

'Don't tell anyone I have it.'

Kjarri's jaw drops. 'Do you hear yourself?'

'I'm just asking you not to say anything.'

'You could go to jail for this.'

'Please.'

'I could go to jail for this.'

When Kjarri and I were kids his mum once said to Dad that she didn't want the two of us hanging out together. She thought that I was a bad influence on her son. She said that the bus trip we took to the town centre – that time she thought we'd been kidnapped – had been my idea. She would be right.

Kjarri grabs his office chair and rolls it over to my desk.

'You probably don't have very long before the police come back. I'll help you.'

I wrap my arms around his shoulders. 'Thank you, thank you, thank you.'

'Don't thank me. Just promise to bail me out if I get arrested.'

I plonk myself down on my chair. We have no time to lose. I rummage through my backpack looking for Imogen's phone. I find it underneath a squashed banana Rósa handed me when I left for work this morning. 'Stable blood sugar levels for a stable mood,' she'd said. *What was that supposed to mean?*

I grab the phone, don't bother wiping off the banana goo, and press the home button.

Shit. It's out of battery.

I go into my bag, find my iPhone charger and plug it in. After a few seconds the phone springs to life. It asks for a six-digit passcode.

'The first thing we need to do is crack the code.'

Kjarri bursts out laughing. 'Oh, okay then, 007.'

'It's Imogen's mum's birthday. But I don't know the exact date.'

Kjarri reaches for the keyboard on my computer and types in: 'Imogen Collins Facebook'.

Imogen Collins's Facebook page appears at the top. He clicks on it and goes into the 'About' section. There he finds 'Family and Relationships':

Annabel Collins
Mother.

Kjarri clicks on the name and 'About'.

'Oh my God,' I gasp. 'It can't have been this easy.'

There it is. Annabel Collins's date of birth. I press the home button on Imogen's phone. *Here goes nothing.* I type in: 230464.

Imogen's home screen appears like a magical world out of thin air. We're in.

Kjarri and I stare at the screen huddled up against each other.

It looks underwhelming – like any other home screen. I don't know what else I was expecting.

I have no idea what to do next, where to start. What am I looking for?

'So,' Kjarri says. 'What do we do now?'

It's hard to be organised when you don't know how much time you have. It's hard to think when you're expecting the police to show up any minute.

'What if we just copy all the content of the phone on to my computer? Then we can take as much time as we need to go through it all.'

'Sounds good to me.'

'Do you know how to copy a phone? Do you need a cable? Or an app?'

'I have no idea. I'll google it.'

'No. We don't know how much time we've got. We can't waste it on something that might not pan out.'

There's no time for a plan. I start opening things at random. Instagram. *Okay, why would there be clues about a murder on her Instagram account?* I close it again.

WhatsApp. I scan the list of conversations. There's a message from someone called Sigurlína Ólafsdóttir. The profile picture is of a woman with long and beautiful grizzled hair.

S: I was thinking of making meatballs for dinner. How does that sound?
I: Sounds wonderful. See you tonight.

There's another one from Anna Tilbury.

A: Hi, babe. Hope you're having a fabulous time in Iceland. I've got a pile of your mail. Do you want me to forward it to you? It's mostly just ads and crap.

I: Having an amazing time. No need to forward any mail. If an envelope looks important, you can open it and maybe message me a photo of it. Thanks, babe. Give my love to Steph and Josh.

The latest conversation is with someone called Orri Sigurlínuson. A profile picture of a guitar. The date is yesterday. The day of Imogen's arrest.

O: I'm at the embassy. You here yet?

I: Already inside. Find me at the bar.

O: OK.

I: Btw, the creep is here. Just try to act normal.

They must have been arranging to meet up at the cocktail party before Imogen's talk at Harpa. *Orri.* Could that be Imogen's friend? The one I saw her with at the party?

I read the message again. *The creep. The creep is here.*

I have no idea what to do with that. I grab my own phone from the desk and take a photo of the screen.

'Good thinking,' Kjarri says.

The office is filling up with the sound of footsteps. It's just our colleagues arriving for work but it's making me nervous. I keep imagining the police showing up and arresting me.

I close WhatsApp.

I have no idea what I'm doing.

I tap Gmail. At the top there's an unread email from Mark Reynolds. I open it.

From: mark.reynolds@londonanalytica.co.uk
To: imogen.collins@londonanalytica.co.uk

Hi, Immie.

A quick update on the Slimline meeting. The clients loved your work on the dashboards. Their only complaint was the colour scheme – it needs to reflect the brand's identity a bit better. Our designer is having a look at this and we'll update you with a new colour palette next week at the latest.

Great work, Immie.

All best,
Mark

Immie. She's known as Immie?

I open another one. It's a reply to an email Imogen sent to a social media agency that seems to send sponsorship deals her way.

Hi Imogen.

Good to hear from you. I hope you're well. Unfortunately we have nothing for you at the moment. We'll be in touch if something comes up.

This is hopeless. I'm not going to find anything. Not when I haven't got a clue where to look and my time is limited.

I see an email from the University of Iceland admin office. The subject is 'Your personal entrance code to the DataPsych lab'. I open it. The code is 375090. I snap a photo of it.

I skim the emails. One catches my attention.

It's an email from someone called Victoria King. The name rings a bell but I can't place it. The subject is 'We're not running the piece – Please stop calling me'.

Kjarri leans in. He smells nice: soap and sweets. 'Click on that one,' he says.

From: v.king@theherald.co.uk
To: imogen.collins@londonanalytica.co.uk

Imogen, I know you're disappointed. But you have to let this go. I'm not in a position to work on this. I beg you, stop harassing me.

I look at the signature at the bottom of the email.

Victoria King
Technology correspondent
The *Herald*

That's where I know the name from. Granny Jo sometimes buys the *Herald*. And I think I've seen Victoria King appear on *Newsnight* or *Question Time* or some show like that.

There's a phone number included in the signature.

'I'm going to call her,' I say to Kjarri.

'What! Why?'

I ignore Kjarri. It might not have anything to do with the murder. But it might. I grab my mobile and dial the number. It only rings twice before there is an answer.

'Victoria King.'

'Yes, hello. My name is Hannah Eiríksdóttir. I'm calling from a newspaper in Iceland called *Dagblaðið*. I'm looking into the murder of a university professor called Mörður Þórðarson. I understand that you have been in communication with Imogen Collins and I just wanted to quickly ask you—'

'Don't you ever call me again.' The line goes dead.

I turn to Kjarri. 'Did you hear that?'

'Yeah. That was weird.'

I snap a photo of the email from Victoria King and go back to the inbox.

I immediately notice an email a couple of rows down. I don't understand why I didn't see it before. The subject is written in capital letters: I HOPE YOU DIE.

I click on it.

From: sara.gunnarsdottir@fco.gov.uk
To: imogen.collins@londonanalytica.co.uk

I hope you realise what you've done. I hope you realise that you've ruined my life. Is that what you came here for? I hope you rot in hell.

'Hannah!'

It's Dad.

Kjarri freezes. It's as if he thinks that if he doesn't move he might not to be noticed.

For a second, I'm paralysed with fear – Dad is going to kill me. I snap out of it long enough to take one last photo; a photo of an email in which the wife of a murder victim threatens the suspected killer of her husband.

That is something. That's definitely something.

I feel Dad's presence as soon as he steps into my cubicle. I have my back to him but I sense his burning rage, his scorching disappointment and his freezing terror. I know what he's thinking: *She's got it, she's got the curse.*

'Hannah. In my office. Now.'

Photo: A delicate yellow buttercup reaches out of a crack in a concrete pavement, facing cold wind and icy rain with serenity and strength.
Filter: Perpetua.

Caption: That flower may be bent but it's not broken. Something may look fragile on the surface but that doesn't mean that it's weak. I am like that flower.

❤621

What the caption should have been . . .

Option one: I'm flirting with the truth now. I know you don't like it. I know the truth makes you uncomfortable. But tough luck. I'm sick of pretending.
Option two: I lost forty-three followers yesterday.
Option three: Where have all the sponsors gone?

Chapter Twelve

Imogen

The bar is so dark Imogen can hardly see the drink in front of her. Orri is telling her how it came about that he started working for the British Embassy.

'It was here, in this bar, that I first met the ambassador.'

Imogen is trying to act normal. But it's hard when she can still feel Sara's embrace on her shoulders and back, when she can smell the perfume he might have bought her on her clothes, when her smile of gratitude is etched on her brain.

It had taken Orri ages to fix Sara's computer. The whole time Sara had been chatting to Imogen about fashion, the secret obsession with all things Instagram she shares with her 'middle-aged girlfriends' and her time living in the UK – 'I lived in Cambridge, such a wonderful city'.

At one point Sara had asked: 'Didn't you study at Cambridge?'

Imogen could only hope that her foundation contained the redness of her face. 'Only briefly,' she'd mumbled. 'I left to move to London.'

Thankfully, Orri wasn't listening, otherwise he definitely would have explained that Imogen and Mörður had first met at Cambridge and that was a conversation Imogen did not want to have.

Sara couldn't have been nicer and under normal circumstances Imogen would have loved to get to know her better. But her presence was like breathing in toxic air.

The gin and tonic has made Orri unusually chatty. 'Did I tell you that the ambassador was out celebrating his new post with the embassy staff when I met him? It's weird; this doesn't exactly look like a place where ambassadors hang out.'

'Nor does it smell like it.'

Orri laughs. Imogen loves it when she makes Orri laugh. He smiles all the time but he doesn't laugh out loud very much, so when he does Imogen knows she's earned it.

'I got to know Sara very well pretty quickly. As you saw earlier you don't really get a choice in whether you get to know her or not.' A wry smile. 'She's great, though. She got me the job with Mörður at DataPsych. Mörður was looking for a student to work for him for credits but Sara made him pay me enough to get a place of my own. I've talked to her a lot about the problems I have with my mum.' Orri looks down into his drink. 'I'm guessing you've figured out by now that we're not all that close.'

'I heard you arguing this morning if that's what you mean.'

'That was nothing. It used to be even worse. When I still lived at home we fought all the time. I feel guilty about leaving Mum, though.'

'Children move out all the time.'

'I know. But it's always just been the two of us. She doesn't really have anyone but me. I think she's been lonely since I left. She keeps renting out my room to students but most of them are only in the country for a few months. She puts all this effort into getting to know them and taking care of them and then they just leave.'

'So you're responsible for the floral wallpaper in my room. I didn't see it at first but now I do: You do look like a flower kind of guy.'

Orri laughs for the second time. 'Mum redecorated the room after I moved out, papering over the embarrassments of my youth. I used to be really into posters and I'd covered the walls with things I'd been into.'

'I thought people only did that in eighties movies about American teenagers.'

'What can I say? I'm a living, breathing cliché.'

'Let me guess: Taylor Swift, One Direction, Spiderman and Pamela Anderson.'

'Eww, she's older than my mum!'

'Okay, let me try again: Nickelback, Justin Timberlake, X-Men and Coldplay.'

'Coldplay? Give me back Pamela Anderson.'

'She's all yours.'

Imogen and Orri look at each other. They don't say anything for a while. It's a comfortable silence. Imogen reaches for her mojito. (They were out of mint, so technically it isn't a mojito, but it tastes delicious so who cares.)

Orri is looking back at her. Sadness glistens in his crystalline-blue eyes.

'Are you thinking about your mum?'

He shrugs. 'I guess.'

Imogen gets a sudden craving to make Orri feel better. It's

instinctive and urgent, like hunger after not having eaten for more than a day. 'You shouldn't feel bad. These things happen. I haven't spoken with either of my parents in six months.'

'Wow. What happened?'

'Nothing. Everything. It wasn't any one thing.' *Or maybe it was.* 'They didn't approve of me dropping out of school or moving to London for a job. They never liked my social media career – "I can't understand why you'd want to expose yourself like that," they kept saying, as if I was a flasher walking the streets naked for pleasure.

'I was a quiet child; I didn't give them any grief as a teenager. I was going to uni; I was going to become a psychologist. We'd always been on the same page. But when suddenly we weren't, they couldn't deal with it. They couldn't understand that I needed to do things my way.'

'That's exactly like my mum. She can't see things from any other perspective but her own.'

'It's not that I don't love my parents. I do. But sometimes you just see things so differently that you can't help hurting each other.'

'That's my life in a nutshell.'

'And secrets are the cancer of relationships—' Imogen stops herself. She has no intention of revealing all. Just enough to help Orri see that it isn't just him – it's everyone. But he's caught on.

'You and your parents have secrets too.'

'Not a wilful secret. There are just some things you can't share with your parents.'

He doesn't insist on more details and Imogen is grateful for that.

Orri looks at Imogen from under his brow. 'Do you miss them?'

Imogen doesn't answer. She wants to say something mature like: *Of course, but c'est la vie.* But the pain in her chest gets the better of her. Her heart feels like a pomegranate fruit that is being ripped open by two starving monsters called grief and anger, and they're sinking their big, sharp teeth into the delicate clusters of gem-shaped seeds hidden inside, and there is blood-red juice splattering all over her insignificant little existence. She's grieving for her parents but at the same time she's furious with them. She's furious with them for not seeing what's really going on in her life, in her head. They're her parents, they should know that things aren't okay with her. And – irrationally, she knows – she's angry at them because she can't tell them what happened.

The noise levels at Kaffibarinn are rising. All the tables are occupied. Guys with beards and man buns, and girls with round glasses wearing boyfriend shirts line the bar. There's quite a lot of denim on denim, a whole herd of leather jackets, blazers matched with trainers. This is clearly the place where the hipsters of Reykjavík hang out.

It's getting difficult to hear.

A girl comes up to Imogen and asks for a selfie with her – she's a fan of her Instagram account. Imogen obliges with a smile. The girl disappears back into the crowd.

Orri rests his elbows on the table and leans forward. 'Did you know that this bar was once partly owned by Damon Albarn, the front man of Blur?'

'I did not know that.'

'It was during the original Cool Britannia era.'

Sara. For a brief moment Imogen had forgotten all about the promise she'd made to her. She wouldn't have agreed to take part in Sara's conference if she'd known who she was. It was all so messed up.

A waiter places a small glass tea-light holder on their table. The flame from the candle casts an orange glow on Orri's face. His smile turns crooked.

'How likely is it, do you think, that bureaucrats in British embassies across the world will be able to bring Cool Britannia back from the dead?'

Imogen wasn't even born during the era. Still, she has a picture of it in her head: battle of the Britpop bands, Tony Blair grinning like the Cheshire Cat, Geri Halliwell dressed in the Union Jack.

'Zombies are hot right now. They might just pull it off. Just imagine it, *Shaun of the Dead: Return of the Spice Girl*s. Noel and Liam Gallagher battle it out in *Zombie Fight Club*.'

Orri bursts out laughing.

Third time's the charm.

They look each other in the eye. It's a small table and they're close enough for Imogen to see herself reflected in Orri's eyes. She looks – happy. Come to think of it, despite everything, she feels it too.

Imogen's phone buzzes once, then it starts ringing. It's a UK number.

Imogen hopes it's an agency. Iceland is expensive and she's started dipping into her savings. She hasn't been maintaining her social media career as she should since she arrived in Iceland. She actually lost just under five hundred followers last month. In influencer terms, that's a disaster. But she hasn't felt like posting photos of herself pretending to her followers that she's on some exotic adventure. Her being here is all about being true to herself and making the world around her see the truth of what she's been through. Carrying on pretending on social media feels like she's somehow undermining everything she's trying to achieve.

'Sorry, I have to take this.'

Orri grabs his drink and leans back in his chair to give Imogen privacy.

'Hello.'

'Is this Imogen Collins?' It's a woman's voice.

'Yes, this is she.'

'Hi. My name is Victoria King.'

Victoria King. Imogen doesn't know anyone by that name.

'You sent me an email this morning.'

V. King. *The Herald*'s technology correspondent. Imogen had just assumed that it would be a man.

'Are you available to talk?'

Imogen looks at Orri. 'Erm . . .'

His cheeks are flushed from the gin and tonic. Bathed in the soft light of the bar, sitting next to a worn brick column with a hand under his chin, wearing a denim shirt and with his blond hair covering the right side of his face, he looks like he should be on the cover of *GQ* magazine.

The voice on the phone grows impatient. 'Imogen, are you there?'

184

'Yes, yes, I'm here. I'm available to talk. Just give me a minute.'

Imogen lowers the phone. She has to force the words out of her mouth – hearing them breaks her heart. 'I'm sorry, Orri. I'll need to take a rain check on the rest of our evening.'

Photo: A row of tacos, topped with freshly made guacamole, drizzled with sour cream and sprinkled with coriander and pomegranate seeds.
Filter: Sierra.

Possible captions . . .

Option one: #foodporn #foodpic #foodgasm
Option two: Family dinner.
Option three: Families: They're like a life sentence without parole.
Option four: I'm thinking about stabbing myself in the eye with my fork just to get out of this.

Actual caption . . .

#yum

♥26

Chapter Thirteen

Hannah

It's almost five o'clock. Dad and I spent the whole day at the police station. Dad is completely silent on the drive home.

I take out my mobile and send Granny Jo a quick email. 'Miss you. I'll call you tonight.'

When we arrive at the house Rósa is in the kitchen and, judging by the smell of fried beef mixed with cumin and coriander, she's making her famous tacos. My eyes water. She's gone heavy on the spices. Does no one but me think cumin smells like old sweat?

Rósa is a partner at a law firm. She went part-time when she had the twins and is usually home by four to take Ísabella and Gabríel to football practice and piano lessons and karate and ballet and computer classes and gymnastics . . . the list is never-ending. The twins treat Rósa like their slave. I bet it was Ísabella who wanted the tacos and Rósa ran out to the store to buy the ingredients.

The twins are in the living room watching TV. This morning Ísabella told me that the two of them have a bet on how long it will be until I'm sent back to London and they never have to see me again. Gabríel is generously giving it twelve months. Ísabella predicts I'll be gone before the end of the year.

I fear she may be right.

Cold wind slips into the house before Dad manages to close the door.

Rósa pops her head out of the kitchen. 'This is a pleasant surprise,' she says, but despite the thick layer of foundation on her face and what I suspect is a regular injection of Botox, a worried frown escapes through the mask of her beauty regime. Dad never comes home early from work. Something must be the matter.

Dad ignores Rósa and looks at me for the first time since we left the police station. His eyes are swollen. The volcano is about to erupt.

'I can't believe you did that to me!' he screams.

To him? Is he seriously going to make this all about him?

Rósa scuttles back into the kitchen. I hear a snigger coming from the living room. What did I ever do to them?

Dad pulls off his blazer and throws it on the floor. 'Do you realise how this looks?'

Sometimes I can't believe that my dad and I are related.

'What have appearances got to do with anything?'

His face turns bright red. He thinks I'm taunting him. Maybe I am.

It's as if the earth is shaking.

'Hannah!' Dad thunders. The laughter in the living room dies down. 'Do you not realise how it looks when I hire my teenage daughter who has no qualifications and no skills to do an internship that hundreds of university graduates applied for? Do you not realise I put my reputation on the line when I hired you? Do you know what this does to my integrity?'

I stare at him, confused and surprised. I hadn't really thought about it like that. I never saw the internship as a favour. I never saw it as something nice Dad was doing for me. Everything Dad ever does I see as punishment.

Dad loves nothing more than his job. If he put it on the line for me, maybe he cares after all.

'Who else knows?'

'About the phone? Just Kjarri.'

'I'll talk to Kjarri. You don't tell anyone else about this.'

I stare at the floor. I feel deflated. Stupid. My limbs are heavy and it's like gravity is pulling my shoulders to the floor. I enjoy working as a journalist. I don't want to lose my job.

At the police station Dad had done all the talking. He'd explained away my action as a clash of cultures. He said that I'd just arrived in the country after losing my mother to cancer and I didn't understand the language properly and hadn't understood what was happening. They let me go with a caution.

Dad's shoulders curl and he bends down to get his jacket. He looks deflated. The volcano is dormant again. He looks at me with a quiver of his mouth; I'm left wondering whether it was meant to be a smile.

'We can only hope that we got away with it,' he says as he leaves for work.

At the editorial meeting the next morning I have every intention of being on my best behaviour. I truly, honestly do.

It's the same as usual. Dad hands out assignments. The staff gives their input and suggests their own topics. I stay quiet.

189

Heiða, the paper's investigative journalist who's covering the murder of Mörður Þórðarson, gives a special briefing.

It's been two days since Imogen's arrest. She appeared before a judge last night and has been remanded into custody for four weeks – the maximum that can be given at a time.

'Who's her lawyer?' Dad asks.

'Valur Vilhjálmsson,' Heiða says.

Dad makes a face.

'I know,' Heiða says.

Kjarri is sitting next to me. He arrived late to the meeting and we haven't spoken since yesterday when Dad and two police officers escorted me out of our cubicle. He looks awful. His eyes are red, like he hasn't slept. His dirty blond hair has no product in it and is hanging limply down his forehead. His stubble is overgrown and he isn't wearing his thick-rimmed glasses, which seems to completely strip him of the air of grown-up certainty he usually has about him.

'What's wrong with Valur Vilhjálmsson?' Kjarri asks.

Heiða is the type of reporter who has the fabric of news interwoven in her DNA. She dropped out of school when she was sixteen and has been a journalist ever since. She knows everyone and everything. She's heard all the rumours and instinctively knows which ones are true and which are false. She can smell when something doesn't add up.

'Nothing,' Heiða says monotonously. She's surprisingly unassuming in both character and appearance – if she were a colour, she'd be grey. But maybe that's the key to her success – she blends in to the point you barely know she's there. 'It's a perfectly good choice – if you're charged with tax fraud or if you're overdue on child support payments, that is.' Heiða turns to Dad. 'The British Embassy organised it. I guess they're not used to helping their nationals fight murder charges.'

Dad reaches for his iPad. 'Anything else?'

Heiða shrugs. 'Not really. Apparently, she isn't talking.'

I bite my tongue. *I'm staying quiet. I'm staying out of it.*

But by some magic, it's as if Kjarri reads my mind.

'Why isn't she talking?' he asks.

I'm so grateful for his meddling I feel like I should buy him a thank you gift.

Heiða turns her head with what appears to be a herculean effort. The look on her face firmly states that she doesn't have time for stupid questions. 'Well, she's not obliged to. It's her right not to talk.'

Dad is checking his email. 'Has her family been notified?' he asks as he scrolls through the inbox like he does at the end of every editorial meeting to see if there are any last-minute press releases that they need to tackle.

'She's over eighteen so the police aren't required to contact them unless she specifically asks them to. Valur said she doesn't want them involved. She says she's not that close with her parents. But I'd be surprised if they haven't heard. Her arrest has been on the news in the UK and it's all over the internet.'

'Find them,' Dad orders with his eyes on the iPad. 'Try to get them to comment.' He stops scrolling and opens one of the emails.

Heiða pushes her chair back. 'Anything interesting?'

'No. Just a missing person's report.'

Everyone starts getting up to leave.

Dad puts the iPad down. The missing person's report is still open. There's a photo included.

I glance at it. *Oh my God.* I recognise the face. *Hannah, stay out of it.* My heart is racing. I lean a little closer. It's him. It's definitely him.

'Isn't anyone going to cover this?' I ask as innocently as I can.

Dad is gathering up his things: his Montblanc pen Rósa gave him when he became editor, his leather-bound notebook. 'It's just a missing person's report. It happens all the time; kids stay at their friend's house and don't bother telling their parents. I bet he's been found already.'

I stare at Dad. He doesn't know. I look for Heiða. She's out the door. None of them know who the missing guy is. None of them realise that this isn't just a missing person's report.

I manage another look at the report before Dad snaps up the iPad.

Name: Orri Sigurlínuson
Age: 22
Description: Blue eyes. Blond, shoulder-length hair. He was last seen wearing a green parka, black jeans, a denim shirt and black boots with yellow stitching around the sole.

'When was he last seen?'
Dad glances at the iPad.
'Monday evening.'
The evening of Imogen's arrest. 'That's two days ago.'
Dad shrugs.
'Can I cover this?'

192

'We put it on the website the way we get it. But I guess you can translate the report into English and put it up on IceNews as well.'

'So, you're giving this to me?' I want him to say it. To spell it out. I want to be able to quote him directly when he realises what I've done. 'You're giving me this as an assignment.'

'Sure.'

That's everything I needed.

When I step into my cubicle Kjarri is waiting for me. I get a flashback to the previous day: Dad's anger radiating from him like a shockwave from an explosion; the two police officers standing behind him, dressed in black like executioners from the Middle Ages.

'I'm sorry,' I say. 'I didn't mean to drag you into this. Taking the phone was stupid. I told the police you didn't have anything to do with it. I told them it was all me.'

He suddenly grabs my hand. 'I should have done more. I should have been more into this. I should have thought of things that would have helped us keep the phone for longer. I should have suggested we leave the office, go to my house. That would have bought us a couple of hours.

'I realise that when you're trying to get to the truth it's sometimes necessary to bend the idea of right and wrong. Sometimes the end justifies the means.

'I've been thinking . . . I want to become a better journalist. I simply need to start thinking outside the box like you. I need to find a balance between the values I've been taught – right and wrong and stuff like that – and doing what needs to be done. I know things aren't always black and white.'

He sounds genuine.

'Okay. You can help me out with my new assignment. But it does require thinking outside the box.'

Tracking down Orri's mum is as easy as tracking down Imogen's mum was. I start by finding Orri on Facebook. I click on 'About' and get his overview.

Works at DataPsych
Studied at University of Iceland
Lives in Reykjavík, Iceland
Single

Then I click on 'Family and Relationships'. There is only one relative to show:

Sigurlína Ólafsdóttir
Mother

Next, I open the online version of the Icelandic phonebook. In Iceland everyone is in the phonebook. Literally. Even the prime minister. Sometimes Iceland is cute like that.

There it is. Her name, her address and her phone number.

We take Kjarri's car. I'm so relieved that I'm not driving. There's heavy snowfall, and although the snowflakes look pretty, like cotton balls in a Christmas decoration, they completely cloud our view. But it doesn't seem to bother Kjarri. He tells me that he passed his driving test in a blizzard.

Kjarri parks in front of a small red cottage-like house which looks like a cartoon version of living quarters from the olden days. It would actually be a good fit for that Christmas decoration.

I knock on the door. The woman who answers looks like a cross between an elf and a hippy. She's got long blonde/grey hair, a make-up-free face and piercing grey eyes. She's wearing a floating gold robe and she reminds me of Cate Blanchett in *The Lord of the Rings*.

She looks at us, slightly confused.

I take the lead. 'Hi. My name is Hannah Eiríksdóttir. Are you Sigurlína Ólafsdóttir?'

The woman nods.

'I'm from *Dagblaðið*,' I say, kind of expecting her to slam the door in my face.

'Oh, of course you are. You must be Eiríkur's daughter.'

Now it's my turn to be confused.

The woman smiles. 'I went to primary school with your dad. You look a lot like him when he was younger. I haven't seen him for years. How is he?'

I'd forgotten how everyone knows everyone in Iceland.

'Erm . . . he's . . . good.'

'Don't just stand out there in the cold. Come in, come in.'

We follow Sigurlína into her house, which is as cosy on the inside as it's cute on the outside. She takes us to the kitchen.

'Have a seat. What can I get you? I just made some mint tea.'

She does not look like a woman whose son is missing.

'Or better yet: I can make you some hot cocoa. You look like you need it. Let me just get some cinnamon buns out of the freezer and warm them up.'

'Oh, just a glass of water would be good,' I say, knowing that if I don't accept something, she will bring out everything edible in the house and won't let us leave until we've tried it all. That's the Icelandic way.

'I'll have some water as well,' Kjarri says. It appears that he's going to dutifully follow my lead in every aspect this morning.

Sigurlína fills up two glasses from the tap and comes to sit with us at a diner-like kitchen table with a cream coloured plastic tabletop and chrome edges. The design and the condition of the table indicate it was made in the fifties. 'So, what can I do for you?'

I suddenly get tongue-tied. I thought I'd have to coax her into talking to us. I didn't think she'd just roll out the red carpet like this.

'It's about . . .' I suddenly feel bad. What kind of job requires you to deceive a nice lady like Sigurlína? *Shut up, Hannah.* It's what needs to be done. It's like Kjarri said: Sometimes the end justifies the means.

'It's about your son. It's about Orri. I just wanted to ask you a few questions. We're going to publish the missing person's report on *IceNews* and I just wanted to get a fuller picture of him. You know, to increase the chances of him being found quickly.'

I feel slightly nauseous. I try to swallow the disgust I feel towards myself. I grab my bag from the floor and take out a notebook and a pen I got from the stationery cupboard at the office.

To my surprise, Sigurlína shrugs indifferently. 'Even if someone can't be found, it doesn't necessarily mean he's missing.'

196

I look up from the blank page of my notebook. 'Orri isn't lost?'

'Oh, Orri is lost all right.'

My pen hovers uncertainly over the page.

Sigurlína sips her mint tea. The cup looks as old as the table. 'He's been lost since he was a teenager.'

I glance at Kjarri to see if he knows what she's on about. He looks as confused as I am.

'I'm talking metaphorically lost,' Sigurlína explains as she puts her cup down. I notice that it's cracked; it's got a line running through it, splitting in two a faded bouquet of blue violets. 'He says he doesn't know who he is and he's constantly trying to find himself. I'm just saying that someone can be lost without missing.'

I'm no closer to understanding the facts. 'So, is Orri missing or isn't he missing? You know, in the literal sense. Do you know his whereabouts?'

'No and no.'

My head is starting to hurt. 'So he isn't missing. But you don't know where he is.'

'Right.'

Talking to Sigurlína is like solving a Sudoku puzzle with a Confucian twist. Is she deliberately trying to be vague?

'But then why have the police launched a missing persons appeal?'

'I don't know. His friends must have called the police. It wasn't me.'

'So you're not concerned about him?'

A cloud of worry shadows Sigurlína's stoic elfin face and for the first time since we arrived she looks like a mother whose son is missing. 'Of course I am. I've been watching him, worrying about him for years. But he's on a mission to find himself, all the while getting more and more lost.'

'So there's nothing in his life – apart from his troubles finding himself – that have been a cause for concern.'

'Well. There is of course this business with DataPsych. I assume you know all about the murder of Orri's boss, Mörður Þórðarson.'

Kjarri and I nod. My guilt starts gnawing at my heartstrings again. I feel awful about questioning Sigurlína under false pretences. *The end justifies the means, the end justifies the means . . .*

'Something's been going on at DataPsych. Well before the murder. For the past few weeks Orri has been unusually wired. He says it's just stress. The lab is in demand with companies across the globe and things can get very busy. But I've had the sense that it's something more than that. Maybe he fears that he'll lose his job if he doesn't keep up with the demands. Or maybe the situation has to do with Imogen – I kind of suspect that he fancies her.'

Imogen. Now we're getting somewhere. 'Have you met Imogen?'

'Of course. She lives here. She rents Orri's old room. The police came knocking on my door the evening she was arrested; they had a search warrant and everything. They searched the whole house.'

'Did they find anything?'

'They took her laptop and some of her things. Clothing. Some jewellery. Not much really.'

Sigurlína shakes her head. 'I didn't want Orri to take the job at DataPsych in the first place. I wanted him to focus on his PhD. He's my only child and I've always found it hard to order him around. Sometimes I feel we're more like friends than mother and son. I guess he needed a mother figure. At least judging by how he has taken to that Sara woman at the British Embassy.'

'Sara. That's their events organiser, right?'

'Something like that. I detest that woman. Orri is the embassy's go-to computer guy. They became friends or whatever. I'm pretty sure she's the one who put the idea in Orri's head that he needed to move out. And she's the one who got him the job at DataPsych which gave him the financial means to move. It's like she's on a mission to steal him away from me.'

Sigurlína's face is flushed. 'You must think I'm heartless. Saying that when her husband has just died. But the truth is the truth. She's a total cow. She was really mean to Imogen at a meeting they had about that conference Imogen was taking part in.'

The kitchen falls silent. I'm thinking of my next question when Kjarri takes a leap.

'Do you think she did it?' he asks matter-of-factly – not aggressively, not apologetically, just like he's doing his job. 'Do you think Imogen is guilty of the murder of Mörður Þórðarson?'

Kjarri is in. He's all in.

Sigurlína averts her eyes. 'It's not for me to judge.' But she knows something. She has an opinion on the matter she isn't sharing.

I realise that it's not an opinion but a mother's worst suspicion when she adds, 'But Orri didn't do it. I'm absolutely sure he had nothing to do with this.'

Who said anything about Orri being involved?

Photo: A close-up of a face, skin without foundation, lashes without mascara, blemishes uncovered.
Filter: Clarendon.

Caption: Be yourself. It's free of charge.

❤374

What the caption should have been . . .

Option one: I once got paid five thousand pounds for wearing slimming pants in a photo on Instagram. I told my followers that I never left home without them but I never wore them again.
Option two: Should I feel dirty?

Chapter Fourteen

Imogen

Imogen steps out of Kaffibarinn with her phone in her hand and the journalist waiting on the line. It's turned dark outside. A gust of freezing wind comes out of nowhere and chokes her with its force. She wants to scream. She wants to cry. Once again, the Beast is controlling her life, preventing her from doing what she wants to be doing and forcing her on to a different path. But this is important. This could end all that.

Imogen can hear the sound of people enjoying themselves coming from Laugavegur, Reykjavík's high street that's lined with restaurants, bars, clubs and shops. She walks in the opposite direction. She needs peace and quiet. But mostly she needs privacy.

She sees a dark alley between two attached residential houses, a short cut to the adjoining street. Common sense tells her she should avoid dark alleys. But Imogen has learned that bad things can just as easily happen in broad daylight, out in the open.

Imogen puts the phone to her ear and heads towards the alley. 'I'm here.'

The alley is pitch black and she can only just make out the graffiti covering the walls. It smells of urine and there's a cat lurking at the other end, its silhouette black against the street lights from the street beyond.

'Are you alone?' a stern woman's voice asks. Victoria King sounds like an angry schoolteacher and Imogen immediately feels like she's done something wrong and is being sent to the headmaster's office.

'Yes.'

'Good.'

The cat is looking at Imogen. Cats give her the creeps. She turns her back on it. 'What happens next?'

'Your email was rather cryptic. Let's start at the beginning. Who are you?'

Imogen has no idea how to talk to journalists. 'I'm Imogen Collins.'

'Yes, I gathered that from your email address and your signature.'

What a fun way to spend an evening. Imogen is sweating despite shivering with cold. *You can do this, Imogen.*

'I'm nineteen. I'm an influencer on Instagram.' *Influencer.* The word suddenly feels so dirty. A thought strikes: *Is what she's doing on Instagram the same as what Mörður and London Analytica are planning to do to all those girls?* The thought is so unbearable that she suppresses it. 'I studied psychology at Cambridge University, but a year ago I quit and went to work for London Analytica.'

'And that's a marketing firm, right?'

'Yes. Ms Kendrick, the founder, says that what we do at London Analytica is the future of marketing. And I think she may be right.

'Behavioural microtargeting is definitely the future. But it's not the utopian, sunny future she makes it sound like in her pitches. Rather, it's the future of *Terminator* and *1984* and *Minority Report* and *The War of the Worlds* and *Blade Runner* and *The Matrix* and—'

'Okay, thank you, I get it.'

The cat meows and it sends shivers down Imogen's spine.

There's noise on the other end of the phone line, voices in the background. 'Victoria, your dinner is here,' someone calls out.

Imogen realises something. This may mean everything to Imogen. But to Victoria King, this is just another day at the office.

Imogen knows what she needs to do. It sounds repugnant, vulgar and vile, but she needs to *sell* Victoria the horror of the story.

She may not know anything about journalism, but she works in marketing, and she's got one million followers on Instagram. If there's one thing she knows, it's packaging something to make it appealing, intriguing and interesting. If there's one thing she knows, it's selling.

Victoria is chewing down the phone. 'So, tell me about this Slimline project. How is it different from the other work London Analytica takes on?'

'It isn't. It's exactly the same. We're basically taking a product and targeting it directly at individuals who are likely to buy it. It's the audience that's the problem. It's the audience that I have issues with.

'A few months ago, the pharmaceutical company Frexer came to us with some slimming pills they've been making and selling over the counter for years. The sales had dropped recently so they rebranded them, redesigned the packaging and gave them a new name: Slimline.

'To tie in with the rebrand they wanted to do a targeted campaign. This happens all the time. Companies rebrand something and want to get the word out to the right people. That's fine. But it's how their target audience has been defined that I find absolutely sickening. In London Analytica's work for Frexer it's stated that the targets of the campaign are to be – and this is a direct quote – sixteen- to twenty-four-year-old girls with body image issues and eating disorders.

'It's all a secret, of course. I could go to jail for just telling you this. The staff sign a nondisclosure agreement for every project. But I don't care. This is just unacceptable.'

There's silence on the other end of the line. *Damn.* Imogen had thought that she'd been so persuasive. She clearly needs to do better.

'Look,' Imogen says, changing her tone from enraged to measured. 'You've probably seen a lot as a journalist. War zones, violence, banking crises, people dying from incurable diseases. This in comparison may not sound like anything important. But let me ask you this: if you could search every social media account in the world and find accounts of people who've had suicidal thoughts in the past month, would you think it okay to target them with ads from a gun store?'

A thought she's been trying to keep from surfacing chokes her up and fills her with horror. Is that what she's been doing?

As an influencer Imogen gets paid for smiling at a camera while wearing a particular item of clothing or make-up or jewellery. When you think about it, she's a living, breathing billboard. She has sometimes pretended that what she does has more to do with art than business – it often feels creative, designing the shoots and taking the photographs; she sometimes feels she's composing a short story when she writes the captions. But it's total self-delusion.

Imogen remembers her date in London with Callum – it feels like a lifetime ago. He'd talked about how marketing was all about making people feel bad about themselves so companies could sell them a quick fix and make a quick buck. It's like the Slimline project; it's all about using people's weaknesses against them. But there's more to it than that.

When Imogen promotes a fashion brand, a cosmetic product, a toothpaste, she presents an ideal, a mould, a picture of what the perfect life/look/person is meant to be. In doing so, she's giving people goals; she's encouraging them to aspire to be like her; aim for it; compete for it. But how are people meant to reach that goal when the bar is set so high – no, not high – when the bar is so far removed from reality that not even Imogen Collins, the person, stands a chance of achieving the life of Imogen Collins, the social media influencer?

Is this the reason Imogen hasn't been posting on Instagram lately?

Imogen's thoughts are interrupted by Victoria King chewing. 'What have you got?' she says, clearly with her mouth full.

'What do you mean?'

'What proof do you have?'

'Other than the fact that I'm working on this project right now?'

'Yes, so you tell me. But for me to pursue this further I need something concrete. I have to know that this project actually exists. No one will just take your word for it. I need proof.'

Imogen can't believe what she's hearing. She lowers the phone. The blood is pounding in her ears. These words. Not only has she heard them before but they've haunted her for the past year of her life.

No one will just take your word for it. That's what Mörður said to her.

'Imogen, Imogen, are you still there?'

Victoria King's voice sounds thin and metallic through the receiver of Imogen's phone. The acoustics of the alley, with its concrete walls and arched ceiling, give it a hollow, haunting, ghostly quality as it seeps through the tunnel and disappears into the night. The cat meows whingeingly, as if offended by this intrusion into his hangout, and runs off.

Imogen is left alone in her hiding place. She pushes the phone back up against her ear. It feels cold against her skin.

Victoria King and the Beast may be right. Perhaps no one will take her word for it. But Imogen is on a mission. Nothing is going to stop her getting justice – or better yet: revenge. She will do what needs to be done. Whatever it takes.

'Imogen? Imogen?'

'Don't worry, I'll get you your proof.'

Photo: A photo of an article in a newspaper.
Filter: Inkwell.

Possible captions . . .

Option one: I'm in print **#lovemyjob #dreamcometrue**
Option two: I thought I'd be changing the world as a journalist – instead I'm writing about a lost cat . . .
Option three: . . . and the alleged vermin of the skies.
Option four: Seagulls may not be as cute as swans but do they not have the right to exist? And what's the deal with cans of 'dolphin-friendly tuna'? There are no cans of 'tuna-friendly dolphin'. Is it because the dolphin is cute while the tuna is butt ugly?

Actual caption . . .

My first real job **#grownup**

♥37

Chapter Fifteen

Hannah

At the morning's editorial meeting I'm given such a mundane assignment that I'm finding it hard to stay awake writing it. My article is about a group of seagulls that have set upon Tjörnin, a pond in the city centre which is a popular destination for families with children who bring bread to feed the ducks. The bread is starting to attract seagulls to the pond which some say are threatening other birdlife. The City Council is about to debate whether to cull the seagulls with poison or firearms in the hope they'll stay away.

Yawn.

Not all journalists are given such mundane assignments as mine. Heiða is doing a feature on the life of Imogen Collins. She called Imogen's parents. They didn't want to give a comment but they said they would respect their daughter's wishes for the time being and not fly over to Iceland. Apparently Imogen's lawyer had said that Imogen wouldn't want to see them if they came over, so really there was no point. They might be over for the trial though.

I begged Dad to let me and Kjarri work on a special piece about the murder for *IceNews*. He looked at me as if he'd never heard anything so ridiculous in his whole life. But I'm not giving up. If I present him with a finding – a scoop – about the murder that Heiða has missed, I might convince him to let me do it.

Why am I so obsessed with this case? Why do I feel that I'm meant to solve it? A shocking thought enters my mind. Is it the curse? I go through the list of symptoms: false beliefs, delusions of grandeur, voices in your head.

But the voice in my head telling me to do this is my own. And I didn't imagine Imogen giving me her phone. That actually happened. All of this is happening. I'm just being paranoid.

That logic, however, makes me feel even worse. The word arouses another bout of anxiety.

Paranoia is an early symptom of the curse.

It doesn't have to mean anything, I tell myself as I fight a burst of panic. Sometimes I feel like my body is stuffed with bubble wrap. The kind you squeeze with your fingers and the plastic bubbles pop, except the bubbles inside me aren't filled with air but anxiety which splashes through me with each explosion.

It doesn't mean anything. It doesn't mean anything. You are not your mother.

I need to think about something else. I need to fill my head with thoughts, keep my brain busy to prevent it from conjuring up memories I want to keep buried like dead bodies in a cemetery. Maybe that's why I'm so obsessed with Imogen Collins and the murder of Mörður Þórðarson. It keeps those zombie thoughts at bay.

I suddenly get an idea. I reach for my mobile and open the contacts. At the top is Alda. I click her name and the phone starts ringing.

'Hi, darling,' she drawls in her husky voice and I can hear that she's got a cigarette hanging from the corner of her mouth.

'Are you free for lunch?'

'For you: always.'

'I see you've changed your hair,' Alda says when we sit down in the cafeteria at Oddi, the social science building, each with a cellophane-wrapped sandwich and a glass of lukewarm tap water. Alda's office is in Árnagarður, the humanities building, but I told her that I'd prefer eating in Oddi because someone had told me the food is better there.

'I decided to take Rósa up on her offer.' The purple stripe is gone and I'm back to my original red hair colour. When I glanced at myself in the mirror this morning I looked eerily like Mum.

'I read your interview with that internet girl,' Alda says.

'That *internet girl*.' I snort.

'I don't get it.'

'You don't get what?'

'Why is everyone so obsessed about being noticed, talked about, seen? Why does everybody want to be famous?'

I unwrap my sandwich. 'I don't know. I suppose it gives your life meaning. I mean, there's no meaning to any of this, but if you're famous at least you leave a mark.'

'What do you mean, there is no meaning? I've never heard anything so stupid in my life.'

'Aren't you the vice-chair of the Atheist Society?' Alda is the only person related to Dad that Granny Jo approves of. I have

211

the feeling that it's their mutual loathing of a higher power that brings them so divinely together.

'Meaning has nothing to do with religion. You should know that better than anyone.'

'Why should I know that?'

'You've recently had to face up to the finitude of life. Let me tell you something I recently read about heartbeats. A typical human heart beats somewhere between sixty and one hundred times a minute. That means that in a lifetime a human heart beats around three billion times. Each of us gets three billion heartbeats. That doesn't sound much at all, does it? You can either get depressed about it or you can use each and every heartbeat you get to the fullest. Three billion heartbeats. Ready, set, go.'

'That might tell me something about urgency but it tells me nothing about meaning.' I bite into the sandwich. The filling appears to be ninety-five per cent mayo, one per cent prawns, and four per cent egg.

'So,' Alda says as she takes her tuna mayo sandwich apart. The filling is all gathered in a lump in the middle. She starts spreading it evenly towards the edges of the slice. 'Why are you here? Certainly not for the sandwiches.'

'Can't I have lunch with my aunt for no particular reason?'

Alda puts the sandwich back together and takes a bite. 'I'm guessing that it's no coincidence that we're eating in the same building where your friend, "the internet girl", worked.'

Am I that transparent?

Alda suddenly jumps up from her chair. She waves to a guy with a pimply face and shaved head, wearing a brown shearling jacket, just paying for a cup of coffee at the till.

'Máni,' she calls out. 'Could you come here for a second?'

The guy strides over. He's noticeably tall and slim. His shoulders are hunched as if gravity is trying to get the better of his tallness.

'This is Hannah, my niece. She just moved here from the UK.'

The guy nods at me. I nod back.

'This is Máni Jónsson. He's a psychology major and he kindly keeps me up to date on the latest news in the School of Health and Sciences.'

Máni gives a snorty laugh. 'That's a nice way of putting it.' He turns to me. 'Your aunt is known as the gossip queen of the history department. Her colleagues say that she's more interested in present events, especially those taking place in the hallways of the university, than the past; they say that maybe she should switch to the anthropology department.'

Alda and Máni laugh heartily as if he said something funny. I guess it's one of those jokes that's only amusing in academic circles.

Alda grabs her satchel from the floor, slams it on the table and takes out her nicotine gum. 'Hannah is very talented. She works for *Dagblaðið*. I want you to tell Hannah what you told me about Mörður Þórðarson. About what you saw a couple of days before his murder.'

Máni immediately obliges. 'It happened here in the cafeteria. It was late. Most of the students had gone home. Mörður was having coffee with some guy I'd never seen before. He was slightly porky, wearing a huge leather jacket. They were speaking in English but the man had an accent.

'All of a sudden Mörður's wife bounded in. She was screaming and crying and stumbling. For a moment I thought she might be drunk. But I think she was just seriously mad. She ran over to where Mörður and the man were sitting and hit Mörður over the head with a big leather laptop bag. He jumped up from his chair, screaming out in pain. She threw the bag on the floor and slapped him. Then she began punching him all over and screaming at him.'

I don't blink as I stare up at Máni. 'What did she say?'

'Nothing that made any sense. "You lousy bastard. I can't believe you did that to me again." Something like that. The man in the leather jacket got caught in the crossfire when the woman's fist hit him right in the eye.'

'How did the fight end?'

'Mörður grabbed his wife by the wrists and manoeuvred her out of the cafeteria into the DataPsych lab. That was the last time I saw him.'

There's a sombre silence. Máni takes a sip of his coffee then looks at his watch. 'It's been nice talking to you ladies but I've got a class.'

Alda gets up and gives Máni a hug. 'Say hi to your mum for me.'

'Will do,' he says and he's off.

Alda sits back down again. 'Good kid. I went to school with his mum. I'm keeping an eye on him for her.'

'Did you know Mörður?' I ask without trying to hide my intentions; Alda knows what I'm up to – although she doesn't know the full extent of it.

'Not really. I sometimes said hello to him in the hallway, but he wouldn't have been interested in a longer conversation.'

214

'Why not?'

'My boobs aren't big enough. Allegedly he was quite the ladies' man.'

My phone buzzes. It's Daisy.

D: Miss you. Call me when you get home from work.

Alda is staring at me with a cheeky grin on her face. 'Does your dad know what you're doing?'

'I'm not doing anything.'

'If you say so. But be careful. Iceland is like a small town. You step on someone's toes in such a tight-knit community and you'll invoke the wrath of the rest of their clan. Blood runs thicker than water and in Iceland everyone is related.'

I can't look her in the eye when I ask the question. 'Are you having coffee?'

'I don't know. Probably. Why?'

'I was just wondering whether you could get me an orange juice. I feel like my blood sugar levels need a boost.'

Alda gets up. 'Anything for my favourite niece.'

As soon as Alda turns her back I bend down, slip my hand into her bag on the floor and rummage blindly through the contents until my fingers find what I'm looking for. With a swift movement I pull out Alda's university badge, which she refuses to wear around her neck 'because she is not a branded sheep'.

Alda is just reaching the counter when I raise myself up again and slide the badge into the pocket of my coat hanging on the back of my chair.

Alda grabs a juice from the fridge and joins the queue for the till. She smiles at me. I smile back, feeling awful about what I just did – what I'm about to do – while at the same time chanting a mantra in my head: *The end justifies the means; the end justifies the means.*

Photo: A white door.
Filter: Willow.

Caption: This is the door to my office. Does it look scary to
you?

❤301

What the caption should have been . . .

Option one: Stepping through that door every morning is like
putting my soul into a shredder.
Option two: I cried myself to sleep last night out of fear of
having to get up in the morning to go through that shredder
once again.
Option three: Sharing an office with the Beast causes me to
relive what he did to me every single day. My life is like a
horror version of that film Groundhog Day.
Option four: Do you care? Do any of you want to know?
Sponsors? Followers?

Chapter Sixteen

Imogen

Imogen is alone in the DataPsych lab. Mörður is out in meetings and Orri went to lunch with his mum. 'I feel guilty about shouting at her the other day,' he explained to Imogen. 'I should make it up to her.' He invited Imogen along but she declined. This is exactly what she needs: the office to herself.

Imogen waits a little while after Orri leaves – he's always forgetting something: his car keys, his phone, his jacket. When she's sure he isn't returning she gets up from her desk and heads for Mörður's office.

She opens the door. Immediately the smell of Mörður attacks her senses. His aftershave, sickly sweet and aggressively peppery, fills the room. She stops herself gagging by imagining the smell of victory. *Flowers, happiness, revenge.*

She sits down at his desk. His computer is in sleep mode. The thought of touching anything he's touched repulses her but she forces herself to lay her hand on the mouse. The monitor springs to life.

Mörður's computer is password-protected. But Imogen has come prepared. The other day Mörður had asked Imogen to set the room up for a presentation he was giving to the faculty staff about the lab's work. While Mörður logged in on the computer, Imogen was standing behind him, making a note of his password.

Imogen starts typing: baz00ka.

The spinning wheel appears. For a brief moment she worries that Mörður has changed his password.

But he hasn't. Of course he hasn't. Who changes their password?

Imogen isn't sure what she's looking for exactly. She isn't looking for evidence. She's got plenty of that. Mörður hasn't been at all secretive about the Slimline project. He just treats it as any other client work. Imogen and Orri have both signed a non-disclosure agreement for commercial purposes (it has nothing to do with moral ambiguity; the client just doesn't want any trade secrets to leak to the competition). So Mörður has forwarded most of the documents to Imogen to use in her work.

She's got the original proposal branded with the DataPsych logo and signed by Mörður, which outlines the services DataPsych will provide to London Analytica on behalf of Frexer. It lists the costs, defines the scope of their analyses, determines their target audience (sixteen- to twenty-four-year-old girls with body image issues and eating disorders) and stipulates the delivery date.

She's also got emails between DataPsych and third-party companies which provide them with data for their analysis – at a steep price, Imogen came to realise when she was sent the invoices for the purchase. Data mining is clearly the new gold rush.

Finally, she's got emails from Ms Kendrick and Mark in which they discuss the project with Imogen and communicate to her the client's wishes on things that Mörður doesn't care to be involved in, such as the design of the final report, the colour scheme and the delivery method: PDF? PowerPoint slides? Cloud-based reports? Imogen managed to convince them to go with the last option. 'You do claim to be the future of marketing, don't you?' she'd said and got a massive kick out of it when Ms Kendrick got all defensive and sensitive about her age or her tech know-how – Imogen wasn't sure which.

So, Imogen's got enough evidence ready for Victoria King to wallpaper the entire offices of the *Herald*. But something is missing. Imogen doesn't want Victoria's exposé to be only about morally dodgy business practices; she doesn't want it to be a piece about a faceless corporation taking advantage of faceless victims. No. This needs to be more personal. This *is* personal.

Imogen opens a folder on Mörður's computer named 'London Analytica'. She's looking for a motive. Not the obvious financial gain but an underlying one. She needs the news article to show intent: intent to hurt, intent to be cruel. She's looking for proof of Mörður's malevolence. This has to ruin him. Not only professionally. That's not enough. She wants this to be a shadow on his character for all eternity. She wants the whole world to see Mörður for the beast that he is.

Imogen scrolls through the contents of the folder. Mörður isn't very organised and it's filled with documents with undescriptive names such as 'doc1.pdf' and 'dataset5.xlsx' and subfolders named 'New Client' and 'Marketing Analysis'. How can the man work like this? It's a miracle that his laboratory functions at all. How is Imogen meant to find anything amidst this chaos? It's not like Imogen was expecting to find a document neatly titled 'my_evil_plans.doc'. But she thought she could at least narrow her search down to one folder.

She does have one thing she can use against him. The email he'd meant to send to Ms Kendrick but accidentally sent to Imogen. The subject had been rather offensive: 'Youth + Insecurities = A Shitload of Money'. It definitely bore witness to his callousness. Imogen had studied the email last night and included it in the ZIP file she was preparing for Victoria King. It appeared to be a follow-up to a phone conversation between Mörður and Ms Kendrick about whether identifying the target group to which Frexer wanted to market their slimming pills was technically possible.

'I've done some preliminary tests and it can most certainly be done,' Mörður had said in the email. 'All those silly girls think that they can hide the truth about their sad little lives behind lipstick, filters and pretty pouts, but the data doesn't lie. Data reveals the real person behind the fake smile.'

The email is good. It proves Mörður is a vulgar old fart. But Imogen is looking to prove that he's pure evil.

She's sometimes wondered what all the people working on the project think about it. Ms Kendrick. Mark. The designers. The data providers. Even Mörður. They all know what's going on. They all know that they're searching the digital community for the weakest, most vulnerable individuals, people who genuinely need help, and exploiting their weakness, their sickness and disease to make money. Do they think it's okay because it's just business? Or do they simply choose to look the other way and let it happen – like Samuel Pearce did the day the old Imogen died?

This isn't helping. Imogen has less than thirty minutes until Orri returns from lunch. She needs a different strategy.

She goes back to 'All my files'. She moves the mouse and the cursor glides towards the search box. She types in 'Youth +

Insecurities = A Shitload of Money'. Nothing comes up. If she only knew better what she was looking for. *What to type, what to type . . . ?*

She types in the word 'girls'. A list of results appears. A lot of them are Excel documents, data used for research. But although data always reveals the truth, according to Mörður, Imogen doesn't need data. She has plenty of data. She's looking to add colour to her truth. She excludes all Excel documents from the search results. All that's left is one Word document and a couple of JPEGs. She highlights them and presses 'open'.

The Word document is titled 'In the Middle of the Night' and it turns out to be a half-finished novel Mörður is working on. Anger surges inside Imogen. He shouldn't be allowed to have hopes and ambitions. He took all that away from her. She wants to press 'delete', as if wiping out his novel would somehow destroy his dream like he had destroyed hers. It isn't the same, of course – but if it was, it wouldn't be any good; his dream is backed up on Dropbox.

Imogen closes the novel. She jolts back when one of the JPEGs she's opened stares her in the face – literally. It's a photo of two smiling girls. They must be around five years old – one is a little older than the other. They're blonde with blue eyes and they're dressed up as the princesses from the movie *Frozen*. One is Elsa, the other Anna. They must be Mörður's daughters.

Imogen starts to shake. Her eyes are watering. They look so happy. So innocent. Who is she to destroy all that?

That is not your problem, Imogen.

But how can she tell herself that? Isn't that exactly what Ms Kendrick, Mark and everyone who's working on the Slimline project tells themselves? Not my problem. Not my doing.

222

But she is not targeting them specifically. Not like Mörður targeted her. Not like young women are being targeted by Frexer with the help of London Analytica and DataPsych. In every tragedy there is collateral damage. Imogen wasn't the only one who got hurt in Mörður's attack. Just ask her parents.

She needs to stay strong if she's going to complete her mission. It isn't Imogen who's hurting those innocent little girls. It's their dad who's hurting them. Actions have consequences.

She closes the photo along with the rest of the JPEGs.

Twenty minutes. Focus, Imogen, focus.

Imogen types in a new search word: 'young'.

The results consist of a few Word documents and a single PowerPoint document titled 'discord_among_the_young_CONFIDENTIAL.pptx'.

She clicks on it.

It looks like a slide show for a sales pitch. The first slide is branded with the DataPsych logo:

Behavioural Microtargeting and How it Applies to the Petroleum Business

A presentation for Smertoil
CONFIDENTIAL

Imogen moves to the next slide.

What We Offer

• Psychographic microtargeting.

- Access to a unique model that predicts the personality of social media users in the UK and the West.
- In reverse our model serves as a personality search engine.

This all sounds familiar. This is basically London Analytica's sales pitch in a nutshell. But there is no mention of London Analytica anywhere. That's strange. DataPsych recently signed a five-year exclusivity agreement with London Analytica. It isn't allowed to work for anyone else in that period of time.

Imogen quickly scrolls through the slides on the sidebar. There's one about the OCEAN system; there's one that explains how data can be used to identify different types of people; there's one about DataPsych's glowing track record. It explains how, as an example, it helped a clothing retailer increase its revenue by forty per cent in just three months using targeted ads and a viral social media campaign. Imogen remembers the campaign. It was for Wareshop, one of London Analytica's biggest clients – DataPsych only served as a technology provider.

Imogen scrolls back to the first slide. Smertoil. She opens Chrome and types in the name in the address bar. The browser searches Google. There are hundreds of search results. She clicks on a post on Wikipedia: 'Smertoil is a Russian energy corporation with headquarters in Moscow specialising in the business of the extraction, production, transport and sale of petroleum.'

Why would a Russian oil company want to target individual consumers with ads?

She keeps on reading. 'Smertoil is the tenth largest company in Russia and one of the largest global producers of crude oil.'

Imogen types 'crude oil' into Google. According to www.thefreedictionary.com, crude oil is 'petroleum as it comes from the ground, before refining'.

All the deals Imogen has worked on with London Analytica and DataPsych have been to promote consumer-based products. It's not like many people are likely buyers of unrefined petroleum. It at least has to be turned into gasoline or diesel or whatever before it can be targeted at consumers. Why would anyone want to sell crude oil on Facebook?

Imogen scrolls through the slide show again. She stops to look at the next-to-last slide.

DataPsych and Smertoil

In addition to consultation and analysis, DataPsych offers tailored services to meet our clients' more complicated needs. We offer:

- Covert campaigns
- Disinformation campaigns
- The spreading of viral discord among targeted groups defined by both demographics (gender, age, ethnicity, education) and psychometrics (intelligence, aptitude, attitudes and personality traits)
- Political warfare
- Platform manipulation (Twitter, Facebook, YouTube and Instagram)

Imogen is trying to add 1 + 1 but she can't for the life of her get it to result in the number 2. Why is Mörður pitching to a Russian oil company? Why isn't London Analytica in on the deal? And why does the slide-show list services that have nothing to do with marketing? Covert campaigns. Political warfare. What has that got to do with selling crude oil?

Imogen clicks the last slide.

The team

- Dr Mörður Þórðarson, principal investigator and CEO of DataPsych laboratories
- Orri Sigurlínuson, PhD student and sessional teacher at the Department of Computer Science at the University of Iceland

Sitting inside Mörður's office, Imogen doesn't hear the lab door open. She's so engrossed in her snooping that she doesn't detect the footsteps approaching; she doesn't notice a shadow clouding the desk.

'Imogen!'

It's a voice she knows well, a voice that's usually soft, unassuming, reassuring; the sound equivalent of a blanket, hot cocoa, the sofa and a sitcom. She almost doesn't recognise it laced with anger and aggression, sounding so accusatory.

Imogen looks up. Orri's face, usually the picture of stoicism, is rippling with fury.

The sight, the setting: it's an instant trigger. Her body goes into fight-or-flight mode. Her heart pulses, counting down the

226

seconds to a moment that will determine the difference between life and death. Her senses heighten like a radio that is turned all the way up. It's as if she starts hearing with her eyes and seeing with her skin; she can feel the air and smell the danger.

She hits the edge of the desk with the heels of her palms. The office chair she's sitting on wheels back. She jumps up and runs away from Orri. She slams into a wall. She's trapped. She's prey. It all comes crashing back down on her: the lab, the slithering hand, the pinch; her skin is blistering, her soul is dying.

She pushes her back up against the wall. Orri's presence is getting bigger, bigger; he towers over her like the dark end of the world. He growls, roars, rages – like a grizzly bear boding her demise – or that's how her hyper-alert senses perceive the situation.

She cowers from his words.

'What do you think you're doing?'

Photo: White frost on a car window, shaped like snow crystals blown up under a microscope.
Filter: Clarendon.

Possible captions . . .

Option one: Chestnuts roasting on an open fire . . .
Option two: **#beautiful**
Option three: Scraping a car window when you left your gloves at the office should be defined as torture according to human rights law.
Option four: My feet are so cold I can't feel my toes any more.

Actual caption . . .

Craving mince pies and mulled wine.

♥28

Chapter Seventeen

Hannah

'Are you doing anything this evening?' I ask Kjarri when I get back to the office after my lunch with Alda.

'Free as a bird,' he answers slightly too enthusiastically. Expectation gleams in his eyes. I immediately realise that he thinks I'm about to ask him out.

I'm taken aback. I hadn't really thought about him like that. Had he thought about me like that?

I extinguish his hope as quickly as I can. 'Remember when you said that the end justifies the means?'

Kjarri just stares at me, incomprehension widening his face – it is a handsome face. But that's not what this is about. This is not the time to think about Kjarri's face: his blue eyes, playfully weaved with strands of grey; his exceptionally well-trimmed stubble; his smile that embraces you like a hug from a teddy bear.

Focus, Hannah. Focus.

'I need a favour.'

Kjarri and I are inside Oddi, the university's social science building where I met up with Alda earlier that day. I can't feel my toes. Why didn't I wear more weather-appropriate shoes?

Am I turning into a proper Icelander? It's after eleven and the building is completely dark.

We slowly climb the stairs to the upper floor, using our mobiles as torches.

I think of Alda. Has she realised that her badge is gone? Has she realised that her university ID, which doubles as an electronic key to the university buildings to which she has been assigned access, is missing? Probably not. She probably won't realise until tomorrow morning when she arrives at work. Will she immediately know that I took it?

We reach the upper floor. Kjarri aims his light down a corridor lined with identical white doors – identical, except for one. Blocking the entrance of DataPsych laboratories, marked Room 4, is yellow police tape.

'Are we seriously doing this?' Kjarri asks.

'If you don't want to you don't have to,' I say, knowing deep down that he doesn't want to, yet hoping he won't back out.

'Do you think it's illegal?'

'What?' I ask, running through all the things we're doing that might be illegal: stealing your aunt's university entrance pass; using it to break into a university building under the darkness of night.

'Breaking a police barrier,' he clarifies.

'I don't know.'

'I mean, it's just tape. It's not like we're cutting through a steel lock or anything.'

'I'm sure the judge will take that into consideration.'

Kjarri smiles. 'You're mad.'

Usually I'd get defensive if someone said that about me. But the way Kjarri says it, it sounds like a compliment. Maybe it's okay to be slightly off the normal spectrum.

We make our way to the DataPsych lab. When we reach the door Kjarri raises his hand, preparing to remove the police tape blocking the door.

'Wait,' I say. 'I'll do it.' If this is a crime I want to be the one who commits it. This was, after all, my idea. The tape is stuck to the doorframe on each side of the door. It's easy to peel off. We bought a glue stick on our way here to make sure we'd be able to stick it back on once we leave. I feel like we're a couple of seasoned crooks.

Next, I take out my phone and find the photo of the lab code I'd discovered in Imogen's inbox. I only hope they haven't disabled her access.

There's a silver keypad next to the door. I type in the code: 375090.

There's a click and we're in.

We step inside and close the door behind us. The lab is pitch-black but the feeble light from our mobiles will have to do.

My hope of finding something useful suddenly evaporates. The computers are all gone. The police must have taken them to have them examined.

Kjarri looks around the room. There's nothing left but tables and chairs. 'We can go to the cinema instead,' he says. 'There's a new film starring Keanu Reeves. He was voted the sexiest man alive by *People* magazine in 1994. Who can say no to that?'

'As tempting as it sounds, let's just take a quick look.'

I feel my way past the furniture and find myself inside a small kitchen corner which consists of a plate with mouldy fruit on a table and a tiny fridge. I open the fridge. It's empty except for a few cans of Diet Coke. I close it again.

I point my torch towards the back of the room. 'There's a door over there.'

Kjarri fumbles his way towards it. He turns the knob. 'It's locked.'

Of course it is.

I'm half resigned to the fact that this mission has been a big fat failure when I spot that underneath each desk, attached to the tabletop, is a steel safe with a keypad. The possibility is remote, but we've got nothing to lose.

'Which desk do you think is Imogen's?'

Kjarri starts walking between the desks pointing his light at them. 'Probably not this one,' he says and holds up a small Yoda figurine.

'Don't stereotype,' I say, even though I'm pretty sure he's right.

I see something that looks like a tube of lip balm on one of the tables. 'I'm guessing this one.'

'Don't stereotype,' Kjarri replies.

I grin at him. 'Touché.'

I sit down on the floor and point the light at the keypad. 'Here goes nothing.' I type in 230464 – Imogen Collins's mum's date of birth.

A little green light on the keypad turns on. 'No way!'

Kjarri comes running and nearly falls over when he hits his foot on a desk chair.

'Open it,' he yelps.

'What did you think I was going to do? Sit here and admire it?'

I pull the door open. For a whole second, I think the safe is completely empty. But then I spot a single A4 sheet of paper lying folded at the bottom.

Kjarri reaches forward and grabs it.

'Hey,' I exclaim, but secretly I'm pleased. He's into this too.

I lean closer to Kjarri as he unfolds the paper. It's a text-only document. The type is small and it's longer than the one-sheet format would suggest.

It has a date at the top. It's dated a couple of weeks ago. And it's got a heading. I gasp in shock:

An Account of a Crime

I can't help myself. I snatch the sheet of paper from Kjarri's hands and start reading.

My name is Imogen Collins. This is a statement of how on July 12th last year Mörður Þórðarson sexually assaulted me. The attack took place in the then DataPsych laboratory at the Department of Psychology at the University of Cambridge – the lab has since moved to Iceland.
The events of that day have haunted me. It's because of these events that I left the university, and lost all contact with my family and control over my own destiny.
The day Mörður Þórðarson tried to rape me, a part of me died. Following is my account of these events.

Photo: Dog poo in the shape of a sausage resting on a side walk with ice crystals forming on the surface.
Filter: Hudson.

Caption: Why do people on the internet feel the need to shit over someone else's life?

❤174

What the caption should have been . . .

Option one: For the past few days I've been inundated with negative comments here on Instagram. I'm used to getting the occasional 'die you cow' or 'you look ugly today'. But those have always been the exception. I've managed to ignore them. But now it's like the whole world hates me. What happened? What did I do wrong? Can any of you explain to me what I did to piss you all off?
Option two: Maybe I should just bow out and close all my social media accounts. I never meant to become an

influencer. When the number of my followers suddenly snowballed after a hashtag I invented – **#fashionfreakyfriday** – went viral and everyone began posting photos of themselves wearing ball gowns while doing the dishes or their pyjamas in Tesco's, my friends said I should cash in on it. Maybe I should simply quit.

Chapter Eighteen

Imogen

Imogen is cowering on the floor, up against the wall. A sharp wailing sound, like a siren, is hurting her ears. She suddenly realises it's coming from her.

'Imogen. Imogen.' Someone is shaking her. It's Orri. 'Imogen, are you okay? Do you need an ambulance? I'm going to call an ambulance.'

Fear clouds his usually transparent eyes, like white frost on a window. He lets go of her shoulders and pulls out his phone.

The siren stops. 'No.' She doesn't need an ambulance. She needs a time machine. She needs to go back to the summer of last year. If only she could go back in time and change things, as if she were editing a story. But changing the past is not an option. Neither, however, is doing nothing. If she can't change the past, she needs to face it – and conquer it.

Imogen untangles the knot that is her shrunken body. 'I'm okay. I'll be okay.'

Orri stares at her, frozen with uncertainty and shock. 'What was that?'

Imogen suddenly feels embarrassed. Orri must think she's completely mad.

'It's nothing. It's just . . .' Her lame attempt at making up an excuse fizzles out.

For the past few weeks Imogen and Orri have become good friends. Last night, at the pub, Imogen got the sense that they were on the brink of becoming something more than just friends. But now she's blown it.

She stares into Orri's eyes. How can something as beautiful exist in a world that's so ugly and cruel? Some people say the eyes are the window to the soul. Imogen thinks that's a seriously stupid and superficial idea. But in Orri's case, it's true. He's just as calm, kind and tender as his eyes reflect.

She can't let this happen. She can't lose him. The Beast has taken everything from her. He isn't taking Orri as well.

There is only one thing she can do. Imogen tells Orri the truth.

Orri stays silent for a while after. Imogen can't help wondering: Is he disgusted by her?

Then he takes her hands and says, 'I'm going to kill him.'

Imogen laughs with relief. 'Yes, well, join the queue.'

'Why didn't you go to the police after he attacked you?'

Imogen thinks back to the days after Mörður assaulted her. They're all a bit of a blur but she tries to recount to Orri what happened after the attack.

Imogen remembers being unable to sleep, lying in bed crying, sitting at her desk trying to study for her exams but unable to concentrate. She remembers forcing herself to smile and act normal at the dinner table. She remembers her sister walking in on her in the bathroom where she was kneeling in front of the toilet throwing up and asking Imogen if everything was all right. 'Yes, just exam nerves,' Imogen had replied. And she remembers futile attempts to thinking the problem away, to chase her pain away with perspective: *You're lucky. You weren't hurt. You weren't killed. There's no blood, no broken bones. This could have been so much worse. Nothing happened, not really.*

But something had happened. And although the bruises faded, her mind kept bleeding. She felt dirty, violated and sad to the core of her being. Her life had been derailed. Her whole future had been rewritten in the course of a mere two minutes. She was mourning what she'd lost. A part of her had died. Her life would never be the same again. She would never be the same again.

On top of all that she kept blaming herself. Imogen had been flattered when Mörður offered her a place on his team and she'd enjoyed his attention – but only in a professional capacity. She'd been flattered by the attention in the same way Mörður took pride in his statue of a golden lion, a trophy he'd won for his work at an advertising convention in Cannes – it stood on his desk and he showed it to everyone who visited the lab. Had she tempted him somehow? Sent out the wrong signals?

Of course not. She knew she hadn't done anything wrong. But still she couldn't lose the shame over what he'd done to her.

The day of her first exam Imogen called in sick. With her second one, she didn't even bother calling. She simply didn't show up. What was the point?

Then Mörður called her out of the blue. He sounded upbeat. Excited even. 'I've just heard back from London Analytica and we've got the deal. They're actually looking for a social media campaigns executive and I've recommended you. I think you would be perfect for the job. Jobs like this don't come around that often. I think it's a really good opportunity. Having practical experience is very important these days. It gives you an edge. You can return to your studies later. Uni will always be there. I should also say that I'm not sure I can offer you a place at the lab next year; our budget is tight and I have to give other students the same opportunity you got this year. So, what shall I tell them? Will you take the job?'

She might as well. She was failing. He was pushing her.

When Imogen told her parents that she was quitting uni they lost it. There was screaming and crying and slamming of doors. They couldn't understand why she was throwing her life away like that.

What she couldn't tell them was that she had no say over her own life any more. She was a reed in a breeze, blowing in whichever direction the wind decided to send her.

Imogen doesn't realise that she's crying until Orri leans forward and wipes a tear away.

'I'm so sorry you had to go through this,' he says. 'I have a friend who went through something similar. She was studying at a university in the States when a fellow student sexually assaulted her at a party. She went to the school authorities and they allocated her a lawyer and referred her to a counsellor. She was asked to write a detailed report about the incident. She said it was painful and cathartic at the same time. But most of all it was important to document what happened while she still remembered it clearly.'

Orri takes Imogen's hand. 'Have you ever written down what you just told me?'

'No.'

'Do you want to?'

Imogen realises that she does. She really does. She gets up to go to her desk. 'Can you sit with me while I do it?'

'Of course.'

She writes and she cries and Orri wraps his arm around her without speaking, without interrupting the flow of words she's been keeping bottled up for so long.

Once she's finished she doesn't save the document – it's her work computer and she doesn't want Mörður to find it – but prints it out and puts it in the locked safe underneath her desk. One day she might decide to go to the police with her statement.

Orri gets up, goes into the kitchen and gets a glass of water. He hands it to Imogen.

'Thanks.' She doesn't know whether she feels empty or lighter after unburdening her thoughts on to the page like that.

Orri sits back down. 'What were you looking for on Mörður's computer? Something to give to the journalist at the *Herald*?'

'Yes.'

'And did you find anything?' Orri's voice turns hard. Is he angry with her?

'Not really. Technically, I've already got what I need. But I want something more. I want this to be big.'

'I saw what you were reading on his computer. I think you've found what you are looking for.'

'Smertoil?'

Orri nods. 'It's explosive.'

'Really? That's great.'

Orri sits down on the office chair, places his elbows on the table and rests his head in his palms.

'What's wrong?'

'I could get into trouble.'

'Are you involved?'

'Mörður said he'd pay me extra. A lot extra.'

'I don't have to use it. Not if it hurts you in some way. I won't use it.'

Orri is staring down at the tabletop. 'Use it.'

'There's no need. The Slimline project is plenty.'

'Use it. I don't care if it gets me into trouble. Mörður deserves to rot in hell.'

At eight o'clock, Imogen and Orri are sitting in the DataPsych lab waiting for Victoria King to video call them.

'What's she like?' Orri asks. It's obvious that he's nervous.

'I don't know ... From a glass-half-full perspective, I'd describe her as efficient. If the glass were half empty I'd say she's brusque.'

Imogen's laptop starts ringing. Imogen accepts the call. The face of a women in her thirties with blonde, shoulder-length hair and red lipstick appears on the screen. Her nose is hooked like an eagle's beak. Her skin is pale and seductively smooth.

'Hi, Victoria.'

Efficient or brusque, Victoria does not appear to have time for niceties. 'Who's that?' she asks, looking at Orri and drawing together her eyebrows, two sharp lines shaped like knife blades.

That afternoon, Imogen had emailed Victoria all the documents she had collected on the Slimline project. She'd pointed out things she wanted to feature prominently in the news article.

'Mörður refers to the target group he's working with as "silly girls",' she'd written in the email. 'That shows massive disrespect towards young women.' And just to make sure Mörður's immorality came across clearly she added, 'And he absolutely knows that he's seeking out vulnerable individuals. In an email he accidentally sent to me where he talks about the target market, he admits that their smiles are fake and that they are hiding "the truth about their sad little lives behind lipstick, filters and pretty pouts". He knows what he's doing. He can't wriggle his way out of this.'

Victoria had got back to her half an hour later and said that she would do the story. She said that it would never become front-page news, but on the paper's website the article might make waves on social media if it went viral.

Imogen had emailed her right back and asked for a meeting on FaceTime. There was something more she needed to tell her but she didn't want to put it in writing. Not just yet.

Imogen hopes Orri isn't getting second thoughts as she notices him sink in his chair.

'This is my colleague at DataPsych,' Imogen says, looking into the laptop camera. 'Orri Sigurlínuson.' Trying to pronounce Orri's full name is still a challenge.

Victoria makes a face. She clearly did not catch that.

Imogen turns to Orri for help.

'Hi. My name is Orri. I do all the technical work at DataPsych. I think you are wrong. I think this might be a front-page story after all.'

Victoria does not seem fazed by Orri's confrontational statement. 'Go on.'

'A couple of months ago Mörður came to me—'

'The CEO of DataPsych?' Victoria interjects.

'Yes. He came to me with a proposition. He'd been approached directly by a new client. Usually, our work comes through marketing agencies, like in the case of the Slimline deal, which came to us through London Analytica. But this new client wanted as few people involved as possible and he demanded complete confidentiality.'

'Who is this client?'

Orri sucks in his lips.

Again, Imogen fears that he is about to change his mind.

But he goes on. 'Smertoil.'

Through the camera they can see Victoria start typing on her keyboard. 'Never heard of them.' Click, click, click. She's looking at her screen. She starts reading out loud. 'Russia's tenth largest company and one of the largest global producers of crude oil?'

'That's them,' Orri confirms.

Victoria looks back into the camera. 'So, what's so unusual about them needing marketing consultancy services?'

'Nothing, I suppose. Except the outline they sent us had nothing to do with oil.'

'What do you mean?'

'DataPsych's software is designed to search for individuals based on personality traits.'

'Yes, Imogen has explained the OCEAN model.'

'Until now, our services to companies have been to search social media platforms for a certain type of individual and then target them with a tailor-made marketing message based on their personality. Are you feeling low? Buy this chocolate bar. Are you an outgoing person in need of more attention? Go to this karaoke bar.'

'I get the drift.'

'Technically, that's what Smertoil wanted us to do; they wanted us to find specific personalities and target them. The brief was to find unskilled and undereducated introverts under the age of thirty, in the UK and elsewhere in the West, who felt disenfranchised, disgruntled and isolated. But we weren't to target them with a simple marketing message or advertisements. No. The aim was to bombard them with particular links to news items, jokes and tweets. I saw a sample of the things that we were to make go viral within our target group. It looked like fake news: fake stories about politicians going on luxury holidays at the expense of taxpayers; made-up quotes from officials about the poor and the unemployed, saying they were lazy and stupid; false documents; wrong data. Things like that. It felt political. It felt as if we were being hired to conduct a highly targeted disinformation campaign. It wasn't said in so many words in the brief, but I suspect we were meant to spread dissent.'

Victoria takes a moment to think, then asks: 'Why would an oil company want to spread dissent?'

Orri leans closer to the screen. 'I don't know. That makes no sense. Unless it wasn't an oil company.'

'But they *are* an oil company.'

'What if they were buying the service for someone else? Someone who didn't want to be caught buying a disinformation campaign.'

Victoria is so still that for a moment Imogen thinks they have a bad connection and the video has frozen. But suddenly Victoria's porcelain cheeks colour. Her brusqueness – or efficiency – is changed into mania by added enthusiasm. She looks like a drooling dog on the trail of a fox. 'I know what you're getting at and I think you may be on to something. Send me everything you have.'

Orri does a little wiggle on his chair that looks like a victory dance. He's no longer nervous. He even appears excited, as if this is some sort of game and he just got awarded a point.

Imogen, however, does not feel victorious. 'I'm sorry. Am I missing something here? What about the Slimline story?'

Victoria is leafing through papers on her desk. She isn't facing the camera any more. She appears distracted. 'We'll have to put it off. I want to go all out with this more explosive revelation. To immediately grab attention. This could be massive. Just think about it. Smertoil is a Russian company. No one becomes successful in Russia without the blessing of the authorities. But that means you owe them. Russia is waging an information war all over the world. They're trying to influence decisions in other countries, interfering in elections and just generally trying to stir up trouble. This is an important piece in that puzzle. We can do follow-up pieces on the Slimline project and the vulnerable women it targets.'

Imogen stares at the screen. She's trying to hold it together, appear composed, professional. 'Because politics matters more?'

'Excuse me?' Victoria is writing something down. It looks like she's barely listening to Imogen.

Imogen thought a journalist would get it. She thought journalism was all about sticking it to the man and protecting regular people. But Victoria King is like everyone else. She is just like Samuel Pearce, who had found it so easy to look the other way.

Imogen delivers her explanation with the quiet calm of someone who knows their battle is lost. 'What you're saying is that politics matter more than the lives of young, vulnerable women. Someone causing a stir on a political playing field is considered a bigger story, a more important one, than someone trying to ruin the lives of thousands of girls.'

Victoria looks up. Her eyes are two big question marks. Either she wasn't listening or she doesn't get the insinuation.

'Okay, that's it for now,' Victoria says, as if Imogen hadn't been talking at all as if she were voiceless. 'If you can send me all the documents you have this evening – the slides with the pitch, the brief, all communications – I'll get back to you tomorrow.'

The screen goes dark. Another head turns the other way. Quietly. Cruelly. Deliberately. And out of habit.

Photo: The mirror reflection of a silver necklace with a simple heart pendant hanging around a neck.
Filter: Amaro.

Possible captions . . .

Option one: #pretty #jewellery #love #happiness #instajewelry #accessories #envywear #cute
Option two: My mum gave me this for my sixteenth birthday.
Option three: I'm pretty sure Granny Jo bought it, wrapped it and pretended it was from Mum. She has always denied it.
Option four: On my sixteenth birthday my mum didn't bake me a chocolate cake as I'd hoped she would. Instead she drank a case of lager and passed out on the sofa.

Actual caption . . .

Feeling fancy **#bling**

♥42

Chapter Nineteen

Hannah

It's three o'clock in the morning and I'm lying awake in bed. I can't get Imogen's statement out of my head.

He pushed me up against the wall.

The words are swirling around my brain like an angry blizzard.

His hand travelled up my body.

We put the statement back before we left the lab – but not before I'd taken several photos of it.

His fingers pinched my flesh so hard I almost threw up.

Maybe Imogen is guilty after all. She has a motive. Who wouldn't want to kill the person who did those awful things to you?

He unbuttoned my trousers.

I suddenly remember something. I sit up and grab my phone and start scrolling through my photos. I find the snaps I took of the contents of Imogen's phone. There it is. The email Sara Gunnarsdóttir sent her.

I hope you realise what you've done. I hope you realise that you've ruined my life. Is that what you came here for? I hope you rot in hell.

I immediately know what I need to do; I need to talk to Mörður's widow. But how? I can't just go knocking on her door. What if Dad finds out that without his permission I went, as a representative of the paper, and badgered a grieving widow with questions about the recent and tragic death of her husband?

But there is one thing I can do. There is a loophole.

First thing in the morning I call the embassy saying I'm a British citizen in need of consular help.

They say they can offer me an appointment in three weeks. I beg them for an appointment sooner and tell the lady on the phone that it's an emergency.

'What kind of an emergency?'

'It's my mother. She's a British citizen and has died.'

They give me an appointment later that same day.

Technically, it's not a lie. My mother has died. Still, I feel as dirty as muck.

It's only eleven-thirty and I've already finished the work Dad assigned to me at the editorial meeting this morning.

I go to Dad's office and ask if I can borrow his car to go to the shopping centre at lunch to find some new appropriate work clothes. He hands me the car keys along with two five-thousand krona notes. My guilt wraps itself around my neck like a noose. *I'm a bad, bad person.*

To make myself feel better, I vow to make it up to him. I'll make extra effort at the family dinner we're having this evening; I'll be on my very best behaviour. Rósa is taking the day off to prepare a meal of slow-cooked leg of lamb and three-layered cheesecake for dessert. Alda will be there. And Grandma Erla and Grandpa Bjarni. It'll be the first time I've seen *Amma* and *Afi* since my move. I'm dreading it. I never know what to say to them. They always look at me with bafflement and horror. It's like they're looking at an alien that just dropped to Earth from outer space and they're thinking: *How did that thing get here and why did it have to land in our living room?*

I spoke with Granny Jo on the phone last night. I asked her if it would be bad to say that I couldn't make the family dinner and get Kjarri to go to the cinema with me instead. She said it would indeed be bad of me. When I said to her that they hate me, she had replied, 'They don't hate you, Hannah. As a grandmother myself, I can tell you that a grandparent is physically incapable of hating their grandchild. They just don't know you.'

I asked her if she had research to back that up.

Dad's car is freezing. I turn on the ignition and crank up the heat. I hate driving in Iceland and I epically hate driving Dad's car. It's a Range Rover – anyone who's anyone in Iceland drives a Range Rover – and manoeuvring it is like manoeuvring a tank. I prefer driving Rósa's smaller rustic-orange car. I know nothing about cars. To me, the colour of a car is its most distinct feature – the only distinct feature.

The good news is that it has stopped snowing. The bad news is that the sun is shining with the burning ferocity of Judgement Day and its rays reflecting on the crispy layer of snow blanketing the city are scorching my eyes and blinding me. I hope I'm not about to drive over a colleague sneaking out for an early lunch.

Fortunately, the streets are relatively empty, with everyone at work, and it takes me only fifteen minutes to get from the middle of nowhere to the embassy in the town centre.

After finding a parking spot, I stay in the car for a couple of deep breaths to gather my thoughts. I spot a car parked across the street with the engine running. It's a small grey hatchback. A man appears to be sleeping in the driver's seat. I hope for his sake that he isn't homeless and living in his car. A long winter's night in Iceland in such feeble shelter could easily be the death of you.

I get out of the car and close the door. The bang seems to wake the man up. He raises himself in his seat and looks out the window. I can't see his face properly – he's got sunglasses on and is wearing a hood on his head – but I think he's looking at me.

I hurry up the steps leading to the embassy's front door. The cold puts an extra spring in my step. I ring the bell.

A woman's voice echoes from a speaker on the wall: 'Yes?'

'I've got an appointment with Sara Gunnarsdóttir.'

A woman from the reception takes me to Sara. Her office is the first one in a long corridor of closed doors. The woman knocks.

'Come in.'

'Your twelve o'clock is here to see you.'

'Thank you, Ester.'

The woman leaves and I step inside the office.

Sara motions to a chair. 'Have a seat.' She gives me a tender smile which feels surprisingly genuine.

I sit down opposite her. I can hardly see her for stacks of paper, folders and binders. Sara moves a pile to make room for eye contact. 'Hannah, right?'

I nod.

'So, what can I do for you, Hannah? I understand that there has been a death in your family.'

'That's right.'

I don't know what to say next. I was simply going to play it by ear, but Sara's warm demeanour has thrown me off balance. I'd expected a stiff office worker; a handling that had more in common with the mechanically repetitive work at an assembly line than a real human interaction. Suddenly this has become more personal.

'Erm . . . I'm having difficulty . . . erm . . . coping.'

A line of sympathy appears between Sara's eyebrows. 'Oh, sweetie. Tell me what happened. Who has died?'

'My mum.'

'Oh, darling. When did it happen?'

Five weeks, three days and eight hours. 'Around three months ago.'

Sara flinches. She clearly thought it was a recent death.

I need to crank up the urgency. 'I just miss her so much.'

Do I?

'Of course you do, darling. But this is not exactly what we do here at the embassy. We deal more with logistics: how to transport the deceased between countries . . . things like that.'

'Please. I feel like I'm standing on a rock, way out at sea, and the waves are just crashing around me, and there's no one there and no one on their way, and you just know this is how it's going to be for ever and ever: you, alone on that rock, trying not to fall into the sea.'

'Oh, my sweet girl.'

'I just want her back.'

'Of course you do.'

But I can't help thinking again: *Do I?*

The guilt is overwhelming.

Sara is reaching for her mobile. 'I'll tell you what. I have a friend who is a therapist. I'll give her a call and see if she can fit you in for an emergency appointment. She does charge by the hour but I'll get her to give us mates' rates and I have access to a little slush fund here at the embassy that should cover your first few sessions.'

I stare at Sara in disbelief. 'Why are you being so nice? You don't even know me.'

Sara's eyes are misty. 'I know how it feels to be on that rock.'

The door to Sara's office suddenly swings open. I register a suit and a tie before the person wearing them.

'Do you have Orri's—?'

It's the ambassador. I recognise him from the party.

He stops talking as soon as he sees me.

'Sorry. I didn't realise you had someone in here.' He's speaking in English.

I quickly switch language. 'Orri? Did you say Orri? Orri Sigurlínuson? He works here, doesn't he? He helps you with your computers?'

The ambassador stares at me with his mouth open and his words stuck in his throat as if he's choking on his food.

Sara swoops in. 'It's so awful,' she says, drying her eyes on the back of her hand and suddenly sounding a lot less genuine than before – more like the assembly line worker I'd expected.

253

'We're all very worried about him. He's been missing now for . . . what is it, Gerald?'

The ambassador springs back to life. 'Three days.'

'This is Gerald Boothby,' Sara says. 'He's the ambassador. Gerald is just here to look for Orri's manual. Aren't you, Gerald?'

There's no reply from the ambassador.

'Orri keeps writing down things he feels we need to know about our computer systems, instructions that we can follow when he isn't around. He's very organised, that boy.'

Sara reaches for a bright-blue binder on the table. 'There you go, Gerald.'

It takes a moment for Gerald to realise she's handing him the binder. When he does, he rushes towards the desk. Just before he grabs it I manage a glance at its spine. The binder is labelled 'Invoices for Catering Services'. Why would a computer manual be labelled that?

The ambassador bolts back towards the door. 'It was nice meeting you,' he says, before shooting out of the office and slamming the door behind him.

Sara gets up from her chair. 'I'm sorry. I have to cut our meeting short. I promised my daughters I'd pick them up early from nursery today. I'm going to take them out for ice cream for lunch. Sometimes you just need ice cream to make things better – if only for a brief period of time. I recommend it.'

I stand up. Sara ushers me towards the door.

'I believe reception has your number. I'll text you with information about the appointment for the first therapy session.'

Before I can even say thank you, or try to get more out of her, I'm standing outside the embassy in the freezing cold and burning bright Icelandic noon.

That was weird. That was really weird.

I sit down on the embassy steps. I need a breather. I need to think. I'd hoped to come here to prove somehow that Imogen isn't a murderer. I'd hoped to find another suspect. Sara is as far from being the unstable crazy lady the guy at the university cafeteria described as can be.

My mission has been a big fat failure. Why am I doing this? Yes, I'm trying to prove that Imogen Collins is telling the truth; I'm trying to prove that she did not murder Mörður Þórðarson.

We're totally different people: she's successful, pretty and confident while I'm none of those things. But in a weird way I feel like we're kindred spirits.

Or perhaps this has nothing to do with Imogen. Maybe I'm not fighting for absolution for Imogen – but for myself.

The last time I visited Mum in the hospital I hardly recognised her. Her face was so bloated her features looked like she'd been beaten up. She was panting and she kept crying out in pain. Her fingers had turned blue. It was like she was turning into a corpse even though she was still alive.

The day before a nurse took Granny and me aside and asked if her dying wish, to come home, was something that we would consider.

Granny looked at me, seeking my permission.

I nodded.

'You're a good daughter,' Granny said to me.

But I wasn't. I was a horrible, abhorrent daughter who deserved to burn in hell for all eternity.

I didn't want Mum back home. I didn't want her in my life at all. I was sick of having to look out for her every second of the day; I was sick of my life always being about her. I'd had enough. That last day at the hospital I made a wish: I wished she would just die.

And she did. She never came home.

As I sit there on the cold embassy steps, I identify a thought that has been growing, spreading, like Mum's cancer, through my subconscious since her death and has just now reached my brain: *I killed my mother.*

I get up. My joints are stiff from the cold. I lean on the railing as I wobble down the stairs. The sun is searing my eyes. The world is spinning.

Imogen Collins is guilty. I am guilty.

I cross the street without bothering to check for oncoming traffic. I need to get out of here as quickly as possible. I reach the car. *The keys, the keys – where are the keys?* I rummage around in my coat pocket. *There.*

I press the button on the car remote. But as I hear the thump of the car door unlocking I feel a blow from behind. Before I can turn around I find myself pushed up against the car.

I try to scream but before I can make a sound, a hand wearing a leather glove is covering my mouth. I can't help thinking about Imogen's letter and panic overwhelms me.

'Stop sticking your nose where it doesn't belong,' comes a raspy male voice.

I'm screaming on the inside but nothing comes out. I try to wriggle free but the weight of the man's body up against mine keeps me firmly constrained. His hand is squeezing my face so hard it feels like my skull could break.

'Silly little girrrl. You do as I say. If not, you will meet the same fate as that prrrissy little college professor. It would give me great pleasure to feed you my poison – just like I did Mörður. I want to see you die, slowly, painfully.' The man is speaking in English but he has a distinct Eastern European accent.

The gloved hand jerks my head back. I'm convinced the man intends to break my neck. But as quickly as he appeared, he's gone.

I lean forward and, with my hands on my knees, I gasp for breath. As soon as I've got enough air in my lungs I raise myself up, rip the car door open, jump inside and lock the doors behind me.

He's walking away. I can only see his back, but that's enough for me to realise that this isn't the first time our paths have crossed.

The man is wearing a leather jacket. Black. Ill-fitting. This is the man I saw at the embassy party; this is the man I saw at Imogen's talk at Harpa.

He stops by a car. The small grey hatchback.

I didn't kill my mother. You can't wish a person dead. It's a fact. And now I know another thing for a fact. Imogen Collins didn't kill Mörður Þórðarson.

But who is this man that did?

Photo: A lone tall birch tree, stripped of its leaves but cloaked by a thin veil of snow.

Filter: Rise.

Caption: A winter coat.

♥241

What the caption should have been . . .

Option one: I have no one to rely on but myself. I'm as alone in the world as this tree. So are you.

Option two: I may have been wrong. Yes, social media can be superficial, cruel, pointless and degrading. But it doesn't have to be.

Option three: Social media isn't the big threat. Silence is.

Option four: They want you to stay silent. They want to keep you in your place. It's only your word against his so it's like it didn't happen. If a tree falls in a forest and no one is around to hear it, does it make a sound? – To hell with the tree. I'm using my voice.

Chapter Twenty

Imogen

Sara is everything Imogen hoped she wouldn't be: warm, open, kind and funny. Now, Imogen feels even worse about what she's about to do.

They're sitting in Sara's living room having a home-brewed flat white accompanied by cocoa and date raw bites. Imogen feels like she's been transported back to a trendy café in Shoreditch.

The meeting about Imogen's talk at the Cool Britannia conference was meant to take place at the embassy. But Sara called to say her daughters were off sick from nursery and she was working from home.

'Thank you so much for agreeing to meet me here,' Sara says and pushes the golden box containing the individually-wrapped bites of allegedly healthy heaven towards Imogen. Imogen has already had two and they're so delicious she finds it hard to believe that they're good for you – *Simply natural goodness*, it says on the box.

'We could have rescheduled but I've been dying to meet up with you and have a chat. Not in the internet-celebrity-stalking kind of way,' she says and makes a face. 'Just the human-interest kind of way. I love meeting people and hearing about their lives.

I'm so curious to hear what brings you here. Who is Imogen Collins? What have you been up to? I'm sorry. I talk a lot. I ramble. That's the other thing I love doing – or that's what my husband says.'

The mention of Mörður makes Imogen's skin crawl. She tries not to let it show.

'Thank you for inviting me to take part in the conference,' Imogen says. 'I'm so grateful for the opportunity.'

Twenty-four hours ago, that statement would have been a lie. Imogen hadn't wanted to be part of the conference. She'd actually been annoyed with herself for saying yes to it. She doesn't like public speaking after her terrible freeze-up in London before she left, and she intended to keep a low profile. But then the universe taught her a lesson. Each and every one of us is alone in the world. When it comes down to it, the only person you can rely on is yourself.

When Victoria King downgraded the Slimline story to a 'possible follow-up piece' Imogen felt as if her own trauma had been trivialised. Mörður assaulted her. Big deal. It happens. That's just part of life. But it shouldn't be part of life.

So, Imogen made a decision. She has stopped relying on others. She is taking matters into her own hands. She is going to reveal the truth about Mörður in her talk at Harpa. She could, of course, do it straight away on her Instagram account or in a video on YouTube. But she doesn't want her revelation to become just another internet accusation that is printed in the sidebar of the *Daily Mail*; she doesn't want it to simply reverberate within a bubble of her peers who already know that the structure of power is stacked against them; that because they don't have money and they don't have power, no one cares to listen. She wants the truth to travel beyond the echo chambers. She wants it to reach the ears of people who aren't used to being shown the harsh reality of how things really are beyond their neat little semi-detached lives.

There's going to be a lot of people at the Cool Britannia event. Respectable people. The establishment. The elite. And there will be media there. Imogen is going to tell everyone about the Slimline project. And then she's going to tell them what Mörður did to her. The symmetry is eerie.

Imogen is going to make sure her story is catapulted into the respectability of the mainstream where it cannot be ignored. She's going for maximum impact to make sure she gets the revenge she came here for. She's going to record the talk and post it online as well, of course: on YouTube; some photos and a short post on Instagram. And then she will leave and never come back. Last night she booked her ticket back to London. It's for the day after the talk. She emailed Anna and let her know she was coming home. A friend of Steph's has been staying in Imogen's room while she's been away. Anna seemed happy enough to tell her that she will need to find another place to stay.

It is therefore essential that the meeting with Sara goes well. Imogen needs to butter her up. She can't lose her slot.

'Where are your girls?' Imogen asks. She'd expected mayhem: children running around, toys everywhere. But the place is quiet. It's a small but elegant flat with a sloping ceiling at the top of a weathered apartment building in the old west side of town. It's not far from Sigurlína's. Sigurlína had told her that the neighbourhood was the first district to develop when Reykjavík started to grow from a small village to a town in the late nineteenth century. The lighting is soft and the furniture is made of teak. There's a worn Chesterfield sofa in one corner and under the eaves is a shelf running the length of the wall filled with vinyl records. The flat is cosy – and trendy, in a tribute-to-times-gone-by kind of way.

'The girls are both asleep. Fever. That's what it does to you.' Sara furrows her brow. 'How did you know I had girls?'

Imogen looks away from Sara's interrogative eyes. The photos she saw when she was snooping around on Mörður's computer of little Anna and little Elsa are etched into her brain.

Sara throws her hands up in the air. 'Yes, of course, Mörður told you. I almost forgot that you work with him. He never talks about work at home. I sometimes even forget that Orri works at the lab. It feels like two separate worlds: Orri fixing the computers at the embassy and Orri at work with my husband.'

She takes a quick sip of her coffee. 'So how are you getting on?'

'Fine, thank you.'

'It must be hard to adapt to a new place where you don't know anyone. Trust me, I've been there. I hope you aren't lonely. Research shows that loneliness can have a really bad effect on your health. It's been linked to an increased risk of a heart attack, cancer, stroke, depression. You aren't depressed, are you? If you're feeling down, call me whenever.

'I'm going to introduce you to my girlfriends. You need a support network. They would love to mother you while you're here; bring you home-baked bread and the latest goss. Oh my

God! There's a woman at the embassy who has a daughter who's your age and is a huge Snapchat star in Iceland. I'm going to get you her number. You girls could hang out. Go clubbing or whatever it is that young people do these days.

'I read an article the other day about how sensible millennials are; they don't drink, don't smoke, they save their money – except when it comes to avocado on toast, then they're ready to pay a fortune. What's the deal with avocado on toast? It's so boring. So bland. Anyway, I know you're a millennial but you should have some fun. You're only young once.'

Sara is like a bulldozer and a big warm hug rolled into one; a soft wave heading towards her. Imogen loves it. She wishes she could give in to her power, be swept away, carried, enveloped, taken care of. She *is* lonely, she *is* miserable, she *is* depressed. She wants to whisper, *Please hold me.*

Imogen wishes she could be open with Sara. Sara seems like the confidant she needs. Imogen understands why Orri is so taken with her; why he has relied on her so much. If only she could tell Sara everything: about the assault, how she gave up her studies at Cambridge, how she lost touch with her parents, how she hates herself for letting the attack happen – even though she knows it's stupid and that in no universe could she be blamed.

But she can't tell Sara anything. Because Imogen isn't here for salvation. She is here to ruin Sara's life.

But first she has to win her over.

Sara yawns. 'Oh God, I'm so sorry. You must think I'm so rude. Don't take this personally. I was up all night. The girls kept waking up. Then I had a massive row with Mörður this morning.

He just kept snoring on, didn't go to them once. He can be such a prick sometimes. Stay single. Have fun. That's my advice.' She laughs. Her laughter fills the living room like the smell of apple crumble baking in the oven on a cold winter's day.

Imogen smiles in a way she hopes comes across as sympathetic. 'You said you've been there.'

'Excuse me?'

'In a new place. Alone.'

'Oh, yes. My husband and I lived in Cambridge for a few years. I think I told you that. We only moved back a year ago. Mörður did his PhD at Cambridge and then taught at the school for a few semesters. It's hard to find your footing in a new place.'

'Why did you move back?' Imogen hopes the question sounds innocent and not laced with accusation.

Now it's Sara's turn to look away. She glances at a closed door, the first in a narrow corridor that leads towards the kitchen. Imogen is guessing it's the girls' bedroom.

'I probably shouldn't tell you.' She looks down into her cup of coffee but then raises her eyes again. 'I loved Cambridge. It took me a few months to find my footing, but once I got a job and made some friends it was the best place to live.

'I got a part-time job in admin at the university and got to know the students. I love being around people younger than me. It keeps me on my toes. I went with them for coffee on campus, helped them out and became a shoulder to cry on when they got homesick.

'One day one of the students came to the admin office, a girl I knew but wasn't really close with, and asked if we could talk in private. I thought she might be in some kind of trouble; that maybe she wasn't coping.

'We sat outside one of the university buildings, on a bench on the street. It was a beautiful day; sunny but with a slight chill in the air.

'She told me Mörður was cheating on me. I was caught so off guard I just started laughing. I couldn't believe it. We were so happy. Mörður was enjoying his graduate studies. I liked my job. We spent our weekends exploring a beautiful new city, trying out new restaurants, going to concerts and museums, getting lost in bookstores the size of a palace. What else could we ask for?

'The girl said that she and two other students had walked in on him and a colleague from the psychology department having sex in an empty classroom. If I didn't believe her, she could tell me who the other students were. They could corroborate her story. She said she thought I deserved to know. Because I was a nice person and didn't deserve this being done to me.' Imogen starts to feel clammy.

'I confronted Mörður about it when he got home that evening. I was ready to laugh it off. I was ready for this to be one big misunderstanding; some practical joke that was being played on me. I'd even stopped by M&S to buy some nice ready meals and wine for us to share.

'But he didn't deny it. He'd been having an affair for months. I couldn't believe it. We'd been together since our first year at uni. He wasn't only my husband. He was my best friend.

'That's when I realised how alone you are when you move to a new place. I didn't have family to support me. I didn't have my girlfriends to help me figure out what to do. It was just me. And him.

'He begged me to forgive him. I said I'd give him another chance. But if something like this ever happened again, I would leave him without a second thought. Things were strained for a while. But slowly we found our way back. I fell pregnant with Ella. She's my oldest. She'll be five next month. Within a year of having Ella I fell pregnant with Sylvía.

'Things were going great. Mörður graduated and managed to get the finance to set up a new lab. Then, a year ago, it all started again.'

Imogen has hardly been able to breathe. She's starting to feel faint. 'How did you find out that time?'

'Mörður came home from work one day all flushed and jumpy and smelling of Coco Mademoiselle. I'd recognise that fragrance anywhere; it's my favourite perfume. But we were kind of broke, living off his meagre wages with two small children, and I hadn't had a bottle for more than two years.

'I asked him point blank: "Are you having an affair?" This time he denied it. But I didn't believe him.

'He burst into tears. He said that one of his students had a massive crush on him. That she kept following him around, standing too close to him in the lab, accidentally bumping into him, touching him. That day she'd apparently jumped on him and started kissing him.'

Imogen's heart is burning. It's as if the core of her being, her soul, is being ripped apart once again by the sharp claws of the monstrous Beast that's hunted her, haunted her, every minute of every day for the past year.

Liar.

But she can't let her emotions show. She uses the force of her rage to power her composure. She isn't going to lose control. She isn't going to mess this up.

Sara swallows a lump. 'I'd said I would leave him if he did it again. But I had two children to take care of, no support network and I wasn't working. I didn't feel strong enough to follow through. I insisted that either we moved back to Iceland or I'd divorce him. I didn't want him around his Cambridge tarts.'

Sara's eyes are watering slightly. 'But lately . . .' She breaks off. 'Lately, I've got the feeling that something's up. For the past couple of months things have been different. Mörður has been edgy, distant. He has been coming home late, going to work early. I'm really scared that he's at it again. If he is, I don't think I can cope. It's taken its toll. Mentally. I'm not sure what I might be capable of if I'm put in that situation again.'

Sara runs an index finger under each eye, wiping away mascara-stained tears that are spilling over the lower eyelids.

'Look at me. I should be stronger than this. I want to be stronger than this.' She suddenly laughs her pastry-soft laugh. 'I'm so sorry. I didn't mean to bum you out. I wanted you to think I was fun. I guess I failed. But that's a price I'm willing to pay. I find that if you're open with people, people are open with you in return. I like that.'

Imogen feels that she should comfort Sara but she can't bring herself to. It feels too hypocritical. Imogen is, after all, about to ruin this woman's life.

Imogen is suddenly filled with self-loathing. What gives her the right to ruin Sara's life? She shouldn't be here. She should get up and leave. She should tell Sara that Mörður isn't having an affair but the reason for his late nights at the office is a side project – she could leave out the sickening details of his work. Sara could live happily ever after.

But then what? By staying silent, who is Imogen hurting? The things Mörður did to Imogen – what if he does them to someone else?

No. Backing off is not an option.

Sara forces a smile. 'Talking about fun: shall we have a little discussion about your talk at Harpa? I told my girlfriends that you agreed to take part in my conference and they screamed with excitement. They're all coming to the event. It's absolutely up to you what you talk about, but I was thinking that maybe sharing your experience, your journey, could be interesting. There are so many people who want to do what you do and would love to get some pointers.

'I've noticed that you haven't been posting a lot lately. Are you taking a break?'

'Not officially. Things have just been a bit hectic. As you said, navigating your way in a new place can be exhausting. And work has been busy. At the lab I'm working with new software: DataJuice. It's really cutting-edge, but just like finding your footing in a new place, it takes a lot of mental energy to find your way around new software. I mean, it's not totally new to me. I had started to use it at Cambridge—'

'Oh, yes, you studied at Cambridge.'

'Only for a year. I still have my spot on the Psychological and Behavioural Sciences tripos if I want to return.'

Imogen knows she shouldn't share details of her life with

Sara but the words are just flooding out. Imogen realises she's trying to impress Sara.

'There were only psychologists and psychology students at the DataPsych lab at Cambridge, no computer specialists, so I was in charge of—'

'You worked in Mörður's lab at Cambridge?'

Imogen immediately knows she's said too much. It is Sara. She clearly has this effect on people. She'd even said it: 'If you're open with people, people are open with you in return.'

Sara hadn't known that Imogen worked with Mörður in Cambridge. Why would she? She'd said that Mörður didn't talk about his work life at all with her.

Sara is quicker to speak. 'So when were you at Cambridge?'

There is no way out of this. 'I started two years ago.'

'And when did you drop out?'

'Last summer.'

'When did you come to Iceland?'

'A couple of months ago.'

Sara goes quiet. She bites the skin on her lower lip as she thinks. Her lipstick is very red. Blood red.

Imogen's breathing is getting shallow. She's nervous. Why should she be nervous? Yes, she studied at Cambridge University. Yes, she worked at Mörður's lab. But that's not information that could give away her secret. There's no way Sara can suspect the reason for Imogen being here, in her home, in this country, in this situation.

It's only just getting light outside. Harsh white beams force their way into the living room through a small window in the sloping ceiling. During winter, the days are short in Iceland.

Although the clock is approaching ten in the morning, the sun is just rising. Autumn is giving way to the darkness of winter, which leads to the darkest day of the year, in late December, when the sun only shines for four hours before night descends again.

Sara suddenly looks up. Dawn drains the colour from her face – in Iceland the start of the day has a deadly whiteness to it, tinted with blue. The cold hue of a corpse.

Slowly, Sara leans forward, closer to Imogen.

Imogen is too afraid to move.

Sara sniffs the air. Her face is pale. Fine wrinkles cut her skin like cracks in a snow crust.

What is she doing?

Sara draws her chin back into her neck. What looks like disgust reaches her eyes. 'Is that . . .' *Sniff. Sniff.* 'Is that Coco Mademoiselle you're wearing?'

No. She's got it all wrong. Imogen realises that Sara putting together the clues and finding out the truth isn't what she should be worried about. What she should be worried about is Sara trying to solve the puzzle but putting the pieces together wrongly.

Imogen knows there's no point in denying it. She reeks of Coco Mademoiselle and guilt.

'It's not what you think,' Imogen pleads. Her voice breaks. She's about to start crying.

Sara shoots up from her chair, which falls backward, hitting the wooden floor with a massive bang.

'Get out of my house!'

Imogen doesn't get up. 'Please, let me explain.'

Sara grabs the shoulder of Imogen's chiffon dress and tries to pull her up off the chair. Imogen doesn't budge but there's a ripping sound when the seam under the arm splits and a huge tear opens up, running right down the sleeve of the dress.

'Get the hell out of my house or I'll strangle you right here with my bare hands.'

Imogen doesn't care if Sara strangles her. The only thing Imogen craves at that moment is for people to believe her. 'It's not what you think.'

'I can't believe you followed him here.'

'I didn't.'

'What's wrong with you? I'm going to kill him.'

'I beg you, just listen to me. Let me explain.'

Sara takes a step towards Imogen.

Imogen shrinks in the shadow of her fury.

Sara leans closer. 'You don't want to test me. You don't want to see what I'm capable of. Get. Out. Now.'

The two women jump with fright when a soft creaking sound reverberates behind them. The closed door in the narrow corridor is slowly opening. The noise from the hinges pierces the soul like the soundtrack to a horror film.

A pale little face is revealed. Blonde tangled hair. Blue squinting eyes. A pink nightgown with a picture of a unicorn. A drowsy, high-pitched voice, like innocence just awoken. 'What's wrong, Mummy?'

Imogen's lips start to quiver. Her eyes water and tears block out the world around her.

Imogen's heart is bleeding. It's bleeding for that little girl, it's bleeding for Sara, it's bleeding for herself, it's bleeding for girls everywhere.

271

Photo: A dining table strewn with crumbs and dirty plates. The tablecloth is splattered with gravy and the residue of harsh words sputtered.
Filter: Gingham.

Possible captions . . .

Option one: #funtimes
Option two: What a mess.

Actual caption . . .

Life is a party.

♥31

Chapter Twenty-One

Hannah

I'm alive.

As I run up the office stairs the words form a tornado in my head, a column of clouds that swoops up the rest of my thoughts and sends them flying through my brain as debris and chaos.

I need to talk to Dad. I need to give him a hug. I need to tell him I almost got killed. I need to tell him that I'm alive. I need to tell him that I don't hate Rósa, that I appreciate her efforts. I need to tell him that I want to get to know the twins better. I need to tell him that I know who killed Mörður Þórðarson. I need to tell him that I don't know who killed Mörður Þórðarson. I need to tell him that I'm sorry and thank you. Because I'm alive.

The door to Dad's office is open and I slip in.

It's like I've run into a brick wall when I see Heiða there; all my thoughts fall flat on the ground.

The paper's investigative journalist is unusually animated. 'I've just got a tip-off from one of my sources within the Met. Last night they found the murder weapon.'

Dad is sitting behind his desk. They don't seem to have noticed me.

'It's a trophy.'

'A trophy?'

'It's a statue of a big, fat golden lion.'

'Seriously?'

'I've looked into it and the Lion Award is apparently this huge deal in the advertising industry. Cannes Lions is an international festival held every year in Cannes. It's for those working in creative communications, advertising and related fields. They give out awards at the festival and the prize is a trophy in the shape of a lion.'

'And whose is it?'

'The victim's. He won it for a project he worked on with a marketing agency in London called London Analytica. Apparently, DataPsych collaborated with them on quite a few projects. The award was for technological innovation.'

Dad relaxes back in his chair and runs his fingers through his hair. 'Killed with his own trophy; killed with the physical manifestation of his moment of glory.' The corners of Dad's mouth turn up. *Is he smiling?* 'Will you judge me if I tell you that I find it ever so slightly funny?'

Heiða wrinkles her nose. 'I won't judge you if you won't judge me.'

The two of them start laughing, heartily, like old friends gossiping over a cup of coffee.

Look at him. Look at how at ease he is with Heiða. Look at their rapport. *Why is he never like that with me? Why is he never like that at home?*

The laughter fades out into a chummy silence.

'So,' Dad says. 'Do you think she did it? Do you think that Imogen girl is guilty?'

Heiða sits down on Dad's big leather recliner in the corner of his office. He uses it when he needs to work late into the evening. It's his refuge and no one is allowed to sit on it. But apparently Heiða is.

'Yes,' she says, sinking back in the chair. 'I think there's no doubt about it. Her fingerprints are all over the murder weapon. And there appears to be some backstory. Imogen and Mörður apparently knew each other before she came to Iceland.'

'Did she follow him here?'

'I don't know. But it wouldn't surprise me.'

'That leaves some room for reasonable doubt though.'

'There's more. A lot more. My source at the police tells me that Imogen rented a car the day Mörður was killed. She hasn't had a car the whole time she's been here. She lives close to the university and walks to work. They're examining the car and they're pretty sure that it was used to move the body. They're also looking at one of the towels the body was wrapped in when it was found in the crevice. It's very luxurious and has the initials I.C. embroidered on it in gold.'

Dad strokes his stubbly chin. 'I guess she did it.'

Heiða raises the built-in footrest on the chair and leans further back. 'I guess she did.'

Dad lifts his legs up and rests them on his desk. 'Trophy,' he says and the two of them start laughing again.

I back out of the office. I thought I was bringing Dad a scoop. I thought I was about to break the news to him who killed Mörður and how he was killed. The man who attacked me outside the embassy had said that he was going to feed me his poison just like he did Mörður and I was sure that man was the murderer. I was sure he had killed Mörður with poison.

But clearly, I'd jumped to the wrong conclusion. And as for the rest of the things I needed to tell him: everything I was thinking and feeling sixty seconds ago has evaporated into thin air.

The atmosphere around the dining table is as icy as Rósa's table decorations. The tablecloth is crisp white, sprinkled with silver snowflakes to match the silver napkin rings.

'Eiríkur, can you pass me the butter?' Alda says, interrupting the sound of people chewing.

Grandma Erla and Grandpa Bjarni haven't asked me a single question. There's been no, 'What have you been up to? How's the move going? How's work? How are you doing without your mother?' There have, however, been plenty of awkward silences.

'This slow-cooking thing is just a fad,' Grandma Erla suddenly says. 'There's no need to cook a leg of lamb for this long. I don't like the soggy texture. Lamb should always be served medium rare. That's how we've always done it.' She turns to Grandpa Bjarni with a sigh. 'Bjarni, please stop slurping the gravy like that.'

Grandpa ignores her. 'It needs more salt.'

Grandma shakes her head. 'You think everything needs more salt. You know what your doctor says: too much salt will kill you.'

Alda slathers an inch-thick layer of butter on her artfully tiny slice of baguette. 'If so, I could definitely do with some salt right about now,' she mumbles to herself.

I try not to laugh, afraid if I do my mirth might melt the snow queen that is my grandmother.

Grandma puts down her fork. 'You don't need it. I think that butter will do the trick.'

I stare at Grandma, confused by her comeback. Was that a joke or simply a criticism?

Rósa reaches for the irregularly shaped frosted-glass bowl containing the greens. 'Erla, please have some more mangetout.'

'No, thank you.'

Rósa's face falls with disappointment. She's been cooking all day. 'But I thought you liked mangetout.'

'I do. But I don't like that red stuff you've sprinkled on it.'

'The pomegranate seeds?'

'Why does everything have to be sprinkled with something?'

Alda snorts. 'I think you could do with a sprinkle of joy, Mother.'

'Excuse me, but I simply don't care for this fancy sprinkling.'

Rósa grabs her wineglass from the table and gulps half of the wine down in one go.

This evening is turning out to be just as torturous as I'd expected. I make a mental escape and turn my gaze to the window. The dining room faces the back garden. The moon is out and its light is reflected in the dusting of snow covering the leafless shrubs, looking like the setting of a Christmas ad that accidentally went slightly too Halloween.

A branch moves. *What was that?* The snow falls off and glides to the ground, leaving the branches exposed, looking like the crooked fingers of skeletons digging their way up from a grave.

I've been on edge since the incident in front of the embassy. On the drive home from work I kept seeing that car everywhere:

that little grey hatchback. I know I'm being paranoid. But there's a saying, 'Just because you're paranoid doesn't mean they aren't after you.' Or is that just double paranoia?

I was going to tell Dad about what happened but then I changed my mind. I was afraid that he'd think it was all in my head. That it was the curse.

Another branch taps the window. I can't help it. I jump from my seat. 'Did you see that? Did you see that just now? Look.'

I point to the window. But no one's looking out. Everyone is looking at me.

I try again. 'See, just there.'

Dad is glaring at me, his face stiff with frustration and disappointment. Grandma Erla and Grandpa Bjarni ooze silent embarrassment and the twins, for once, aren't smirking.

Oh, I get it. I see it in their eyes. I know what they're thinking. They're thinking about the curse again.

I detect movement outside in the garden again. A shadow passing the window.

'What's wrong with you people? I'm asking you to do a simple thing. What do you think is going to happen? Do you think that once you turn your heads I'm going to start pouring the gravy over your heads? Do you think I'm going to take off my clothes and start dancing on the table?'

Alda gets up. 'I'm going out for a smoke. Why don't you come with me, Hannah? Get some fresh air.'

There's no point in protesting; there's no point in explaining. They've all made up their minds about me. They've decided that I'm my mother's daughter.

I don't want to go out – I'm sure there's someone there,

hiding inside the skeletal shrubs in the garden, but I don't want to be inside either. I'll be safe with Alda. I follow her to the front door feeling humiliated and small. Small like a flea. A nuisance. That's what I am to them. A creature infesting their perfect little lives.

Alda grabs a down coat from the coat rack by the door and hands it to me. It's actually Rósa's but I put it on anyway.

We step out into the freezing, clear night. Alda lights her cigarette.

My heart starts racing. A siren is wailing in my head. Is it happening? Are they right? Am I just like her?

I'm pretty sure that Dad is of the opinion that the reason I got expelled from school, the reason I got sent here, is the fact that I'm turning into Mum.

The cold is bringing tears to my eyes. I turn to Alda, who's taking a slow drag of her cigarette.

'Why do Grandma Erla and Grandpa Bjarni hate me?'

Alda laughs dryly. 'They don't hate you. They're old-school Icelanders. They're just emotionally numb from all the cold.'

I laugh.

'They don't approve of public displays of affection and they keep themselves warm by nagging. They drive me crazy but when it comes down to it they're good people. They have your back. Trust me.'

My phone buzzes in my pocket. I take it out. It's a message from Daisy.

D: Going to Nandos with Mum and Dad for supper. I'll call you when I get back.

I don't reply. I tell myself that it's because my fingers are too cold. But it's not that. I love Daisy, but sometimes I can't help being jealous of her. She has the perfect family.

While growing up I'd visit other kids' houses and notice how different their lives were; everything was tidy, quiet, peaceful and consistently the same. In periodic bursts of optimism, I'd try to recreate that for me, Mum and Granny Jo by preparing dinner from scratch in the hope that the power of a home-cooked meal would bring some stability to our unpredictable household. *How stupid.*

Alda finishes her cigarette, throws the stub on the ground and steps on it. Dad's going to go mental when he sees it. She gives me a quick cuddle. 'Shall we go back inside?'

Alda's short embrace makes me feel slightly better. I should give Grandma Erla and Grandpa Bjarni the benefit of the doubt. Maybe they don't hate me.

When we arrive back in the living room Rósa is clearing the table. No one is helping her.

'You guys ready for dessert?' she asks and gives me a smile which looks a bit stiff but I think is meant to be reassuring.

She's making an effort.

I smile back at her and start removing plates from the table.

Gabríel aims a piece of baguette at the bread basket at the other end of the table and throws it. It's a near miss.

'Gabríel!' Dad barks.

But Gabríel is immune to Dad's barking sounds. 'Can I play with the iPad?'

'If Gabríel is having the iPad, so am I,' Ísabella says in the uniquely whiny voice of a twelve-year-old.

Rósa reaches for the bowl of mangetout on the table.

'I don't understand why you let them play with the iPad this much, Rósa,' Grandma Erla says, as if Ísabella and Gabríel are the products of a virgin birth, like Jesus, and Dad has absolutely nothing to do with any of this. 'Don't you read the papers? Don't you know how bad it is for them?'

Alda snorts. 'Mum, remember when I was twelve and you let me and Eiríkur rent *The Shining* on VHS and spend an evening home alone with a whole bar of Toblerone each for dinner, because you had a meet-up planned with your girlfriends and Dad was on a fishing trip with some mates out in the country, and the babysitter fell through?'

'That never happened.'

'It so did. Ask Eiríkur. He was so afraid of Jack Nicholson he weed himself.'

'I did not,' Dad says, but smiles.

The phone rings.

'I'll get it,' Rósa yelps, clearly desperate to get away from the living, breathing Spanish Inquisition, aka my grandmother.

'Hello?' Silence. 'Yes, this is her place of residence.' Silence. 'Can you tell me what this is in reference to?' More silence.

Rósa lowers the phone. She looks at me. Her made-up eyes are wide, like on one of those prim, old-fashioned porcelain dolls.

'Hannah. It's for you. It's the police.'

And there goes down the drain any chance of proving to everyone that I'm not the black sheep of this family.

Photo: A girl with long dark hair, wearing a black leather pencil skirt, a red cashmere crew-neck jumper and a lipstick in a shade called *Hope*.
Filter: Valencia.

Caption: This is not a sponsored post. This is just me.

💜387

What the caption should have been . . .

Option one: I don't want to care about what you say about me; what you think of me.
Option two: But I do.

Chapter Twenty-Two

Imogen

Imogen can't go back to the lab looking like this. Her face is stained with mascara and tears. Her dress is ripped and her body is shaking.

When Imogen gets home after her meeting with Sara, Sigurlína is sitting at the kitchen table eating a bowl of muesli and reading the paper.

Shit. Imogen had hoped Sigurlína would be out in her shed. She wanted to be alone.

Imogen's phone beeps. It's an email. From Sara. She opens it.

I hope you realise what you've done. I hope you realise that you've ruined my life. Is that what you came here for? I hope you rot in hell.

Imogen turns off her phone for the first time in what feels like for ever.

'How did the meeting go?' Sigurlína asks, her eyes still resting on the paper. She finishes what she's reading and looks up. 'Oh my God! What happened to you?'

Sigurlína jumps up and rushes over to Imogen. She grabs her

by the shoulders and starts looking her up and down, up and down, frantically inspecting the state of her.

'Did you have an accident? Did someone do something to you? Was it that Sara woman?'

Imogen doesn't manage a single word. She's in shock. Or she's blocked. Or she's simply given up. She isn't sure exactly. The only thing she knows is that she feels cold and numb and she wants to lie down and sleep for one hundred years like that princess in *Sleeping Beauty*. Or maybe it would simply be best to never wake up again.

Sigurlína turns Imogen gently around and guides her into the living room, where she makes her sit down on the sofa. Sigurlína sits down next to her.

'Do you want to talk about it?'

She has no idea what she wants and what she doesn't want.

Sigurlína wraps an arm around Imogen's shoulders, pulls her towards her and leans back on the sofa. Imogen rests her head on Sigurlína's shoulder.

Sigurlína's robe smells of perfume and laundry detergent. The overwhelming scent is lavender. Imogen closes her eyes and takes a deep breath. Lavender is her mum's favourite flower.

When Imogen was younger the two of them sometimes walked to a lavender field just outside Cambridge. When they got home they put the flowers in little vases in every room in the house. It made her dad sneeze but he never complained. To Imogen the smell of lavender is the smell of happiness.

Burning tears sting Imogen's eyes. She starts crying, sobbing, howling, wailing like an animal. She doesn't recognise these sounds. She's never heard them before. They don't sound like her. They don't even sound human.

Sigurlína squeezes her tighter.

Tears are streaming down Imogen's face on to Sigurlína's golden robe. She cries and cries and cries while Sigurlína just holds her. Sigurlína doesn't ask any questions. She doesn't demand an explanation. She just lets Imogen weep in the safety of her embrace.

It's seven o'clock in the evening when Sigurlína knocks on Imogen's bedroom door.

Imogen's been fast asleep since she stopped crying and decided she was going to take a quick nap before going back to work. Sigurlína said that Imogen was in no state to go to work, she needed to take care of herself, and she was going to text Orri and have him tell their boss that Imogen wasn't coming in today.

'How are you feeling?' Sigurlína asks as she sticks her head around the doorframe.

Imogen sits up in her bed. It's turned dark outside. 'Better. Much better. Thank you. For everything.'

Sigurlína smiles. 'All part of the service.' Her face turns sombre. 'You know I'm here if you want to talk.'

'Thank you.'

Sigurlína opens the door wider. Yellow light seeps into Imogen's room, pushing away the darkness. 'On a brighter note, Orri is on his way here. I've made some lamb stew we can have. Then he's taking you to the cinema. You guys can borrow my car. You can, of course, say no, but I think it would do you good

285

to get out of the house and just forget about things for a couple of hours. What do you think?'

Imogen looks around her. She feels like she's been asleep for a hundred years and now she is wide awake. She certainly won't be going to bed at a sensible hour this evening. She needs to kill time. 'Lamb stew and a trip to the cinema sound great.'

She smiles at Sigurlína. She is feeling better. Her soul is calm and her head is clear. She has a plan and she's going to stick to it. The meeting with Sara isn't going to change that. If Sara bans Imogen from her conference, Imogen will find another way to expose Mörður. But right now, she's just going to enjoy herself. Right now, she's just going to live a little.

Imogen puts on her black leather pencil skirt and a red cashmere crew-neck jumper. She wants to look nice for Orri. The realisation causes a swirl of warmth inside her.

Sigurlína's lamb stew is delicious and the company is even better. Sigurlína and Orri are on their best behaviour. They banter with each other and laugh at each other's jokes. Despite their differences, it's clear they love each other.

Sigurlína gives Orri her car keys. Imogen puts on knee-high leather boots and a grey wrap coat with a faux-fur collar. She might be a little overdressed for the cinema but she doesn't care. She feels fabulous for the first time in ages.

Imogen hugs Sigurlína goodbye. 'Thank you for being there for me today,' she whispers in her ear. She knows it's a bit melodramatic but again, she doesn't care.

'Don't stay out too late, kids,' Sigurlína says, waving from the doorway. 'And don't do anything I wouldn't do.'

Orri snorts. 'Is there anything you wouldn't do, Mother?'

'I'm sure there's something . . . I know! Join the Conservative Party. I would never join the Conservative Party.'

'We won't go join the Conservatives this evening then.'

'Have a lovely time.'

Imogen and Orri get into Sigurlína's green Volvo. It has several dents and the paintwork is peeling off. It looks the same age as Orri.

'I need to quickly stop by the lab. I forgot my glasses. I don't wear them all the time, you'll have noticed, but I definitely need them for the cinema.'

It takes Orri three attempts to start the car.

Imogen asks, 'Did your mum tell you anything? About why I didn't show up for work?'

Orri gives a sarcastic laugh. 'My mother is the queen of secrets. She didn't tell me a thing. She just said that you were feeling a bit under the weather, that you needed a rest, and if our boss didn't think that was a good enough reason for you to get the day off, she would come down to the lab herself and give him a piece of her mind.'

Imogen smiles. She's pretty sure Sigurlína would have made good on the threat if prompted.

'I had my meeting with Sara this morning.'

'I see. How did it go?'

Imogen doesn't even hesitate. She tells Orri everything, ending with the moment Sara tried to throw Imogen out and ripped her dress.

'She thought we were having an affair.'

'Wow. Talk about getting it wrong.'

'It was so awful.'

'Did you tell her what really happened?'

'No. I couldn't do it.'

They've reached the campus. Orri parks in the car park outside Oddi. There's only a handful of other cars there.

They step outside. It's a still, crisp evening. The moon is out and the Northern Lights are visible in the night sky. *Wow.* Imogen can't help but stop and stare. They look like a green life force doing a dance of joy. Somehow, they make her think of Sigurlína and her wild, uninhibited character.

Orri has reached the door. How can he not stop and look at all this beauty? Maybe you start taking the Northern Lights for granted when you grow up with them just there, above your head, every time you look up at the sky.

Imogen catches up with him. Orri pushes open the thick wooden door.

Imogen's phone beeps. She pulls it out. It's a text.

'That's weird,' she says to Orri.

'What?'

'It's Victoria King. She's backing out of the article.'

'Seriously! Why?'

'Her text says: "Will not be doing the article. I suggest you let the matter lie; it's not worth the risk. I hope you'll heed my advice. If you decide not to, be careful."'

'Shit.'

'I'm going to text her back.'

Orri holds the door open while Imogen replies to Victoria and pleads with her to reconsider.

288

'I guess we can find someone else,' he says.

'I guess,' Imogen says as she presses send. 'But let's think about that tomorrow let's just enjoy ourselves this evening.'

The light inside Oddi is soft. The corridors are empty. The place feels different without the students and their frantic chatter, their innocent laughter and their vibrant hope for the future.

Imogen and Orri walk up the stairs. The cafeteria is closed. The door to the lab is locked. Orri enters his passcode into the keypad on the wall next to the door. The lab is completely dark. But when they step inside, they see light coming through a crack in the door to Mörður's office. They can hear a voice in there speaking in agitated, angry bursts.

That's Mörður. That's definitely Mörður. Imogen is filled with a familiar feeling of dread. But who is he talking to? There's a pause before he starts shouting again. It sounds like he's on the phone.

Imogen looks at Orri, waiting for him to take the lead. He stands there looking unsure.

Mörður is speaking in English.

'I told you: I don't know how anyone could know.'

Silence.

'I do realise what confidential means.'

Silence.

'No, I'm not available right now. I'm not in the office. This will have to wait.'

Orri clears his throat. He has decided to alert Mörður to their presence.

Imogen was half hoping that Orri would just tiptoe over to

his desk and get his glasses and they would then sneak out of there without having to face Mörður.

His voice falls silent. A few seconds pass. Then the door to Mörður's office opens.

Mörður is standing in the doorway.

'Oh, hi.' He looks a bit flustered, distant even. 'What are you guys doing here?'

'I forgot my glasses,' Orri explains.

Mörður's eyes slide over to Imogen. 'I hope you're feeling better.'

Imogen doesn't know what to say. Has he talked to Sara? Did she say anything to him about their meeting this morning? Or perhaps he hasn't been home yet. Imogen notices a scratch on his face running all the way from his temple to his lip. It wasn't there yesterday.

'Much better, thank you,' Imogen replies without looking directly at him. She never looks directly at him if she can help it.

Orri scuttles over to his desk to get his glasses. *Thank God.* They can finally get out of there.

'We're going to the cinema,' Orri says, filling the pained silence in the lab. 'Without my glasses George Clooney is just a big blob.'

Orri is rummaging through his desk.

Imogen imagines he can't see a thing in the darkness of the lab. She's about to walk over to the door where the light switch is located when Orri calls out: 'Found them.'

At the exact same time the lights turn on. For a brief moment Imogen is confused: *Did I just do that?* She laughs internally at the absurdity of that thought.

It's only when Mörður rushes out of his office that Imogen realises they've got company.

'Stan,' Mörður says, stalking past Imogen. 'What are you doing here? I told you this would have to wait.'

It takes a while for Imogen's eyes to adapt to the lab's stabbing-white fluorescent lights. But when she starts seeing past the black spots swimming in her line of vision she notices a man standing in the doorway to the lab.

He looks familiar. He's stocky, with a round, troll-like face, and he's wearing a baggy leather jacket and acid-washed jeans that look like they belong in the 1980s. She suddenly remembers. The first day Imogen arrived at the lab Mörður was just finishing up a meeting with an angry-looking man who spoke to him in English with an Eastern European accent. That's him.

Mörður places an arm around the man's shoulders and lightly pushes him towards the door. 'Stan, I don't think this is the right time to talk business. Why don't you come back tomorrow? During business hours.'

With a surprisingly swift movements the man slaps Mörður's hand off him.

The shock of the blow makes Mörður lose his footing and stumble backwards.

'So, we arrre having a party, arrre we?' Stan says with his heavy accent. 'That is verrry good then that I brought a friend.'

In steps another man: tall, bulky, bald and eerily expressionless. He's wearing a thick black down coat with a furry hood. He crosses his arms on his chest.

291

The bizarreness of the moment suddenly turns into a wailing siren in Imogen's head. 'Careful! He's got a gun.'

A silver handgun rests casually on top of the man's forearm, denting the down sleeve like death napping in a comfy bed. His finger is wrapped around the trigger.

Stan's angry frown rises into an angry smirk. 'This is Nikita Ivanov.'

Mörður raises his hands. His palms face Stan as if he's trying to calm a crazed dog. 'There's no need for this. Let's talk in the morning. I'm sure everything will seem clearer in the light of day.'

'Aren't you going to introduce me to your friends?'

'Please, Stan.'

The man with the gun uncrosses his arms. It doesn't take more for Mörður to give in. 'This is Orri. This is Imogen. Everyone, this is Stanislav Khrushchev. He's from Russia and he's a client of DataPsych. A very valued client.'

Stan's smirk fades. 'You lie.'

'Excuse me?'

'You say I'm a valued client.'

'You are.'

'Then why you brrreak your promise?'

Mörður looks away. As he stands there facing this leather-clad savage, himself wearing his juvenile little T-shirt with the picture of the Joker, he looks feeble and ridiculous. Up against the raw threat of the Russian, his bleach-white Adidas trainers and his self-consciously tidy, fashionable beard make him look like a child. 'I didn't break your confidence.'

'Then why I get a phone call from my bosses in Russia telling me that some journalist in England is asking them questions about Smertoil hiring DataPsych for a secret project?'

The words hit Imogen like a punch in the gut.

Mörður starts flailing his hands. 'I don't know. You have to believe me.'

Imogen looks over at Orri, who's standing by his desk. Recognition stains his face with red blotches of guilt.

What have we done? What the hell have we done?

Stan's angry, troll-like features look like they're hewn out of stone. 'Do you have anything to drrrink?'

Mörður's voice is a quivering whisper. 'What?'

Stan growls with impatience. 'Drrrink! Drrrink! To put in mouth. Swallow into stomach.'

'Yes, of course.' Mörður scuttles towards the little fridge in the kitchen corner. He opens it and takes out a can of Diet Coke.

Stan goes after him and snatches the can from Mörður's hands.

He cracks the can open with a fizzy bang. Imogen's heart pounds with fright; for a fraction of a second, she thought that the gun had gone off. Seeing Orri's pale face confirms she's not the only one.

Stan places the can on the kitchen table. He reaches into an inside pocket of his jacket and takes out a small plastic bag containing yellowish-white powder. He opens the grip seal and pours the contents of the bag into the Coke can. Then he passes it to Mörður again.

'Here. You drink.'

Mörður jumps back. 'What? No.'

'I have my orders.'

Mörður is looking over his shoulder at the lab door.

The man with the gun takes a step towards it, closes it, then locks it.

Mörður turns back to Stan. 'There's no need for this. We can talk about this. We can sort this out.'

'I have my orders. I always follow orders. I am not like you. I don't brrreak promise.'

'Seriously. We must be able to come to some sort of an arrangement. Please. Please show mercy. I have a family. I have two little girls.'

'Therrre is no leniency. Leniency breeds disloyalty. We need to set an example. We cannot have this happen again. Now drrrink.'

Mörður wrinkles his nose, turning into that child again. 'I won't. And you can't make me.'

Stan turns his head. His double chin doesn't follow and is left hanging around his neck thick as a tyre. He raises his straw-like eyebrows at his friend. 'Nikita.'

The next thing Imogen knows is that she's got an arm wrapped around her whole upper body with the surprising strength of a cobra and a gun pointed at her temple.

'You drrrink or he kill the girl.'

Imogen tries to break free but she's like the constricted prey of a snake stuck in its coils. She can't move a muscle.

Orri shoots forward.

Imogen feels the cold pressure lift off her temple as Nikita points the gun at Orri.

He abruptly stops.

'Now drink.'

Mörður's shoulders slump and his body crumples into the shape of a question mark.

Orri starts shouting at Mörður. 'Do something!'

Mörður is whimpering.

'You owe her, you dirty coward.'

Mörður rubs his face and screams into the palms of his hands. 'Grrrrwaaaaa!'

Stan's shouting. 'Drink! Drink!'

Orri is screaming. 'Do something! Do something!'

'Drink! Drink!'

'Do something! Do something!'

'Drink! Drink!'

'Do something! Do something!'

The different voices harmonise like a choir made up of ambulance sirens.

'Grrrrwaaaaa!' Mörður removes his hands to reveal a red, bloated face. He grabs the can from Stan.

Imogen feels the gun on her temple again.

Stan smirks. 'Now drink.'

Mörður's eyes are wild with fear. 'I can't. I can't. I can't. My family. My girls. Ella. Sylvía. My wife. My lovely Sara. I love her so much.'

But Stan has run out of patience. He turns on his heel, marches towards Nikita, grabs the gun from him and paces back to the kitchen.

Imogen feels the man's grip on her loosen. She uses the opportunity to break free. She runs to Orri, who wraps his arms around her, squeezing her tight.

Imogen watches as Stan raises the gun. He aims it at Mörður. 'Drink.'

Mörður raises the can to his mouth. His hand is shaking. Tears are streaming down his face. He's emitting sounds that can only usually be heard in the animal kingdom. He's howling, wailing, whining, barking; he's crying like a wounded animal. Like a dying animal.

The sounds feel familiar to Imogen. They're the same sounds she made that morning while crying on Sigurlína's shoulder, feeling like there was no tomorrow. It gives her no satisfaction to hear them coming from Mörður.

Mörður takes a sip of the Diet Coke. 'Awwww!'

'More,' Stan orders.

'Please, let me go.'

Stan pushes the barrel of the gun to Mörður's forehead. 'More.'

Mörður raises the can, places it on his lower lip, opens his mouth, lifts the can and pours in the dark fizzy liquid. He swallows with another wailing cry.

Stan nods with hateful satisfaction on his face. 'Now finish it all.'

With each gulp Mörður's face gets more bloated. Sweat is oozing from his pores, forming little drops that run down his face, becoming one with his tears. The fizzy drink froths at the corners of his mouth, staining his beard with the sweet dark drink he always loved but is now going to be the death of him.

He finally finishes it all.

With one last scream Mörður crushes the can in his hand. His fist turns blue. His hand is shaking. His whole body is shaking. He lets go of the can, which falls to the floor with a hollow thump.

He stands for a moment with his head hung like a man who's just faced his judgement. His legs wobble, and he collapses to the floor, where he crouches on his knees rocking back and forth, staring into an invisible distance.

Stan reaches for one of the foldable plastic kitchen chairs and takes a seat. 'In eight hours you will start to die.'

Photo: A small glass of water on a steel tabletop.
Filter: Lark.

Possible captions . . .

Option one: This is a glass of water.
Option two: This is not *just* a glass of water . . .
Option three: No, it's not an M&S glass of water.
Option four: This is a glass of water inside a prison.

Actual caption . . .

#jailbird

♥19

Chapter Twenty-Three

Hannah

I can't wait to get to the office. I can't wait to start work. I wish Dad would park the car a little quicker. This is taking for ever.

The car stops and Dad switches off the ignition.

Finally. I grab the door handle. We're parked right in front of the entrance of the paper's headquarters and I'm ready to run inside.

'Wait.'

No. 'What?' I growl at him.

Oops. I shouldn't irk him. Not today. I try to make up for my tone of voice with a smile. I don't want him to change his mind.

It turned out that when the police called last night, it wasn't because I was in trouble. It wasn't because they'd found out about the break in into Oddi as I thought. They were calling on behalf of Imogen Collins, who is being held at the Hólmsheiði prison on the outskirts of Reykjavík and who has asked to see me.

Dad immediately said that it was completely out of the question; that my obsession with this case was unhealthy and it had nearly got me into serious trouble already. *Good thing I didn't tell him about the incident outside the British Embassy.* It was Rósa who eventually managed to convince him to let me go and see Imogen. 'If you want Hannah to behave like an adult, you need to treat her like one.'

Dad doesn't look at me when he speaks. 'Kjarri is coming with you.'

'What! Why?' So much for treating me like an adult. He thinks I need handholding.

'I don't trust you.'

'What can I possibly do wrong in a visitors' room inside a prison?'

'It's not what you can do.'

'Then what?'

'It's the fact you don't tell me anything. I'm responsible for you, Hannah. I need to know what you're up to. I need to know where you are. I need to know about your life. I can't have you getting mixed up in some murder case.'

Dad rubs his face. He's clearly tired. We all went to bed late last night, after arguing about Imogen Collins and cleaning up after Rósa's feast.

'Hannah, I don't understand why you're so obsessed with this murder case. It's not even interesting. It's just a tragedy. Gossip column material at best. I want Kjarri there because I don't trust that you'll tell me what truly takes place inside that visitors' room.'

I choose not to respond to his words. Mostly because they're true. 'Shall we go?' I say.

Dad sighs before opening the door.

Maybe I can sneak out of the office before Dad has time to fill Kjarri in. I don't need Dad's car to get to the prison. I'll just take a cab.

When we walk into the office I see Kjarri standing in the lobby looking overly respectable in a black blazer and knitted crew-neck jumper over a white shirt. I realise that Dad is one step ahead of me: he has already talked to Kjarri.

The prison isn't far from our offices. It's only a quiet ten-minute drive through a landscape of frosty grass cut off by the shadows of monstrous mountains in the distance. I make a point of sulking the whole way.

The prison is a brand-new low-rise building that clings to the flat, scrubby landscape. Its many different wings, clad with rust-coloured steel plates, slither through the snowy lava and grass like octopus tentacles.

We drive through a gate in the steel fence and park the car.

As we're standing outside, waiting to be buzzed in to the prison, Kjarri says, 'Don't worry. I won't tell your dad anything you don't want him to know.'

It's a relief not feeling like a resident of some dystopian surveillance state any more. I smile at him. 'Thank you.'

In the prison's lobby we go through an airport-style security check. Then a woman wearing a black shirt, black tie and black trousers leads us silently along a corridor painted bright white. She stops in front of a white steel door with a small round window. She opens it and waves us in.

We step inside a small room with a big window revealing the wild landscape outside. It looks nice, considering it's a prison.

Imogen is sitting with her hands clasped on top of a round steel table, looking down into a sad little glass of water.

The door closes behind us.

Imogen looks up.

Her face is so much paler than when I last saw her. She doesn't have any make-up on – but it's more than that. Her cheeks seem to have shrunk and the colour has drained even from her lips. Her long dark hair is tied back in a ponytail. She's wearing a simple, light-grey jumper. Despite the circumstances, however, prison does nothing to diminish her natural beauty. Incarceration has simply added a mysteriously tragic edge to it.

Imogen smiles but the smile does not reach her eyes.

'Thank you for coming, Hannah,' she says before looking at Kjarri. 'I'm sorry, I've forgotten your name.'

Kjarri blushes. 'It's Kja-kja-kjarri.'

He's nervous. Or embarrassed. His stutter is back.

I sit down opposite Imogen on a black plastic chair with chrome steel legs. Kjarri sits down next to me.

I suddenly find myself lost for words. I'd been so eager to get here and dive into the mystery that is the murder of Mörður Þórðarson that I got ahead of myself and didn't think about how you greet someone in prison. 'How are you?' sounds too personal under the circumstances; why would I be wondering how she is when I so clearly know the answer? 'Good morning', sounds so formal, like I'm her lawyer or someone who's here to perform a strip-search on her.

Imogen offers me absolution. 'I guess you're wondering what you're doing here?'

'I guess,' I mumble, suddenly thinking that maybe I should have brought her something. Chocolates? Flowers? Are you even allowed to bring people things in prison? *Cigarettes*. That's what I should have brought. That's what people always bring on TV.

She's looking me straight in the eye. 'I'm going to plead guilty.'

I almost fall off my chair. 'What! Why?'

'It's the only solution.'

I stare at Imogen. Her face remains expressionless. It's as if we're talking about something mundane, like the weather. *Do you know if it's going to rain today? I think the forecast is light drizzle. Oh, by the way, I'm going to prison for life.*

How can she say these words with such emotional detachment? This is weird. Something is up. She looks like a member of a cult who's been brainwashed and is just monotonously repeating words that have been violently drilled into her. Or am I simply seeing what I want to see?

'You can't,' I say. 'You didn't do it. You didn't do it, right?'

Imogen drones on like that cult member. 'That has nothing to do with it.'

How can she say that? 'That has everything to do with it.'

'Reality isn't black and white.'

What is this crap? I want to jump over the table, grab Imogen's sweatshirt and shake her until she wakes up from this trance. Who is this woman?

I try to decipher her mad ravings. *Reality isn't black and white.* What does that even mean?

Imogen shrugs as if she doesn't care.

I turn to Kjarri. 'A little help here.'

Kjarri leans on the table and looks at Imogen from under his brow. 'Are they offering you a deal? Is it because they're offering you a deal?'

'There might be a deal.'

I take a deep breath. 'But you didn't do it. You didn't murder Mörður.'

'Yes. Well. I may not have pulled the trigger. But I had a hand in it.'

'That makes no sense.'

Imogen's robotic mannerisms ease slightly. Her cheeks colour. 'I heard about what happened to you in front of the British Embassy yesterday morning.'

How? I glance at Kjarri. I haven't told anyone about what happened. I don't want Dad to find out.

'I asked you here because I owe you an apology. I should never have got you involved. I should never have given you the phone.'

My head is hurting with incomprehension and unanswered questions. 'Why did you?'

Imogen looks down at the table. 'The less you know, the better.'

I suddenly slam the table with my open palms. It's completely involuntary. My anger scares me. I can't control it. 'You got me involved. It's too late to undo that.'

Kjarri touches my shoulder. 'Cool it,' he says, sounding like a character in a gangster film.

I shake him off. 'Who killed him? Who killed Mörður?'

'That's the thing,' Imogen says. 'I'm not completely sure who they are exactly.'

'They?'

'We were working for some dodgy clients at DataPsych. They might be Russia's military intelligence service; they might be a criminal gang; they might belong to the Eastern European mafia. It all went belly-up and they killed Mörður.' She looks up at me, either annoyed or pleadingly. 'There. You've solved the mystery. Now let it go.'

'I don't get it.' I can't let it go. 'Why did you give me your phone? If there was evidence on it that proved your innocence, why didn't you give it to the police?'

'Keeping quiet was the only protection I had. The only protection me and Orri had.'

'What was on your phone that was meant to prove your innocence to me?'

'There was an attachment in my sent messages folder. I'd emailed all the documents about the deal to a journalist in the UK. The clients seemed to have gotten wind of it and that's why they killed Mörður. So, it wasn't Mörður who blabbed. It was me. I guess in a way you could say that I killed him.'

She says this with remarkable emotional detachment. As if she neither cares that he's dead nor that she played a part in it – she's simply stating a fact. To be fair, why should she care given what he did to her?

'I'm so sorry I gave you the phone. I'm so sorry I put you in harm's way.' 'At my talk at Harpa, when I saw the police coming for me, I panicked. Then I spotted you and for a fraction of a second I thought that there might be a way out.

'I couldn't say anything about the dodgy DataPsych client to the police. If I told the police the truth and they released me from prison, I would have been killed within five minutes, so would Orri. But in my crazed state I thought that if someone else discovered the truth – someone on the outside with no connection to me, someone I couldn't have told – I would somehow get out of this mess. I wouldn't go to jail for murder and we wouldn't be killed either.'

I take a moment to think. I guess it makes sense. It does sound credible. And the evidence does back up the story. The man who attacked me in front of the embassy and, I assumed, had something to do with the murder, sounded Russian – Imogen had said that this dodgy client was very possibly a member of Russia's military intelligence service.

Imogen smiles and I can see that brainwashed cultish look on her face again.

'But everything is going to be okay. You will be safe. When I confess to the murder, the case will be closed. Then those crazy DataPsych clients don't need to worry about being implicated and they can simply go back to where they came from. The end.'

'Why do you assume that?'

'My lawyer explained it to me. He told me how organisations such as government intelligence services and the mafia work. They use violence to keep up loyalty and discipline. They murdered Mörður to make it known to everyone else they work with that they do not tolerate disloyalty, that they do not tolerate blabbermouths. Their methodology is stay loyal, stay silent, stay safe. He pointed out to me that if I pleaded guilty I'd be declaring my loyalty and I'd be safe. If I pleaded guilty, everyone else at DataPsych and their families would be safe. There are so many more people who could get hurt if this case isn't closed.'

I can't take my eyes off Imogen. She's sitting with her back straight and demented determination on her face.

'Like who?'

'A lot of people. Like Sara. Sara Gunnarsdóttir and her daughters.'

'Excuse me.' I must have misheard. 'The wife of the man who sexually abused you? I read her email to you – it was horrendous.'

Imogen's serene expression crumples slightly but she quickly recovers. 'I bear her no ill will. She is a victim of circumstance just like me.'

A question suddenly pops into my head like a smack in the face. 'How did you know that I was attacked outside the embassy yesterday?'

Kjarri shrieks in horror. 'You were attacked?'

I ignore him. I'll explain later.

'How did you know?' I say again.

Imogen's mouth shoots to the side in a pout of reluctance. 'Someone saw it.'

'But no one came to my rescue. No one from the embassy came out to see if I was okay.'

Imogen is frowning. *In anger? Protectively?* 'He couldn't.'

'He couldn't?'

'He can't leave.'

'What?'

'He would have helped you if he could. Orri is the kindest person I know.'

'Orri?' I suddenly remember my visit to the embassy. 'Oh my God. He's hiding in the embassy, isn't he?'

Imogen shrinks. 'Please leave him out of this. It's the only place he's safe. Please don't tell anyone. I beg you.'

'Are you together?'

Imogen looks down on the table. 'I don't know what we are. The only thing I know is that I don't want anything bad to happen to him. He's been great through all of this. He's supported me every step of the way. His letters are what keep me sane in here. Every time I have a meeting with my lawyer or the ambassador they bring me a new letter. No one has come to visit me for four or five days now. I'm really starting to crave a new letter. I sound pathetic, don't I?'

It's obvious that Imogen is not going to change her mind about pleading guilty. But how will it work?

'To plead guilty, don't you have to know how the crime was committed? Don't you have to describe what it is that you're admitting to? How can you do that if you didn't commit the murder?'

'A lot of it has been in the papers.'

'So, you're just going to recount what you read in the papers?'

'Not exactly. I'm not allowed to read the papers in here. The ambassador has mentioned a few things on his visits. But it's mostly Orri who keeps me up to date in his letters.' Imogen leans back in her chair.

'Things like, how the police believe that Mörður was killed inside the lab and that his body was then driven out of Reykjavík and tossed into a crevice. That he'd been wearing a T-shirt with the Joker printed on it. That he died from a head injury after being hit over the head with a blunt object and that the murder weapon was Mörður's precious Cannes Lions trophy—'

'Excuse me?' I interrupt.

'The murder weapon. It was a trophy. It was in the papers.'

Kjarri wiggles on his chair. 'Yes. It was. It was in *our* paper, actually. It was our scoop.' He says this with the pride of a man whose football team just won a match. 'The trophy was discovered in a dumpster outside the university's main building.'

I, however, couldn't care less about the glory of our team's goal. I'm confused. Something doesn't add up. 'You said that the last time you got a letter from Orri was four or five days ago.'

'Yes.'

'But how did you know about what happened outside the embassy yesterday?'

'Orri called while I was in the gym and left a message with the warden. It said: Hannah met Stan. I saw it out the window. Something needs to be done.'

'The message didn't say anything else?'

'No, why?'

I look away. I can't do this. I can't take away the only good thing left in Imogen's life. I can't take away the last glimmer of hope from someone who has lost everything.

'Nothing.' I reply.

But it is something. It's definitely something. The police only discovered the murder weapon two days ago. It looks like Imogen's precious boyfriend isn't all that he seems.

Photo: A shadow of a hand.
Filter: Reyes.

Caption: Where there's a shadow, there's also light.

♥257

What the caption should have been . . .

Option one: If I could only find that light . . .
Option two: I want to find that light . . .

Chapter Twenty-Four

Imogen

It's six in the morning and Mörður is still alive.

That, however, is clearly not according to the plan. Earlier in the night, Stan had been drooling with murderous anticipation, like a vulture watching hungrily as his prey bleeds to death. But with every minute that passes, more of his theatrical thuggishness falls away. And with every ounce of confidence Stan loses, Mörður looks more alive. His tears have dried and his face is no longer puffy. He's sitting on the floor up against the wall, his back straight and a hopeful glint in his eyes.

Stan looks once again at his wristwatch, a grotesquely flashy diamond-encrusted Rolex with a leopard strap. For distraction, Imogen has been staring at the watch for the past hour, inspecting it, trying to determine whether it's authentic or fake. The jury is still out.

Stan gets up from the kitchen chair. 'I don't understand.' He looks at his friend. 'The abrin has always worrrked before.'

Stan's troll-like face has lost its wicked edge and now looks like the face of a child who doesn't understand why his mummy hasn't come to collect him from school yet.

'Nikita.'

Stan's friend is sitting on one of the office chairs in front of the door, making sure no one gets out. The gun is resting on his lap.

'*Da*,' the man answers.

Stan says something in what Imogen assumes is Russian.

Nikita raises himself in the chair, slips the gun into the inside pocket of the down coat he still has on, and gets up.

Stan grabs his leather jacket from the kitchen table, flings it on and strides across the room in a huff.

Nikita opens the door.

They're leaving. Imogen can hardly believe it. *This is over. This is actually over.*

Imogen is just thinking what an anti-climactic end this is to the second-worst moment of her life when Stan stops and turns around in the doorway.

He looks at every single one of them. Then a poisonous smile crosses his lips, exposing yellowing teeth mixed with gold veneers. As if he'd been reading Imogen's mind, he says: 'This is *not* over.'

The door slams shut.

Imogen isn't sure how long they sit there, without moving, without saying a word.

All of a sudden Mörður shoots up from the floor. 'It was you two, wasn't it?' His face is red and the words spew from his lips, burning with rage. He's like a volcano that has started to erupt without any warning. 'It was you who contacted that journalist.'

Imogen and Orri are still on the floor, huddled together up

against a radiator. Imogen feels Orri squeeze her upper arm. She turns to look at him and sees that his guilt is written all over his face. There's no point in denying it.

'You bloody fools. You stupid children. Do you know what you've done? Do you realise the danger you've put us all in? You pathetic little millennials with your simple minds and your high-minded morals. It's easy to be principled when you're just a kid. It's easy being principled when you don't have mouths to feed, when you don't have a mortgage on your back, when you don't have the noose around your neck called reality. You lazy, good-for-nothing, whimpering snowflakes, all wrapped up in cotton wool with your smashed avocados and your ethical coffee and your safe spaces and—'

Orri lets go of Imogen and jumps up. 'Shut the hell up, Mörður,' he shouts. 'If anyone is to blame, it's you. You got us into this mess.'

'Oh, look who's talking. If I remember correctly you did not say no to the money either. You're no different to me.'

Orri suddenly runs towards Mörður, grabs him by the shirt, slams him up against the wall and starts screaming. 'I'm nothing like you! I don't abuse women like you. You sick, disgusting bastard.'

Mörður stares at Orri, his eyes wide as if he's standing in the middle of a road looking at oncoming traffic.

'How could you do this to her? How could you do this to anyone?'

Mörður gathers some composure. 'You have no idea what you're talking about, you stupid boy. If anything, she came after me. Always smiling, always laughing at everything I said, always wearing those low-cut T-shirts with her bra on show. She wanted it. She was asking for it.'

With the quick movements of a cobra, Orri pulls his head back, hurls it forward and headbutts Mörður.

Mörður cries out in pain.

Imogen jumps to her feet. 'Orri, this is not the time. We need to figure out what to do. They're going to come back. We need to call the police.'

Orri shoots Mörður a dirty look as he reluctantly lets go of him.

Mörður rubs his forehead. 'We can't get the police involved.'

Imogen hopes he's in pain. 'Of course we can get the police involved. Who else would we get involved?'

'This is too big for the police.'

'How can anything be too big for the police?'

'These are no regular criminals.'

'Smertoil isn't an oil company?'

'Smertoil is an oil company and on paper Smertoil is our client.'

'And in reality?'

'I'm not sure. But I have my suspicions. I think they might be members of the GRU.'

'GRU?'

'Russia's military intelligence service.'

Orri digs his fingers into his hair. 'We have to call the police.'

Now it's Mörður's turn to shout at Orri. 'Don't you get it? The Icelandic police is like that cute country cop you see on British cop shows like *Midsomer Murders* or *Inspector Morse*.

Calling them would be like asking the Suffolk police to take care of the Cold War. They just don't have the resources or the know-how. Getting them involved is more likely to get us killed than provide us with protection.'

Imogen covers her ears. She can't listen to any more of this.

'We need to stay calm,' Orri says, his tone suddenly slightly more measured. 'We need to put our heads together and figure this out. There's no alternative.'

Mörður frowns like a child. 'There's nothing we can do. They're everywhere. They've got their dirty tentacles woven into the fabric of organised crime in Iceland. They've got a massive pull within the Eastern European mafia, whose presence in this country is growing by the day. We need the protection of a big player, the highest power. We need the protection of a government. But the government of Iceland is just as feeble as the police.'

Orri yelps out a word. 'Sara!'

'What about Sara?'

'She works at the British Embassy. You need to call her. She needs to get the ambassador to help us. She needs to get him down here right now.'

Mörður is already pulling out his mobile. He punches at the screen and places the phone up against his ear.

The metallic echo of Sara's voice escapes into the lab. But they can't make out words.

Mörður switches to Icelandic. 'I'm at the lab,' Imogen manages to understand. She's become pretty good at understanding Icelandic but – because she can't speak it for the life of her – people don't realise that she can quite often understand what they're saying.

Orri sits back down next to Imogen and starts translating Mörður's side of the conversation in a quiet whisper.

'Yes, she's here.'

Mörður glances at Imogen for a fraction of a second – long enough for Imogen to register the hate he feels for her.

'Nothing happened.'

Sara is shouting.

'We're not having an affair,' Mörður shouts back at her. 'Sara, will you please—'

He's cut off.

'Sara, listen to me. This is an emergency. We've been attacked. I've been attacked. They tried to kill—'

His lips quiver. He shakes it off.

'I can't go into the details right now, but remember the Smertoil deal? It's dodgy. It's really dodgy.'

There's shouting again.

'Did you not say that we needed a bigger place to live? Did you not say that you wanted a second car? Did you not say that the girls needed to have piano lessons?'

More shouting.

'Sara, this is not the time for this. We're talking about life and death here. Do you even care if I live or die? Would you even have grieved for me if those bastards had managed to kill me?'

Mörður lifts the phone from his ear. Imogen isn't sure if it's to protect his hearing from more shouting, or because he doesn't want to know the answer.

They all hear Sara's reply. 'I don't know, Mörður. I don't know anything any more.'

Mörður stays quiet for a while. Then he pushes the mobile back up to his ear. 'Sara. I need your help. We need your help. Orri is here too. Please. Can you call Gerald Boothby? Can you ask him to come to the lab? Now.'

Sara is saying something.

'Thank you. I love you.'

There's a click. Sara has hung up.

Mörður droops his head. Then he looks up. 'She's going to call him. She'll let us know.'

It's hardly been two minutes when Mörður's phone buzzes. It's a text from Sara. Mörður reads it out loud: 'He's on his way.'

They sit around the kitchen table and wait. Mörður makes coffee. Imogen reaches for the biscuit plate, hands a cookie to Orri and takes one for herself.

Half an hour later there's a knock on the door.

Mörður opens it.

The ambassador charges inside. Mörður tries to shake his hand but the ambassador strides right past him. He goes to Orri. 'Are you all right?'

'Fine.'

Mörður follows on the heels of the ambassador.

'You know Orri, of course. And this is Imogen Collins.'

'Yes, we've met briefly before,' Gerald Boothby says and gives Imogen a vague smile.

Imogen tries to smile back but it's hard to express fake emotions under the circumstances, even though politeness calls for it.

Mr Boothby turns to Mörður. He's dressed in jeans and a snow coat. His dark hair is a mess. He must have been asleep when Sara called him. He lowers his thick eyebrows down towards his simmering-blue eyes. 'What the hell is going on here?'

Mörður shrinks back slightly. Then he slumps down on a kitchen chair and tells the ambassador everything.

Imogen doesn't take her eyes off Mr Boothby while he listens to Mörður's account. Although he listens in silence, the whitening of his face as the story progresses and the widening of his eyes reveal the gravity of the situation. She has her conformation. This is as bad as they'd thought.

Mörður concludes his account with the words, 'Then they left, promising to be back.' He looks pleadingly up at Mr Boothby, handing over to him.

The ambassador takes a moment to compose himself. He is visibly startled by the events. Suddenly his face glazes over, closes, like a locked door. 'There's nothing I can do.'

'What?' Mörður yelps.

The ambassador is obviously trying to appear measured, dispassionate, professional, but his voice shoots quite a few units over what would be considered shouting on the decibel scale. 'Why should the British government help someone who's been collaborating with the Russians in their propaganda war? You must realise what you were hired to do. You must realise that you were hired to spread dissent and undermine our political system. The Russians were basically paying you to stir up trouble in the UK. This is a war and you have been fighting for the wrong side.'

Mörður doesn't reply. It's obvious he knows full well what he was doing.

'Please.' Mörður looks as if he's about to cry.

But Mörður is as likely to get blood from a stone as he is to extract sympathy from Mr Boothby. 'You took the money. You take the consequences.'

Mörður suddenly jumps on the ambassador and grabs him by his snow jacket. 'I can give your government information.'

Mr Boothby pushes him off. 'You know nothing that MI6 doesn't know already.'

'What about human kindness? You can appeal to them on humanitarian grounds.'

The ambassador's chest expands as he inhales to emit what Imogen thinks will be laughter but turns out to be scathing contempt. 'You bloody fool. Do you think the British government wants an international incident on their hands? Do you think they'd risk an already fragile relationship with Russia to save a greedy university lecturer from a faraway country? They wouldn't touch you with a bargepole.'

The ambassador looks at Imogen and Orri. Sadness crosses his face. 'I'm sorry.'

He turns, walks to the door and departs without so much as a goodbye or good luck.

He leaves behind him a deathly silence.

After a while Mörður shoots up from his chair. 'I've got an idea.' He runs into his office and returns holding his jacket. 'Sara's parents have a secluded cabin by Þingvallavatn.'

'It's a lake in a national park around forty kilometres northeast of here,' Orri explains to Imogen.

'It can only be reached by a private road. The land is fenced off. It won't keep anyone out but at least we'd see them coming.

We can hide out there while we wait for this to blow over or until we come up with a better idea.'

Imogen gasps with horror. 'I'm not going to some cabin with you.'

Mörður looks her up and down, contempt creasing his face. 'Do you want to get killed?'

Imogen goes cold. *What kind of a choice is that?*

Orri reaches over to her and takes her hand. 'We can find our own hideout.'

Mörður bangs his fist on the kitchen table. 'Why are you being so stubborn?'

'Why do you care if we come with you?' Orri growls back at him.

'There's safety in numbers. And we can work together to find a solution. We all have different connections. If we pool them together we stand a better chance of finding someone who can help.'

Orri looks at Imogen. 'What do you think?'

Do they have a choice?

'I wouldn't leave your side for one moment.'

'Fine,' Imogen whispers. *So the horror continues*, she thinks.

'We'll take my car,' Mörður barks as he buttons up his coat. 'Do any of you have a gun?'

'What?' Orri cries.

'No worries,' Mörður says. 'I've got the shooting rifle I use for my ptarmigan hunting. I'll bring that.'

Mörður looks down at his watch, a super-trendy Daniel Wellington with a striped fabric strap in blue and green. This is not a watch made for a life-and-death situation. This is a watch to be worn in a crisis involving colour palettes and logos and font sizes and photo resolutions, made more bearable by a snack of carrot sticks and hummus, flat whites and wheatgrass shots. 'It's almost eight o'clock. Let's all go home, pack a bag and meet back here in an hour.'

Imogen and Orri get up like robots programmed for synchronisation.

'I'm just going to take care of a couple of things here,' Mörður says. 'You go. I'll be right behind you.'

They leave the lab.

'An hour,' they hear Mörður call after them. 'If you're not here, I leave without you.'

'Jerk,' Orri mumbles.

Sigurlína's car is parked outside Oddi. 'I'll drive you to my mum's,' Orri says to Imogen. 'Then I'll go home, pack and pick you back up.'

He unlocks the Volvo.

They get into the freezing car. It takes them ten minutes to get the engine running and navigate their way out of the busy car park, which is quickly filling up.

It still looks like night outside but the morning rush hour is in full swing. Imogen looks into the cars driving past. The passengers appear gloomy under the dark skies and awaiting tasks of the day ahead. If they only knew how lucky they were. But no one appreciates the glory of mundanity until it's taken from them.

Imogen and Orri arrive at Sigurlína's house. They've driven the whole way in silence.

Orri parks the car without switching off the engine. He turns to face Imogen.

She looks into his eyes. Those watery-blue eyes, clear as a lake on a quiet morning. Endlessly deep and hiding unexplored mysteries. She wishes she could take a dip in them; she wishes she could be the one who got to discover the surprises beneath the surface.

If only things were different. If only they'd met under different circumstances, normal circumstances. As students perhaps, going to the same classes. If only things had been simple: a hello, a drink, dinner.

But their relationship would never be simple. They would always have met for one reason and one reason only: because of what the Beast did to her. Would they ever be able to move out from under that shadow?

Orri's hand is clasped around the handbrake between their seats. Imogen's is resting next to her thigh. Orri reaches out his little finger and strokes the back of her hand.

His touch sends warmth to her heart and light to her head. This little gesture is the biggest sign of hope Imogen can imagine. It offers all the possibility of spring, all the warmth of summer. It says, there is a page after this one.

Maybe. Maybe it is possible to chase the shadow away. Maybe, when this is over, she can stop letting the worst day of her past define her future. She doesn't yet know how they can get out of this mess. But they will find a way. At the cottage they'll put their heads together and come up with a plan. Maybe everything will turn out okay.

Photo: A small red house, on a quiet street, with snow on the roof.
Filter: Slumber.

Possible captions . . .

Option one: Cute.
Option two: Christmassy.
Option three: Home of a happy family.
Option four: Or is it?

Actual caption . . .

Beautiful Reykjavík.

♥14

Chapter Twenty-Five

Hannah

Sigurlína's kitchen smells like burnt toast. She doesn't seem too pleased to see us. She slams a dirty pan into the sink with a massive bang.

Kjarri shoots me a look.

'You need some help with the washing-up?' I say, desperately trying to make things less awkward.

Sigurlína takes a seat at the kitchen table. 'I'm sorry. I'm not a morning person.'

It's almost noon.

'So,' she says, wrapping herself tighter in her golden robe. The house is freezing. 'What can I do for you this time?'

I feel as welcome in her house as the common cold. 'Nothing actually. We've just come from the prison, on Hólmsheiði. We were there to see Imogen.'

I wait for her to say something. But she doesn't. She doesn't ask how Imogen is doing. She doesn't ask what we were doing there.

Sigurlína suddenly shoots up from her chair. 'Sorry. I need coffee. Would you like some coffee? I have a Danish pastry to go with it.'

Sigurlína reaches for a paper bag on the counter and takes out a strip of pastry dripping with sugar, vanilla custard and chocolate. She opens a kitchen drawer and pulls out a carving knife. She turns her back. 'I always need something sweet with my coffee. Life is about balance. It's about yin and yang—'

I interrupt Sigurlína. 'She's going to plead guilty.'

Sigurlína turns around slowly. She's still holding the knife. The harsh noon sun is reflected in its blade.

'I see.'

I try to read her face. Is she upset? Is she surprised? Or did she expect this to happen?

'But she didn't do it,' I say, no closer to figuring out what Sigurlína is thinking. 'She isn't a murderer.'

'Appearances can be deceiving.'

'I know. But the evidence doesn't point to her. I've been looking at the evidence and I think I know who the real murderer is.'

Sigurlína doesn't say a word. She just stands there with her knife. There's a strange glint in her crystalline eyes. Maybe it's lack of caffeine, maybe it's something else, but she looks slightly scary with her elfin hair in her elfin robe holding a carver big enough to cut up a spit-roast.

I had a big fight with Kjarri on our way here. He wanted to go straight to the police after our visit to the prison. But I wanted to make one stop on the way.

'It wasn't Imogen who murdered Mörður,' he shouted at me as if I didn't know that. 'And it wasn't those Russians either. It was Orri. It's obvious. You said it yourself. Only the murderer could have known about the murder weapon before the police discovered it.'

Eventually Kjarri caved and agreed to stop by at Sigurlína's before we went to the police.

I reach for my backpack on the floor by my chair. I take out the letter. I hold it out to Sigurlína.

'Imogen asked me to give you this.'

She doesn't take it straight away. I glance at the envelope in my outstretched hand. It's open. 'So you can look at it,' Imogen had said. 'I don't want you to think that I'm trying to get you into trouble again. I'm not. I just want to do right by everyone.'

Sigurlína finally takes the envelope. I watch as she opens it slowly, reluctantly, like she doesn't want to face what's inside.

Kjarri and I read the letter out in the car in front of the prison. It went like this:

My dearest Sigurlína,

I hope you're well. I hope life is starting to settle after the uproar of the past few weeks.

I'm not sure what you think of me as you read this. I'm sure the papers have been writing some awful things that do not cast me in a favourable light. Some of them are probably true, some of them might not be.

But that's not why I'm writing to you. I'm not writing to you to seek redemption; this is not about penance, this isn't even about me. This is about you. And Orri.

I'm not good at expressing feelings; I've locked mine up for so long I'm not sure if I know how to let them out any more. But I hope my sincerity comes across in the meagre ramblings that follow.

I need to tell you three things (I'm sorry if this sounds like an Excel spreadsheet; I've always been more comfortable with numbers than words). So here goes:

1) I want to thank you. You probably never realised it, and I never told you, but you were there for me at one of the lowest points in my life. You took me in, made me meatballs, let me snuggle up against you while watching Netflix, at a time when I had no one. You were like a mother to me. I will always keep you in my heart.

2) I'm so sorry for complicating your life. I never wanted to cause you grief. Please don't hate me.

3) Orri loves you. And Orri needs you. I know he doesn't always show it but it's true. Take

it from someone who's been there. Even though
you're not talking, even though you're
separated by a thousand miles and the deepest
ocean, you always love your parents, you
always need your parents. So, don't give up
on him.

That's it. That's all. That's curtain call.

When I'm at the end of my life and I look
back at this time, you and Orri will be two
shining lights on an otherwise dark path
paved with nothing but regrets. You are my
two bright stars in the night sky.

Thank you for being on my side.

Yours for ever,
Imogen

Sigurlína lowers the letter.

When she doesn't say anything I decide to fill the silence
with the reason for us being there. 'I think your son murdered
Mörður Þórðarson and that he's letting Imogen Collins take
the blame. We're on our way to the police station to tell them
everything we know. I came here to see if you had any comment
for the paper.'

Suddenly, Sigurlína starts shaking. Tears are rolling down
her cheeks. I have no idea how to act. I have no idea what to do

when a stranger cries right in front of you. But Kjarri does. He gets up, opens one of the kitchen cabinets, grabs a glass, fills it up with water, hands it to Sigurlína and wraps an arm around her shoulders.

Sigurlína sips the water. Then she dries her eyes with the back of the hand holding the letter, reaches for a scruffy mobile lying on the kitchen counter and dials a number.

Photo: A slice of pepperoni pizza on a porcelain plate with blue flowers.
Filter: Aden.

Caption: #hungry

♥312

What the caption should have been . . .

Option one: I should simply enjoy this slice of pizza instead of wasting time taking a photo of it and posting it here while it gets cold.
Option two: But sometimes you don't want to do the things you should.
Option three: Sometimes doing something pointless isn't pointless – it's fun.

Chapter Twenty-Six

Imogen

Imogen and Orri have been standing out in the car park in front of Oddi for forty minutes. Mörður is late.

They should be trying to lie low, be discreet, but Orri is so on edge he might as well be holding a sign saying, SOMETHING UNTOWARD GOING ON HERE.

'You okay?' Imogen asks.

'Do you think he might have left without us?' Orri says, huddled against the cold.

The words trip off Imogen's tongue. 'I wouldn't put it past him.'

'I know why he isn't dead.'

Imogen flinches. 'Excuse me?'

'Mörður. I know why he didn't die.'

'Okay . . .'

'Remember what Stan said? He said, "The abrin has always worked before." I googled it. Abrin is a deadly poison that is found in the seeds of a plant called the rosary pea. It's similar to ricin. There is no antidote. Mörður should be dead.'

'Why isn't he?'

'Because of a massive stroke of luck. While googling, I came across an old news article in *The Times* about a daughter who tried to kill her overbearing and controlling mother. The daughter bought abrin on the Dark Web, laced her mother's Diet Coke with the deadly poison and watched her drink it, expecting her to die. When nothing happened to her mother the daughter assumed she hadn't given her a big enough dose. She went to buy some more, but the police caught on and arrested her. It turned out that the problem wasn't the dose. It was the Diet Coke. The soft drink contains an acid that stops abrin working.'

Imogen is lost for words. Through experience she's come to learn that life is random. As it turns out, so is death.

Orri looks at his watch. 'I'm going to try to call him again.'

No answer.

Imogen can't take this waiting around any more. 'I'll go check for him in the lab.'

When she gets there she enters her passcode and opens the door. The lab is empty. She walks over to Mörður's office. The door is locked. He always locks it when he leaves the lab.

'Anything?' Orri says when she returns.

'He's not there.'

Orri raises his eyebrows. 'So. What do we do?'

'I don't know.'

'It's probably a good idea to lie low for a bit.'

'I guess.'

'Leave town for a few days, maybe.'

'Where would we go?'

'We could rent some place. Find a secluded cottage out in the countryside on Airbnb.'

'That's a start.'

Orri takes out his mobile. 'I'll look for a cottage. You rent a car.'

'What about your mum's car? You don't think she'd let us borrow it?'

'It's falling apart. It will barely get us out of the city centre, let alone over the city line.'

Imogen finds the website of a car rental.

'I've found a cheap cottage in Hvalfjörður on Airbnb. Shall I contact the owner and see if it's available?'

'Sure.'

'Done. I was thinking that maybe Mum should come too? We don't know what these guys are capable of. What if they go to her house looking for us?'

'You're right.'

Imogen finishes renting the car. 'Why don't you drop me off at the car rental – it's not far, it's on Flugvallarvegur 5 – and then I'll meet you back at your mum's.'

Imogen shows Orri the address on her phone.

'Aha. Flugvallarvegur.'

'That's what I just said.'

Orri smiles. 'No, it isn't.'

Icelandic is impossible to pronounce. But Imogen is going to get the hang of it. Because of Orri. After this she wants him to be a part of her life. A big part.

They go back to Sigurlína's car. They'd meant to leave it at Oddi and text Sigurlína later to let her know. There's no need for that now.

Orri leaves Imogen at the car rental.

Imogen signs some papers and is off again.

Driving on the wrong side of the road is hard. Imogen feels like her head is bursting from concentration. At least she doesn't have headspace to worry about the situation; this mess that they're in, all the questions swirling around in her brain. *Did I cause this? Is this all my fault? How can we get out of this? Should I text Victoria King again?* There will be plenty of time to figure stuff out once they're in hiding.

It takes Imogen a while to find a parking space outside Sigurlína's and it takes her even longer to park; parallel parking has never been her strong suit.

When Imogen steps inside the house she can hear voices coming from the kitchen. It's Sigurlína, Orri and a third person whose voice she doesn't recognise.

Imogen freezes for a second. Is it them? Have they found Orri and Imogen already? Instinctively, she turns. She needs to leave. She needs to get out of here. Then she stops. She can't just leave Orri and Sigurlína. They might be in danger.

The door to Imogen's bedroom is ajar. Her room is right between the front door and the kitchen. She tiptoes towards it. She makes sure she doesn't touch the creaky door as she slides inside. Then she places herself up against the wall with her ear to the opening. She needs to find out what's going on.

Sigurlína is saying something. She's speaking in English. And she sounds angry. 'What do you want, Gerald?'

Gerald? Who's Gerald?

'I'm sorry, Sigurlína, this won't take long. But I need to speak with Orri.'

She was wrong. She has heard this voice before. But where?

'Then speak with him.'

'Privately.'

Orri answers the request. 'If it's because of what we told you at the lab, you can talk in front of Mum.'

It's the ambassador!

'I told Mum everything. Imogen and I are leaving town; we're going into hiding for a few days while this whole mess blows over. I was just trying to convince Mum to come with us. You know. Just in case.'

'I think it's good that you're going into hiding,' the ambassador says. 'That's why I'm here. I want you to come to the embassy. I want you to stay there while we figure this out. No one can touch you there. We have security. And there's the Vienna Convention on Diplomatic Relations, the rule of inviolability: no one can enter the embassy, not even local police and security forces, without the permission of the ambassador.'

A few moments pass before Orri answers. 'Wow. Thank you. That's cool. That's definitely better than the cottage I found. Let me just call Imogen and tell her.'

'No,' the ambassador interjects. 'It's just you.'

'Just me.'

'And I guess Sigurlína can come.'

Sigurlína barks, 'I'm not going anywhere with this man.'

Orri sounds confused. 'I don't understand. Why not Imogen?'

'I don't have the authority to do this, Orri. My bosses have not cleared this.'

'But why me, then?'

Sigurlína gives a cutting laugh. 'Yes, *Gerald*. Why him?'

The ambassador is getting agitated. 'Please just trust me.'

'You tell me what's going on or I'm not coming with you.'

There is complete silence in the kitchen for what feels like for ever. Finally, the ambassador speaks. 'Orri. I'm your father.'

'What?' Orri's screech feels sharp enough to bring down the house.

'Your mum and I met when I visited Iceland with my friends one weekend just over twenty years ago. It was meant to be one last weekend of fun – we were all either finishing grad school or starting our first important jobs – before the seriousness of life took over. I met your mum at a Blur concert. I ditched my friends and spent the whole weekend with her.'

'Why now? After all this time?' Orri suddenly gasps. 'Oh my God. You didn't know I existed. You just found out!'

'I knew.'

'Oh.'

'I asked to be posted here. I wanted to get to know you.'

Sigurlína interrupts, her voice dripping with scorn. 'How's Valerie?'

'Good. I think. We've separated.'

Orri suddenly sounds excited. 'Do I have any brothers or sisters?'

'No. We always wanted children but it turned out we couldn't have them.'

Sigurlína snarls like a lioness protecting her cub. 'So now you've come to claim your consolation prize.'

'Mum!' Orri snaps at Sigurlína. 'Don't be like that.'

'I'll be any way I want to be. You are not the only one, my boy, who this man has broken.'

The ambassador's voice turns pleading. 'You know I was already engaged to Valerie. You know that a child out of wedlock could have affected my chances within the civil service. Things need to be a certain way in that world for you to progress; they have to look a certain way. You said you were fine doing this without me. You said you didn't want me to lose out. You said that you didn't want me to ruin my future or my chances of success.'

'I said, I said . . . People say a lot of things. I may well have said those things. But that doesn't mean I wasn't hoping that you'd stay. That doesn't mean I wasn't hoping that you would want to stay. That doesn't mean you should have accepted the get-out-of-jail-free card. That doesn't mean you shouldn't have been a father to your son.'

Again, there's silence.

'I need to get back to the embassy,' the ambassador says, without responding to Sigurlína's admission of decades of heartache because of him. 'Please come with me, Orri.'

Orri suddenly sounds uncharacteristically focused and firm. 'I'm not coming unless Imogen can come too.'

Imogen's heart leaps. She grabs the door. It creaks. No one seems to notice. She wants to run out into the kitchen and wrap her arms around Orri and never let go.

'Who? That girl?' The ambassador sighs. 'That makes things more complicated for me.'

'Oh, for God's sake, Gerald,' Sigurlína groans. 'Think of someone other than yourself for once in your life. Your son is in love. Are you going to leave his girlfriend out here alone with those mobsters on the loose to yet again protect your pathetic little career?'

'Fine.' The ambassador's voice is hard. 'She can come.'

Imogen hears a chair scrape on the floor. Orri is getting up. 'Mum, pack your bag. Imogen and I are already packed.'

'I'm sorry, Orri. I can't go with you. I'm angry. I've kept this man's secret for twenty years – even when it came at the expense of our relationship. I need time. I'll go to the cottage you rented for a few days. It will be fine.'

Imogen realises it's time. She steps out of her room. The floorboards announce her arrival before she can do so herself.

Orri turns around. He's beaming. 'This is my dad.'

Imogen smiles at him. He looks happy. He looks whole. 'I heard.'

'He's going to let us hide in the embassy for a while.'

Imogen looks at the ambassador. His eyes don't meet hers. He doesn't want her there. 'Thank you,' she says.

He just nods. 'Shall we go then?' he says, turning to Orri.

'Oh, wait.' Imogen suddenly remembers there is one thing she needs to do before she can make an earnest attempt to leave the past behind her and take a step towards a brighter future. 'My talk at Harpa.'

'Oh, yes,' the ambassador sighs. 'Cool Britannia is starting tomorrow. I'd forgotten all about it.

'We can cancel your talk. That's no problem. I can call our PR firm now and have them come up with some excuse; the flu, an urgent family matter.'

'I need to do the talk.'

'Once you're in, you're in. You can't just come and go as you like. It's an embassy, not a hotel.'

'I need. To do. The talk.'

Orri gets it. He turns to the ambassador – his dad – and looks at him. A storm rippling the surface of his watery blue eyes. 'She needs to do the talk.'

The ambassador doesn't sound pleased but he seems ready to do anything to get Orri to seek refuge in the embassy. 'If you all stay here, I guess I can have some of the embassy's security team monitor the house tonight and you'll come to the embassy straight after Imogen's talk tomorrow.'

Sigurlína gets up from the kitchen table and walks over to where Imogen and Orri are standing. She wraps one arm around Orri and the other around Imogen. 'So, you have one last night of freedom.' She looks at Imogen. She looks at Orri. 'Make the most of it.'

Orri rolls his eyes at Sigurlína.

She gives him a big kiss on the cheek.

'Mum, you're embarrassing me.'

'I'm going to order some pizza for dinner. You kids just relax and try not to worry about a thing.'

Sigurlína releases them.

Imogen feels Orri slip his hand in hers. His touch is warm and comforting.

Hand in hand, they head for Imogen's room. They close the door on the perils that await. For now, it's just the two of them and the moment.

Photo: A yellowing porcelain cup decorated with blue violets that are fading into oblivion.
Filter: Clarendon.

Possible captions . . .

Option one: A cup of mint tea.
Option two: #refreshing
Option three: People can be cruel.
Option four: Or is it circumstance that is cruel?
Option five: One thing's for sure: Life can be cruel.

Actual caption . . .

A cuppa can make everything right . . . well, almost everything . . .

💙9

Chapter Twenty-Seven

Hannah

I can hear that Sigurlína's call goes straight to voicemail.

'This is Orri. Leave a message.'

Sigurlína's whole body curls in on itself. 'Orri. I'm sorry. I'm so, so sorry. I tried to protect you. But I just can't carry this burden. I just can't. Please forgive me. I love you.'

Sigurlína puts the phone on the table.

'Here's your comment,' she says and glares at me as if this whole situation is somehow my fault. 'It was an act of love.'

Of course it was! The sexual assault. Imogen and Orri were an item. Orri killed Mörður as revenge for what he did to Imogen?

'Sit down,' Sigurlína orders. 'Since you're on your way to the police station you'd better have your facts right.'

We all take a seat at the kitchen table. Sigurlína's face looks gaunt. It's like there's less of her than the last time we saw her. It's like she's slowly disappearing from the world.

She buries her head in her hands. 'It was easier to think of Imogen in prison when I could tell myself that it was only temporary.'

I look at Kjarri. He can't hide the disgust on his face. She knew. She knew the whole time but didn't tell anyone.

'I thought she might get off. I thought she might stand a chance; that the police didn't have enough evidence against her. But if Imogen is pleading guilty, I guess I can't tell myself that any more.'

Kjarri can't hold it in any longer. 'How could you let an innocent person go to prison like that?'

'You won't understand until you have a kid of your own.'

'That's such crap.' Saliva accompanies Kjarri's outburst.

'I had my son to think about. His future.'

I shoot Kjarri a harsh glare. He needs to contain his emotions. He's a journalist. He's meant to report the facts, not his views on right and wrong. I take my phone out of my pocket. 'Do you mind if I tape this?'

Sigurlína's face is flat. 'Go ahead. I'm sick of secrets. I'm sick of lies. It's time that the truth got out.'

'So, if you could start at the beginning.'

'Orri and Imogen came to me with some crazy story about some Russians being after them because of work they'd done for DataPsych – or was it the mafia? I'm not sure. Anyway. They contacted the British ambassador to ask for asylum. But he said no. Then, the ambassador turned up here.'

'Here? In this house?'

'Yes. He offered Orri sanctuary at the embassy.'

'Just Orri.'

'Just Orri. Because Gerald Boothby is Orri's dad.'

Seriously? His dad? This story just gets weirder and weirder.

'Gerald agreed to take them both in: Orri and Imogen. It was all arranged. But then everything fell apart.

'When Orri and Imogen were out of earshot Gerald grabbed my hand so hard I thought my fingers would fracture and whispered in my ear, 'I need your help. Mörður is dead.'

I cried out in horror. He ordered me to stay quiet so Orri and Imogen wouldn't hear. I asked him what happened.

'Gerald said: "He's in his lab. I killed him."'

I gasp. 'What? The ambassador. The ambassador killed Mörður?'

Sigurlína nods. 'He was shaking all over. He said it was an accident, that he didn't mean to do it.

'Mörður, Orri and Imogen had asked him to help them. After he said no he went back to the lab to find Orri. But it was only Mörður there. Gerald wanted a clearer picture. He wanted to know who these people were exactly who were such a danger to them.

'Gerald said that Mörður was rude and full of himself. He said it was none of Gerald's business. Then Gerald came clean. He said that it was most certainly his business; he said that it became his business when Mörður started involving his son in his dodgy dealings.

'Mörður started laughing. As if it was some kind of a joke that Orri's life was in danger. It was as if he wasn't taking this seriously. He just kept on laughing and laughing, frantically, like a madman.

'Gerald said that he didn't know what came over him, that he was angry and scared. He'd just got his son and he wasn't ready to lose him again. He saw some kind of a statue on Mörður's desk. A golden lion. He grabbed it and hit Mörður over the head with it. He'd meant to scare him and stop him

343

laughing. He'd just meant to shut him up. But that was all it took. A single blow.'

Sigurlína looks up at us. 'I believe that Gerald didn't mean to do it. Gerald isn't a violent man. And I believe he loves our son. But actions have consequences. I told him that he needed to go to the police. He said he couldn't because he wouldn't be able to protect Orri if he was arrested.

'He said that the British government could decide to waive diplomatic immunity and have him tried in an Icelandic court. But even with diplomatic immunity, he would be expelled from this country and stripped of all influence. He'd have no way of protecting Orri.'

Sigurlína's face suddenly lights up as if emitting a soft glow. 'Orri looked so happy when Gerald told him that he was his dad. I know what he was feeling. He was finally complete. I couldn't take that away from him. I couldn't be the cause of his unhappiness. Not again. Not any more. I had no choice but to help Gerald.'

I've been holding my breath and I gasp for air as if resurfacing from diving. 'What did he need help with?'

'We went to the lab. He'd left it unlocked so he could return to clean up his mess but he'd locked Mörður's office with a key he'd found on his desk.

'I'd never seen a dead body and I didn't want a dead man's face to be etched into my memory, haunting me for the rest of my life, so I made Gerald go into Mörður's office ahead of me and wrap him up in bath towels and plastic bags. I hadn't realised one of the towels I'd brought was Imogen's.

'We'd meant to take my car to dispose of the body. But that night it wouldn't start. So, we took Imogen's rental instead.

'Neither of us knew how to get rid of a body. We thought it best if Mörður was never found. No body, no crime. It was my idea to have nature take care of the problem. How many times has the wild beast, the cold and harsh island of Iceland, devoured innocent people who were never found again?

'We drove out of the city, parked the car at random, and walked until we found a deep crevice to drop the body in. I'd ask my elves, the hidden people in the big stone in my garden, to have a talk with nature about keeping my secret concealed.

'That was it. The deed was done. At no point did I imagine that Imogen would be arrested for the murder.'

Kjarri gets up from the table. 'I think we need to call the police,' he says.

Sigurlína doesn't object. 'Go ahead.'

Kjarri starts dialling.

So, it wasn't Orri who murdered Mörður; it wasn't Orri who framed Imogen; it wasn't Orri who told Imogen about the murder weapon; it was the ambassador. It was Gerald Boothby.

'Orri had no idea about any of this. He believed Mörður had been killed by this dodgy Russian client.'

Kjarri is talking to the police and giving them Sigurlína's address.

She did a horrible thing. But still I feel sorry for her. 'Do you regret what you did?'

'There is nothing a mother wouldn't do for her son.'

Kjarri is off the phone. They sit in silence for a few minutes.

The doorbell rings. Sigurlína doesn't get up. 'Would either of you mind getting that for me. I'm just going to make myself one last cup of mint tea.'

Photo: A snow-covered lava field as far as the eye can see.
Filter: Moon.

Caption: A new beginning.

♥146

Chapter Twenty-Eight

Imogen

The last time Imogen drove past here was the day she landed in Iceland. That day the grey, barren lava fields that separate the airport and the island's capital were peppered with soft-green vegetation tentatively penetrating the hard rock bed; hope breaking through a wasteland of despair. Now, on her way back to the airport, the landscape is covered with an undisturbed blanket of snow, like a blank sheet of paper just waiting for a story to be written on it. Tabula rasa. An empty page. Clean slate. Just like her future.

The feeling she gets looking out of the window of her taxi, on her way to the airport, is similar to the feeling she got standing on the stage at Harpa looking into the audience. She'd felt as if she was on the cusp of freedom. Every word she spoke had been a step out from under the Beast's shadow towards the light of a new day. But her journey had been cut short. She never got the chance to reveal to the world the truth that would lead to her liberation. The door at the back of the auditorium had opened. Figures dressed in black had started rushing down the stairs towards her, like an angry sea. Once again she was submerged in suffocating darkness.

The last thing she remembers from that evening is turning towards Orri where he was standing below the stage behind the camera – they'd decided to record her talk and upload it to YouTube – and calling out to him, 'Go to him. Go to your dad. Accept his offer. Please, be safe. Be free. Be whole.'

That was the last time she saw him.

He didn't get in touch after she was released from prison, so she didn't get in touch with him. She assumes that he resents her. She assumes that he feels that she's the one who's responsible for depriving him of the father he just gained, the father he's been looking for his whole life, the missing piece of his puzzle. He probably feels that her freedom came at the expense of his father's – or that's how you could interpret things if you really wanted to.

Blame. It has a bad aim.

She hasn't spoken with Sigurlína either. Imogen isn't sure whether it's because Sigurlína is angry with her for the trouble she has brought into her life, or whether it's the other way around: because Imogen is angry with Sigurlína for knowing the truth the whole time and still letting her go to jail for something she didn't do. She understands her motives. But she isn't sure if she can ever forgive her.

Imogen runs her eyes over the white fields of snow. Somewhere out there is where Mörður's body was dumped. She feels nothing. She doesn't even feel sorry for him.

After the murder, Stan had approached Imogen and Orri. It was at the cocktail party at the embassy before her talk. He'd wanted them to keep on working on the Smertoil project. His bosses were apparently very happy with the results so far. He even had a contract for them to sign. 'It's a lot of money,' he'd said with an ugly smirk on his face. 'And it's a way for you to show your loyalty.' Was he buying their silence or did he truly want them to work for him? Imogen didn't know and she didn't want to find out. She wanted nothing to do with Russia's military intelligence services or whoever it was Stan got his orders from.

Imogen's phone beeps. She's sitting in the back seat of the cab. The driver tried to initiate small talk at the start of the journey – 'You've been here on a holiday?' – but she immediately extinguished it. She reaches for her bag, lying on the empty seat next to her and takes out her mobile.

It's a WhatsApp message from Anna.

A: Hi, babe. Just got a message from a girl who wants to rent your room. Are you sure you're moving out? It's been lonely here without you.
I: Absolutely sure. She can have it.

Apart from Anna's message, her phone has been silent all morning. There are no messages on social media. No likes. No deals. No money. Except for a couple of aggressive emails from journalists wanting to sensationalise her life, use her trauma and her pain to sell papers, and a few trolls on Twitter, it's been quiet.

Imogen enjoys the silence. It's all gone. Her sponsors. Her fans. The admiration. It was never really there. It was an illusion. What she presented was fake. The adoration was fake. It was just a plume of nothing.

She considered closing her Instagram account but then decided against it. Even though she's been ambivalent about her own involvement in the business of making people feel bad about themselves, she's come to a realisation: used in the right way, social media can be a force for good. For someone who has no status, no money and no say in the world, social media can be empowering. It gives the voiceless a voice. Who knows, if she hadn't been arrested before she got to the big revelation about how London Analytica intended to exploit fragile minds to make money, maybe the video of her talk might have gone viral and brought down the agency and those paying them for their amoral business practices. No. She isn't going to close her account. That would be a defeat. That would be letting herself be gagged. Instead she is going to take her time and find her true voice.

Imogen can't wait to get home. When she lands she's going to call her parents. They respected her wishes. They didn't come to Iceland when she was arrested. Her lawyer had called them and told them that she wanted them to stay away. They probably think it's personal. They probably think she hates them and wants nothing to do with them. What she would have given to have them there, to have them visit her in prison, to get a single hug from them. But she didn't want to put them in harm's way. She didn't want them mixed up in this.

But now she can finally explain. After she lands in Heathrow she's going straight to Cambridge. She's going to tell them everything.

This isn't over, however. The truth still isn't out. She's organised an interview with a website for next week. She's going to tell them about the Slimline campaign, which London Analytica is launching on Monday.

This morning, Imogen sent an email and resigned from her job. No one has got back to her yet. Ms Kendrick and Mark probably don't even care. They probably gave up on her the moment they heard the news that she'd been arrested for murder.

Imogen can hear a car honking behind them. The driving culture in Iceland is horrible: no one stops for you at a pedestrian crossing, everyone drives over the speed limit, all Icelanders drive too close to the car in front of them and no one gives anyone a pass.

There's another honk. Imogen turns around. It's probably some idiot wanting to overtake them.

Oh, wait. It's a grey hatchback. On the smaller side. Why does she feel like she's seeing this car everywhere? She's sure she saw it outside the prison the day they let her go. She's sure she saw it outside her hotel this morning.

Stop being ridiculous, she tells herself. She's just being paranoid. Who wouldn't be after what she's been through? It's a grey car. The majority of cars in this country are grey in colour. It's nothing.

Imogen turns back around. It's starting to snow. The snowflakes fall softly and quietly to the ground where they disappear without a fuss, without a sound, without impact and blend into the background – still there, yet invisible. They look pretty, innocent, frivolous. But appearances can be deceiving. Snowflakes might look as soft and innocuous as cotton balls. But they are anything but. Snowflakes are crystals, hard, with edges as sharp as needles. And in great enough numbers, snowflakes can be dangerous. They can even be deadly.

Imogen is like a snowflake. She might appear soft, weak, irrelevant. But she has come to a realisation: she isn't. She's tough. She can get through this. Because despite everything, she's still standing. She is going to get through this and she is going to make sure that her story is heard – hers and the stories of all the other snowflakes out there who have been deemed small and lacking and inconsequential – nothing but a target group to be exploited, a body to be used and then tossed aside.

Her story is going to have an impact. She's going to make sure of it.

There's that honking again.

Another asshole trying to take up more space in the world by shoving her aside. But he can honk all he wants. She isn't budging. She has just the same right to be here – on this road, in this world – as he does. He just has to get used to it.

Imogen leans back in her seat and watches the snowflakes fall, quietly, peacefully, with perilously sharp tenacity and grace, as she heads steadfast towards an unknown future.

Photo: A girl with shoulder-length red hair, not straight, not curly, looks into a mirror. On one side the corner of her mouth is turned up, on the other side down. Her expression is as insolvable as the pattern of her freckles.
Filter: Normal.

Possible captions . . .

Option one: Will the real me please stand up.
Option two: Is there really a one real me?
Option three: This face looks eerily familiar.
Option four: This is a photo of me and my burden heading for the light.

Actual caption . . .

Here we go . . .

♥21

Chapter Twenty-Nine

Hannah

It's my first day of school today. A slot at MR, Reykjavík Junior College, suddenly became available. Rósa took me shopping for a new outfit. She bought me skinny jeans, Timberland boots, a bright-green chunky jumper and a black down coat. The look I am going for at this new chapter in my life is normal with a hint of me.

Dad is driving me. Rósa said she could do it, but Dad insisted, even though it meant that he'd be slightly late for work. He said that he wanted to see me off on my first day. I'm not sure if he's being nice or if he just wants to make sure that I show up.

Tomorrow and for the rest of the school year I'll be taking the bus. At least that means I can choose what to listen to on the way. Dad is just turning up the radio, which is playing a song that's as old as Granny and Grandpa, judging by the scratchy sound quality. I don't think he's into the song though. The nine o'clock news is about to start and Dad always has to listen to the news at a volume that falls just short of sonic-weapon levels.

My phone buzzes. It's a message from Daisy.

Daisy and I spoke on the phone for an hour last night. There was some bad news. Her parents are getting a divorce. I still can't believe it. They always seemed to me like the perfect family; the sort of family I dreamed of belonging to. I guess things are never what they seem. Under the surface there are all kinds of stories. Never judge a book by its cover.

I'm starting to realise something: everyone is broken in some way. Daisy and her family were never as perfect as they appeared to be. Imogen Collins – who I've promised Dad I'll stop obsessing about – clearly had some massive issues hidden behind the veil of her social media accounts.

The smiles may seem perfect, but underneath the surface lies all kinds of mess.

Poor Imogen. My heart bleeds for her. She hid it well, but the physical and mental anguish that Mörður Þórðarson caused her is something no one should have to go through.

And speaking of Mörður Þórðarson: Sigurlína told the police everything about the murder. The ambassador was arrested while he was out shopping for groceries. There's a rumour going around that he won't be tried for the murder. Apparently, he has diplomatic immunity, so he might simply be sent back to the UK, where he could actually go free.

The whole of Iceland would be in uproar if that happened. Iceland is a small community, and when something happens to one of their own there's hell to pay. They're kind of like a family. They squabble a lot, but when it comes to the big stuff they stick together.

Just like my family. I got a byline in the paper last week. Well, I shared one with Heiða. We wrote about the ambassador's arrest and Sigurlína's involvement in the cover-up. Seeing my name in the newspaper at the head of a proper story filled me with an unfamiliar feeling which I identified as pride. But not only that. Ísabella came to me and said, 'What you did – solving the murder like that – that was pretty cool.'

Deluded by self-worth, I mustered up the cheek to ask Dad to give me a part-time job at the paper on the weekends. He totally burst my bubble and gave me a flat-out no.

Family. It's not just a word. What it is, however, I'm not sure. I'm still trying to figure that part out.

Grandma Erla and Grandpa Bjarni dropped by unannounced at the house this morning. They said that they wanted to wish me luck on my first day of school and they gave me a present. A beautifully handcrafted leather satchel with my name secretly engraved inside the flap: Hannah Eiríksdóttir. I was on the verge of changing my mind about them hating me when Grandma Erla touched my hair and said, 'Did you know that red hair is a genetic mutation?'

To her I'm an aberration. I'm some weird mutant, like someone from the X-Men, who has invaded her family. She wishes she could have a normal granddaughter.

Normal. What is normal?

Looking at my Instagram account, people might assume the following things about me:

I've got shiny, straight red hair and perfect skin.
I have a fabulous job that I'm successful at.

I drive a Range Rover.

My family is my rock.

I'm normal.

They'd be wrong on all counts. Or would they be?

Granny Jo once said to me that 'normal' is an ugly word.

I didn't agree with her. Being normal has been one of my greatest aspirations in life. I'm not saying that I agree with her now – normal isn't necessarily an ugly word. But maybe it is an unhelpful one.

Normal is just a benchmark that is set too high. Normal has somehow got too close to perfection. But no one is perfect. Everyone is bent, everyone is broken. So, we need to change our perception of normal. Normal isn't any one thing. It's a spectrum, like the rainbow. There is no wrong and no right, just different colours. Normal should include warts and all. Everyone has their burden to bear. The success of our lives should be measured by how well we navigate our journey carrying that burden, not how well we rid ourselves of it. Life is about how happy we are despite everything – not because of everything.

It's our pursuit of perfection that blocks out the light. We let the negative overshadow the positive; because something isn't all good, it's bad. Like my relationship with Mum. She was broken. More than most. Still, she had her own unique version of normalcy. We had some good times together. Like when I was a kid and she spent hours with me at the playground, chasing me around pretending to be a cat; like when she came home from the store with the biggest stretched canvas I'd seen in my life because I'd said I wanted to be an artist when I grew up, and we spent a whole day painting a family portrait of the two of us and Granny Jo; like all the evenings we had Coco Pops for dinner on the sofa and watched cartoons together, while my friends were probably having something sensible like beef and cabbage while their parents listened to *The Archers* on the radio. But the bad memories tend to block out the good ones, like darkness extinguishing light, like night chasing away the day.

But no more. I refuse to let darkness win. I might have the curse. I might not. But either way, I'm going to actively seek out the little blobs of light hiding in the dark as I navigate my humble existence. Because life isn't about the destination, it's about the journey – and treading a good path, a path that interests and excites while carrying our burden, is the closest we can get to perfection.

I loved my mum. And in my own way, I miss her. And I always will, as long as I live.

It's nine o'clock. The news is starting. The first report is about the City Council of Reykjavík having voted against a cull of seagulls on the city's pond.

I'm going to miss working at the paper. But I'm going to work on convincing Dad to give me a part-time job there. I'll wear him down eventually.

Kjarri called me last night. He was just seeing how things are going. He suggested we meet up so he could give me some pointers on my new school. We're meeting up tonight for a burger and then we're going to see a movie. It sounds slightly like a date. But it's not a date. Or I don't think that it's a date. Either way, I'm simply going to go with the flow and see where the light takes me.

The newsreader suddenly falls silent.

Dad reaches for the volume button, as if turning up the radio will somehow make the newsreader start speaking again.

'A missing person's report: The police are looking for Imogen Collins, who was last seen entering a taxi on Tuesday morning. Imogen is nineteen years old with long, dark hair, grey eyes and a slim build. Those who have information on Imogen's whereabouts are asked to contact the Reykjavík Met.'

What?

The car stops. We're at a red light.

Dad shuffles towards me. 'Don't. You promised me. You promised to let this go.'

I feign indignation, as if Dad's distrust of me is seriously unjustified and unfair. 'I have,' I growl at him.

I'm serious about letting this go; I'm serious about this new start. I'm going to school, I'm going to make friends, I'm going to get good grades, I'm going to get a part-time job at Dad's paper and I'm going to find my place within my family – the other day the twins asked me what I wanted for Christmas, so I guess they're no longer betting on me being gone by then. I'm going to be sensible, considerate and obedient. If being normal is a colour spectrum, I will play the part of the colour grey.

I look out of the car window. The blanket of snow that covered the city a couple of days ago is melting, turning into dirt-grey slush. It hasn't snowed since then but suddenly I see a single snowflake fall from the sky on to the car's wing mirror, where it rests for a second before it melts and glides down the mirror like a tear.

Hannah, you're letting this go.

The light turns green. We're off again.

Who am I kidding? I am who I am. There's nothing I can do about it. I'm not going to let this go, am I?